WICKED PRINCE

LAYLAH ROBERTS

Laylah Roberts

Wicked Prince

© 2023, Laylah Roberts

Laylah.roberts@gmail.com

https://laylahroberts.com

ALL RIGHTS RESERVED. This book contains material protected under International and Federal Copyright Laws and Treaties. Any unauthorized reprint or use of this material is prohibited. No part of this book may be reproduced or transmitted in any form or by any means, electronic or mechanical, including photocopying, recording, or by any information storage and retrieval system without express written permission from the author/publisher.

Editing: Woncas Creative

Cover Design by: Allycat's Creations

Photographer: Golden Czermak; FuriousFotog

Model: Nick Bennett

❦ Created with Vellum

LET'S KEEP IN TOUCH!

Don't miss a new release by signing up to my newsletter. You'll get sneak peeks, deleted scenes, and giveaways: https://landing.mailerlite.com/webforms/landing/p7l6g0

You can also join my Facebook readers' group here: https://www.facebook.com/groups/386830425069911/

BOOKS BY LAYLAH ROBERTS

Doms of Decadence

Just for You, Sir

Forever Yours, Sir

For the Love of Sir

Sinfully Yours, Sir

Make me, Sir

A Taste of Sir

To Save Sir

Sir's Redemption

Reveal Me, Sir

Crime Boss Daddies

Daddy's Obsession

Papi's Protection

Papi's Savior

Montana Daddies

Daddy Bear

Daddy's Little Darling

Daddy's Naughty Darling Novella

Daddy's Sweet Girl

Daddy's Lost Love

A Montana Daddies Christmas

Daring Daddy

Warrior Daddy

Daddy's Angel

Heal Me, Daddy

Daddy in Cowboy Boots

A Little Christmas Cheer (crossover with MC Daddies)

Sheriff Daddy

Her Daddies' Saving Grace

Rogue Daddy

A Little Winter Wonderland

Daddy's Sassy Sweetheart

Daddy Dominic

MC Daddies

Motorcycle Daddy

Hero Daddy

Protector Daddy

Untamed Daddy

Her Daddy's Jewel

Fierce Daddy

Savage Daddy

Boss Daddy

Daddy Fox

A Snowy Little Christmas

Saving Daddy

Harem of Daddies

Ruled by her Daddies

Claimed by her Daddies

Stolen by her Daddies

Captured by her Daddies

Haven, Texas Series

Lila's Loves

Laken's Surrender

Saving Savannah

Molly's Man

Saxon's Soul

Mastered by Malone

How West Was Won

Cole's Mistake

Jardin's Gamble

Romanced by the Malones

Twice the Malone

Mending a Malone

Malone's Heart

New Orleans Malones

Damaged Princess

Vengeful Commander

Wicked Prince

Men of Orion

Worlds Apart

Cavan Gang

Rectify

Redemption

Redemption Valley

Audra's Awakening

Old-Fashioned Series

An Old-Fashioned Man

Two Old-Fashioned Men

Her Old-Fashioned Husband

Her Old-Fashioned Boss

His Old-Fashioned Love

An Old-Fashioned Christmas

Bad Boys of Wildeside

Wilde

Sinclair

Luke

Rawhide Ranch Holiday

A Cozy Little Christmas

A Little Easter Escapade

Standalones

Their Christmas Baby

Haley Chronicles

Ally and Jake

TRIGGER WARNINGS

This book contains assault, drugs and criminal activities.

PROLOGUE

Aston pushed herself until her lungs burned.
More! More!
Until the need for air consumed her.
Just a bit longer. You can do it!

Popping her head out of the water, she gasped for air. She rolled onto her back, trying to calm her breathing. She was probably pushing herself too far, but she needed her muscles to burn. She needed to tire herself out so that she might have a chance of quieting her mind and actually getting some sleep tonight.

She couldn't remember the last time she'd gotten more than a few hours of sleep at a time. Too long ago.

When her breathing had slowed, she started swimming lengths of the pool.

Up. Down.

Until exhaustion made her sluggish and she didn't think she could go any farther.

Finished, she grasped hold of the pool's edge and drew

herself up so her chest was out of the water and resting on the concrete.

A pair of bare feet settled in front of her face.

She stiffened.

It was ten at night and usually quiet in the pool at this time. Which was just the way she liked it.

"You know that you're not actually supposed to swim until you nearly pass out, right?" a deep voice asked.

They were good-looking feet. Usually, feet were pretty ugly. Too bony or too hairy. Maybe they had dry heels or toe fungus or overgrown toe nails.

But these feet . . . well, they were kind of sexy.

Then the feet disappeared, and the guy sat next to her. So now she was staring at a thigh, and if she moved her head a bit, some abs.

Holy heck.

Who could sit like that and not have a bit of a fat roll? This guy was *fit*.

You need to move, Aston.

She shouldn't be lying here like this, half dead on the side of the pool. It wasn't safe. This guy could do anything to her. She was as helpless as a babe.

Fuck.

Stupid.

She'd been living in New Orleans for two months now and had let her guard down. She'd started feeling safe.

But Aston knew better than anyone that she should never be careless with her safety.

And so she pushed away from the edge, staring up at the man looking down at her.

Fuck.

How was it possible for someone to be this gorgeous? She likely looked like a wreck. Her normally pale-blonde had been dyed a dark brown. Nothing that would stand out, she wanted to blend in. She also colored her eyebrows. And she knew that the color didn't suit her complexion. So she looked pale and wrung out.

But it didn't matter. She wasn't here to draw attention to herself. All she wanted was to blend in. To be unnoticed.

So why the heck was this gorgeous man coming over to talk to her?

His dark hair was longer on the top and shaved around the sides. He had a sleeve of tattoos down his right arm and over his right pec. She knew this because all he was wearing was a pair of navy blue swimming trunks.

His facial hair was short, which only added to his appeal. Which was nuts because she'd never been attracted to men with facial hair before.

Have you ever been attracted to any men before?

No. Which is what made these feelings even more disturbing.

She needed to get out of the pool.

She just had to find the energy.

"Would you like me to wait so you can get your phone?" he asked.

Huh?

"So you can take a photo." A wicked grin lit up his face and his eyes danced.

What was so amusing? Was he . . . laughing at her?

She could feel her defensiveness rising. She hated being the butt of the joke. Her brothers had done that to her constantly.

And they'd been mean about it.

She knew her skin was too thin, that she was likely reading too much into it, but she couldn't help the small sting of hurt.

"And why would I want a photo of you?"

"Ow. Ouch." Instead of looking insulted, his grin widened as he held a hand to his chest. "That hurts. And here I thought you were checking me out."

She totally had been, but she'd never admit it.

"I just zoned out and you happened to be in my line of sight."

His eyes narrowed as he grew serious. She tensed. Aston was starting to get cold, but she didn't want to leave the pool with him sitting there.

She didn't need to give him more ammo to laugh at her.

Not all men are like your brothers and their friends.

She knew that. Deep down.

But she was utterly drained and her defenses were down.

This was why she never swum to the point of exhaustion when there were other people around. She couldn't keep her guard up in this state.

"This isn't a good time for you to swim," he told her.

What?

Who was he to tell her when she could swim?

"This facility is open twenty-four-hours, and I've paid my dues just like you. I can swim here whenever I like."

Was it just because he wanted the pool to himself? Well, tough.

His eyebrows rose at her tone. Yeah, she knew she could come across as standoffish, but keeping people from getting close was safer.

For them and for her.

"So you really think that swimming on your own at night until you're clearly exhausted is a smart idea?"

Wait, he was warning her from swimming here at night because it wasn't safe for her?

She frowned. When was the last time anyone had cared about her safety? Sure, her father had kept her safe, but only because it was in his best interests.

She'd been an asset. If she'd been a liability, well . . . she hated to think of where she'd have ended up.

"Are you threatening me?" she asked.

His eyes widened. Then, to her shock, he threw his head back and laughed.

This guy was off his rocker.

"Me? Sweetness, no. I don't make it a habit to attack defenseless women."

"I'm not defenseless," she muttered, thinking of the Mace in her handbag. Which was in her locker . . . at least a hundred feet away, in the changing rooms.

Crap.

Maybe he had a point.

He stood and stretched, and yep, her gaze was caught on those abs. And he had those slashes by his hips which drew her gaze to his swimming shorts and the bulge she was certain she could see.

Get your mind out of the gutter, Aston!

"You sure you don't want me to wait here while you get your phone, sweetness?"

"No," she gritted out. Darn it. How had she gotten caught staring again?

This was insane. She never looked at men like this.

But it would be hard not to look. He was ripped, cute, sexy, and confident.

He oozed sex appeal.

Unlike her. She was frumpy and uninteresting.

You really need to leave. Right. Now.

"You should get yourself tested," she told him as she gripped the side of the pool to heave herself out.

In hindsight, she really should have swum over to the ladder.

But that's why hindsight was a pain in the ass.

"Tested for what?" he asked as she attempted to haul herself out.

Shoot. Her arms gave way.

"You're having delusions."

He smiled. "And you've got some drool going on . . . right . . . here." He reached out and touched the corner of her mouth, just as she attempted to heave herself out of the pool again.

Her head smacked right into his, sending him falling back on his ass.

"Shit," he muttered.

"Oh my God! Ouch! What is your head made of? Concrete?" she cried as she slipped back into the water, rubbing at her head.

"Right back at you, sweetness."

"You're the one who bent down when I was clearly trying to get out of the pool."

He removed his hand from his head, which already had a red patch forming on it. Guilt filled her tummy.

Oops.

She really hadn't meant to hurt him. It'd just been unfortunate timing.

"So this is my fault?" he asked.

She wanted to say yes. She really did. But she was trying her best not to lie. Or to make anyone else feel bad. She hated doing that.

"No, it was mine. Are you all right?" she asked in concern.

He gave her a surprised look. "Not your fault, sweetness. Just an accident."

Shoot. Now, she felt even worse because he was being nice. How fair was it that he looked like sex on two legs and he was genuinely nice?

This was bad. Very bad.

"Here, let me help you out." He held out both hands, but she backed away, shaking her head.

No. Nope. Aston didn't trust herself to touch this man and not self-combust or something.

And yes, she knew she was being ridiculous. But she couldn't help it.

He sighed. "Just come here."

"No. I'm fine. I have this." She moved to the ladder and started climbing out, only for her hand to slip, her energy completely zapped.

Fuck. Was she going to have to swim to the other end of the pool? To where the ramp was?

This was too embarrassing.

Then he was there, offering her a hand again. And she knew that she couldn't refuse without looking like a complete idiot.

So she reached up and took it. And yep, it was as bad as she thought. A tingle of awareness moved through her. His hand was warm and dry. His grip firm but not punishing.

And he hauled her out of the water like she weighed nothing.

Which wasn't the case. Once she was standing next to him, she realized he was taller than she'd first thought. Around six feet, since he towered over her own five feet five.

"Thanks."

She shivered and walked quickly over to grab her towel, which she'd left on a bench. She wrapped it around herself. Without looking at him, she muttered her goodbye.

"Bye, Rainbow," he called out. "I'll be seeing you later."

Rainbow? Why the hell would he call her that?

And seeing her soon? Yeah. That wasn't going to happen. She'd just have to come even later at night to the pool or really early in the morning.

Relax. This is a chance encounter.

You're never going to see this guy again.

1

She was going to be late.

Aston hated being late. Everything in her life was scheduled. She had plenty of reminders set on her phone to keep her on track so things like this didn't happen.

But she hadn't accounted for the water in the shower suddenly going cold, meaning she'd had to finish washing her hair in the kitchen sink.

Then, not only did her hairdryer die halfway through blow-drying her hair, but her coffee machine had failed to switch on.

She still had forty minutes to get to work, which was actually plenty. But she liked to always be early. And with her luck this morning, the bus would be late or break down.

Juggling her coffee mug and handbag in one hand, she hit the button for the elevator.

Come on. Come on.

She'd wasted precious moments searching for her coffee travel mug, only to realize she'd lent it to Mr. Logan a few months ago. She needed to add buying a new one to her to-do list.

Finally, the elevator arrived and she picked up the large basket at her feet and got in. Her boss had asked her to bake some blueberry muffins for his meeting today. Which was no hassle.

Wasn't like she had anything else to do.

She was also carrying some mending she'd agreed to do for Mrs. Janssen, one of her neighbor. The older woman didn't have much disposable income and was going blind, so she couldn't do her own sewing anymore. Although Aston thought it would be way easier just to buy some new socks, the other woman wouldn't hear of it.

If she could have juggled everything, she'd have taken the stairs.

The doors opened and she stepped out into the building foyer, right into the path of a man walking into the elevator. Her coffee tilted as she slammed into him.

No. No, no, no.

Turned out that the *Bad Luck Fairy* wasn't finished with her yet this morning. Hot coffee splashed down her dress, making her gasp in pain and horror. At least it had cooled down on the wait for the elevator.

The man jumped back. "Shit! Is that coffee?"

"It's not lava," she snapped without thinking.

After a beat of silence, she glanced up at the man who'd spilled her coffee. All. Over. Her.

Shoot.

She should have known. Only *he* would attempt to walk into an elevator without waiting to see if anyone was exiting.

"You," she gritted out.

He grinned. He was wearing a white shirt with the arms rolled up to reveal tattooed forearm.

She did not find that sexy.

She. Did. Not.

Tattooed, irreverent, thought they were God's gift to women men were not her type.

Face it, Aston, at this point, do you even have a type?

That would be a big fat no.

His grin grew as she ran her gaze up over his face. Really? Who wore sunglasses inside? Not to mention that it was barely light outside.

"You."

"Me," he confirmed.

"Why are you wearing sunglasses inside?" Then it hit her. "Are you hungover? Oh my God. Are you doing a walk of shame right now?"

She didn't understand the jab of pain in her chest. What did she care if he'd been out all night with a woman?

This man meant nothing to her.

Sure, she might acknowledge that he was hot, but that didn't mean she wanted anything to do with him.

He was . . . he was . . . far too full of himself.

He was also known for random acts of kindness and had a smile so sexy she was surprised that her panties hadn't just self-combusted.

"Walk of shame . . . now, that would imply that I feel ashamed."

Urgh, she wished she could wipe that smug look off his face.

Aston didn't know why Maxim Malone riled her up so much . . . he just did. That smile. Those dancing eyes. His gorgeous looks. The way he could charm anyone of any sex . . . it just all pissed her off.

Which made her even more annoyed.

She'd really thought she'd never see him again after she had first moved to New Orleans five months ago.

But as usual, the universe kept showing her just how much it hated her when she'd discovered he lived in her building. She hadn't even had to ask who he was, one of her neighbors had pointed him out to her. As though he was some sort of celebrity.

Everything seemed to come so easily to him. She bet his hot water never ran out while he was washing his gorgeous hair.

Uh. So she guessed she was jealous, which didn't make her feel good about herself.

She needed to be better. Be nicer.

It was just so hard to be nice to *him*. She didn't know why. Most people she didn't have a problem with. She didn't exactly have friends. That wasn't a good idea. But she was a good neighbor, right? Always feeding people's cats when they were away or lending them stuff they needed.

"You're impossible."

"How are you this morning, Rainbow? You seem like you're in an even better mood than usual."

Urgh. Killing him would be illegal, if satisfying.

Although if anyone knew what she suffered around him, she was certain they'd forgive her. Surely, she'd be able to cop an insanity plea with the way he liked to torture her.

"My name is Aston, not Rainbow."

She hated that nickname.

There was nothing rainbowlike about her.

And he damn well knew it.

"And obviously, I'm just peachy now that I've been doused in boiling hot coffee."

"Boiling hot?" He frowned. "Did you burn yourself?" He reached for the top of her dress, as though he was going to start undoing the buttons that ran down the front.

She jumped back. "What are you doing?"

"Checking your skin for burns. Why aren't you using a travel mug? That would have been way smarter."

Now he was insulting her intelligence?

"I lent it to someone, not that it's any of your business. And now, because you couldn't even wait ten seconds for me to get out of the elevator before you barged on in, I'll have to get changed. And I'm going to be late for work. So thanks."

"Whoa, Rainbow, you're the one who walked into me." He held his hands up.

"I did not." Had she, though? She'd had her gaze on her feet, which was pretty typical for her.

She'd learned a long time ago that it was better to keep her head down and her mouth shut—less chance of someone noticing her that way.

"You did. You bumped into me, spilled your coffee out of your mug, and then tried to blame me."

Had she done that? Fudge. Maybe.

Crap. Now, she felt terrible for accusing him.

He leaned around her, hitting the button to open the elevator doors again. "Come on, you need to get out of those wet clothes before you get a chill."

"I'll wait until it comes back down."

He shot her a look that, even with his glasses on, she could tell was filled with impatience.

"Get in, Aston."

She scowled as she stepped into the elevator. Wait. How did he do that? She prided herself on not letting anyone boss her around. She was her own boss now.

But one deep command from him and suddenly, she was following him around like a lamb to the slaughter.

And yes, maybe she was being slightly dramatic.

Unease filled her, so she made sure that she stood as far away from him as possible.

"What's wrong?" he asked with a grin. "Worried I'm going to bite?"

"Yep."

"I promise, if I bite, you'll like it."

"Ew." She made herself look disgusted, but the truth was that heat lit her from the inside out. What was up with this man that he could affect her like this?

That she could both dislike and be attracted to him?

Perhaps part of it was that she didn't really dislike him . . . not deep down.

But she wasn't going to admit that.

"Now, now. Don't judge until you've tried it," he chided.

"That will never . . . eek!" An embarrassingly high-pitched scream escaped her as the elevator suddenly stopped, the lights cutting out.

Shoot. *Fuck*. No.

Everything suddenly closed in on her. The darkness was so thick it felt like it was pressing in against her.

She couldn't breathe.

There was no air in here.

Calm down, Aston. You're being ridiculous.

"Hell," Maxim muttered. "The landlord is going to get a fucking earful about this. I told him to get this piece-of-shit elevator serviced." Something lit up. His phone. "No service. You got any, Rainbow?"

Got any . . . got any . . . she tried to think what he meant, but her vision zeroed in on his cell phone. Well, the light coming from it. She was trembling from a mix of fear and the chill of her wet clothes against her skin.

Her brain tried to figure out what he wanted.

"Rainbow? Why are you breathing like that?"

Like what? Like the way everyone else in the world breathed? But the words stayed trapped in her brain, unable to get them out because she couldn't seem to take a decent breath.

Her lungs grew tight as the world around her disappeared.

All that existed was the light and him.

"Fuck, you're having a panic attack."

Was she?

Oh yeah. She was. She and panic attacks were old friends. Although it had been a few months since her last one.

Damn you, old trauma.

Bad enough that it had reappeared when she'd thought she was finally burying that crap down deep, but it had to reappear in front of *him*.

"Hey, Aston, you're safe. I know this is scary, but I won't let anything happen to you."

What kind of bullshit was that? He couldn't stand her, so why would he want to protect her? And it wasn't like he could protect her if the elevator suddenly plummeted, plunging them to their deaths.

Fuck.

Her legs gave out on her and she slid down the elevator wall to sit on her ass.

"You need to breathe, Rainbow, or you're going to pass out."

Passing out sounded good. She should do that.

"Whoa, no. You're not passing out on me," he said in such a stern voice that surprised her.

Aston hadn't realized that he could actually be stern.

She jumped as she felt him touch her thigh. She stared up into his face, illuminated by his phone.

"Come on, Rainbow. You need to concentrate on calming down and taking a breath. Can you do that for me? Take a nice deep breath."

She couldn't do that.

"Besides, you wouldn't want to pass out in my presence, right? Imagine all the things I could do while you were unconscious. I could get into your phone and change the names of all your contacts. Or grab a pen from your bag and draw a moustache on your face. You don't want me to do any of that, right?"

He sat on his ass in front of her. His voice might be light and joking, but there was a serious look on his face.

"Take a deep breath in and hold it for me. No, don't look away. I want you to follow my breathing. You can do it." He put his phone on the floor and grabbed her hands in his. She tried to snatch them away, but he held on tight. "Your hands are like fucking icicles. Come on, baby. Breathe in. That's right. In with me. Hold. Then out, slowly. And again. No, nope. Don't go into your own head. You're here with me. We're doing this together. In. Hold. Out. Good girl."

She tried to tell herself that she hated him calling her good girl. That she hated everything about him, from his too-perfect hair to his charming grin and straight, white teeth.

But she'd be deluding herself.

"Uh-uh, don't let your mind wander. You keep your attention on me. I'm the only thing you should be thinking about right now."

She'd never admit it, not even under the threat of torture, but she thought about him a lot.

"That's it. Eyes on me. In, nice and slow. Follow my breathing. Hold. Now, out. Good. That was good."

Urgh, his words should have sounded condescending, which should have made her want to nut punch him.

But they didn't, and she found herself unwilling to hurt his nuts.

Nope.

Which was annoying. Because life would be so much easier if she actually disliked him.

But then when had life ever been easy for her?

2

Suddenly, just as Aston was starting to breathe more easily, Maxim's phone cut out and the elevator grew pitch black again.

A tiny, scared sound escaped her. And she *hated* it.

God, she hated it so much.

It was bad enough that she had chinks in her armor, but letting someone else see them?

Not smart.

"It's all right, Rainbow," he murmured. "I'm right here. Fuck, I can feel you shaking. Where's your phone?"

Her phone . . . where was her phone? Why couldn't she remember?

"Fuck it," he muttered. "Do not hate me for this later."

Hate him? Why would she hate him?

He was being incredibly kind right now. Most people would've just ignored her or, more likely, gotten annoyed.

Not Maxim.

Trouble was, she was pretty certain he only knew she was alive when she was standing right in front of him.

She was like a stone in his shoe. Annoying while it was there, but easily forgotten once you threw it away.

Ouch. That was a painful thought.

To her shock, she was suddenly picked up and settled into a wide lap. He wasn't the biggest guy she'd ever met, a lot of the guys she worked with were bigger.

But he was built. She could feel how firm his chest was against her back. How hard his thighs were beneath hers.

And warm... darn, he was warm.

He quickly enveloped her in his embrace. And for the first time in a long time, she felt safe.

Which was completely and utterly terrifying.

Because she had no right to feel safe in his arms. She'd rather not feel anything in his arms. Feeling something for this man would only lead to heartbreak.

He'd been given the title of most eligible bachelor in the state.

He was out almost every night, often not coming home until the early hours. And the reason she knew that was because she barely slept. She spent most of her nights sitting on her balcony, looking out into the city.

So she'd often seen him getting home in the early hours.

And no... she wasn't waiting for him. That would be creepy. She wasn't a fucking stalker.

She was simply doing her bit for the neighborhood watch.

That's all.

In no way was she obsessed with him.

Lord... she was such an idiot. She was utterly obsessed with him, yet he barely knew she was alive.

Which is why she was kind of... sometimes... a bit grouchy around him.

"Let go of me." Fudge, was he some sort of human Xanax? Because she swore all the tension was bleeding from her body and she could actually breathe without panicking, even though it was pitch black in here and she was in a small, confined space.

Without air.

"Nope. Hey, don't go panicking again," he chided. "Breathe in. Nice and slow. Here." He turned her so she was sitting sideways in his lap and grabbed her hand, placing it on his chest.

No, no, no. This was bad. Very bad. She shouldn't be touching him.

Not the son of Satan.

"Did you just call me the Son of Satan?"

"I've called you worse," she said, feeling almost drugged. Definitely human Xanax. She moved her face closer to his neck without thinking. She slid her face between his neck and shoulder.

How did he smell so good when he'd been out all night? It was criminal.

"I've never heard you call me worse."

"I say it in my head. Saying it out loud would be rude."

His chest moved and she grumbled, irritated. "Stay still."

"Sorry, Your Highness."

"You should be. You're so damn irritating."

"Ouch. I'm irritating, and you call me the Son of Satan. In your head, though. Because saying it out loud would be rude."

"Exactly. And I'm always nice."

"You are not nice," he countered.

"Yes, I am. I'm always polite. I use my manners. I help old ladies cross the road, and let pregnant women sit down on the bus. I'm nice, damn it."

How dare he imply otherwise.

For some reason, he'd gone all tense and she didn't like it. She didn't know why she was acting this way . . . almost as though she was drunk.

She'd only been drunk once in her life. Her brother, Benny,

thought it would be funny to get her drunk when she was thirteen.

She'd gotten alcohol poisoning and Benny had gotten a slap around the head. Because her father cared more about his sons than his daughter.

"Benny's a dick," she grumbled.

"Who is Benny?"

Aston buried her face into his chest. Part of her knew this was so wrong. That she was going to have huge regrets when she could finally think again. But right now, he was the one thing keeping her from losing her already fractured mind.

If she fell apart, it was going to be so hard to put herself back together. It got harder every time.

One day, she was worried that she'd fall apart and that there would be no way to put all the pieces back together.

"He's no one," she said quickly. Fudge. Idiot. Talking about her family was the last thing she should or wanted to do. "I feel weird."

"It's the panic attack," he told her. "They take a lot out of you."

"How do you know?" she asked suspiciously. "You've never had a panic attack."

"So sure, are you?"

"Pretty sure."

"You're right. But my sister has. She used to have them a lot."

"You have a sister?" Aston wondered why his sister had panic attacks. Had something happened to her?

She was being a coward. And she hated that. Relying on someone else wasn't the way to get through this crap.

"Yeah, I do. And she went through something pretty traumatic when she was younger. She had trouble with a lot of things afterward."

"Like what?" she asked.

"That's her business." His tone was gentle but firm. And she felt like an idiot for asking.

She'd had to teach herself not to ask too many questions. People didn't like that. Sometimes, she still struggled with social niceties. Things other people took for granted because, as children, they'd learned them from their parents and other relatives.

What had she learned as a child?

Not to piss her father off unless she wanted to be punished.

She shuddered.

"Where's your phone, Rainbow?" he asked, obviously misreading the shudder that had run through her body.

"Stop calling me that, Snickerdoodle."

"Snickerdoodle? Seriously?"

"Yep."

"I think that's worse than Son of Satan," he commented.

"Oh, I'll still call you that. Don't worry. Just up here." She tapped her temple.

"Right, because it's not nice to say it out loud. Tell me, when's the last time you helped an old lady cross the street?"

"Uh. Well, I'm not sure. But if I saw someone struggling, I would."

He snorted.

"I would!" She was frankly insulted by his lack of faith in her.

"I'm sure you would, Rainbow."

Rude.

She tried to slow her breathing, which was picking up again. He might be a human Xanax, but dark, small spaces had been her enemy for a long time.

"When will it be fixed?" she asked.

"Soon," he promised. "Let's find your phone."

Her phone, right. Of course.

Dumbass.

"Why didn't you say anything about my phone before?" she grumbled.

"My bad," he said dryly.

She searched around for her handbag. She should really get off his lap. But she just couldn't do it. Not yet. She found her bag and searched through it. Several items fell out.

She didn't care, though.

Nothing mattered as much as getting her phone. She tapped the screen, lighting it up. She attempted to turn on the flashlight, but her hands were shaking too much.

"Here, let me."

He took it from her and switched on the flashlight. She started breathing easier as it lit up part of the area around them.

"Is it the dark you're afraid of or small spaces?"

She shouldn't tell him. Shouldn't give him ammunition to use against her.

Never show weakness, Aston.

She remembered Grandpop telling her that. In her family, showing a weakness was likely to get you bullied mercilessly.

"Aston," he murmured, surprising her by using her real name.

She blamed that for her lack of filter. "Both."

"Why?"

"Oh no, I'm not telling you that." No way.

"Why not? We've got literally nothing else to do."

"I could think of a thousand other things I'd rather do."

"Oh yeah, like what?" he asked in a suggestive voice that made her shiver.

"Not that!" she squealed.

Yeah, like you wouldn't want that.

"Why, Rainbow, where did your mind just go then? Somewhere interesting, I'm guessing."

She never thought she'd be grateful for the dark. But right now, she was thankful that it hid the red in her cheeks.

"What did you think I was suggesting we do to pass the time and keep you distracted?" he murmured, his breath teasing her ear.

Lord, she wished she hated that.

Idiot.

"Hmm?" he prompted.

"Nothing. Let me go." She shoved herself off his lap, which had her phone slipping from his grasp and landing on the floor, instantly smothering the light.

Panic slid back down her throat, clawing at her breath until she was gasping for air.

Maxim swore and quickly grabbed the phone, turning it over so light filled the elevator once more. Then he reached for her, tugging her back onto his lap.

She tensed, ready to jump out of his hold, but he slapped the side of her thigh. "Stay."

"Excuse me? Did you just tell me to stay? Like I'm a dog?"

"I know you're not a dog," he muttered.

She huffed out a breath. She should hope so.

"A dog would be way more obedient. And grateful."

"Obedient and grateful? Really? Are those personality traits that you admire? Is that what you look for in a woman? That they be obedient and grateful?"

"You want to know what I look for in a woman?"

Nope. Actually, she didn't. Because she didn't want it to hurt when he described someone that wasn't her.

She didn't know what his type was, but she was pretty sure that prickly, stubborn women who wore clothes that covered almost every inch of their bodies weren't it.

"Someone loyal, sweet, kind, funny. Someone who will take my back when I need them to. Who wants me for me."

Oh God. She could be those things. And what was worse . . . she wanted to be those things.

"Let me go."

"No. You're just going to start panicking again and you're far less interesting to be around when you're unconscious."

"How would you know? You've never been around me when I'm unconscious."

"True. Although it would be far quieter, but less entertaining."

"Glad I could entertain you," she muttered.

Because that's all she was. Entertainment.

Fuck. She needed to build herself a tougher skin. This was ridiculous.

She needed a distraction, something else to think about other than how good he felt holding her or how amazing he smelled.

Could this morning have gotten any worse? Getting stuck in a small, dark space was one of her worst nightmares.

Oh, and let's not forget the fact that she'd had a few panic attacks, she stunk like coffee, and her wet dress was clinging to her body, making her shiver.

And she was stuck sitting in this sexy man's lap.

Just perfect.

Shoot! How long had they been sitting here?

"I need to call my boss!" She was going to be late.

Grabbing her phone, she looked at the time and gulped. Then she brought up his contact number. But the darn call wouldn't go through.

"Why won't it go through?"

"I don't think there's any service in the elevator," he told her. "This thing is a piece of shit. It should at least have an emergency button."

"What if . . . what if no one realizes we're in here?" she asked.

"What if they try to lower it down and it plummets? We could die."

"Whoa, there, Negative Nelly. How'd you just go from zero to a hundred? No one is dying."

"You don't know that. It could happen. Maybe we should try and get out of here?"

"And how do you suggest we do that?"

"There's always a trap door at the top, right? We could climb up, stand on the top, and reach the next set of doors. Maybe we should try opening the doors. Maybe we're on a floor already." Safety could be just beyond those doors.

She tried to rise, but he held her with a firm arm across her stomach. "You're not doing any of that."

"But in the movies—"

"This isn't a movie. We're just going to sit here and let the experts get this sorted."

"But what if they don't?" she asked.

"They will."

"How do you know? We could be here for hours. Everyone will just think the elevator is out of order again."

"Because I'm supposed to go to my brother's house tonight for dinner. When I don't show up, he'll reign hell down on this city until he finds me. All right?"

Wow. Must be nice to know that someone gave a hoot about your well-being.

"Okay."

"Strange, I never thought you'd be like this."

"Like what?" she asked suspiciously.

"You know . . . a drama queen."

She gasped in horror. This. Man.

She was going to kill him. It was going to happen.

"If you were going to be hit by a bus, I wouldn't push you out of the way," she told him.

His chest was moving again. What was he doing? Was he laughing?

"I'm serious." She glared up at him.

"Oh, I know. That's what makes it so funny."

"I am not a drama queen. I'm the farthest thing from a drama queen you can get. Whatever is the opposite of a drama queen, that's me. I am chill."

"Rainbow, you're not chill."

"I am chill! Snickerdoodle."

"Drama queen."

She huffed out a breath. Drama queen. What a dipshit.

"It is not being dramatic to worry about dying," she said.

"We're all going to die, Rainbow. No use worrying about the why or how."

God, how she wished she could be like that.

Not worrying about things must make life so much easier. But she just wasn't built that way.

Which is probably why she had so much trouble sleeping. She had to exhaust her body and brain before she could switch it off.

Because the 'what ifs' drove her flipping mad.

"So you just never worry about anything?"

"Didn't say that. But I don't worry about shit I can't control. Like this elevator. Although I will be telling the landlord to get off his ass and fix this immediately."

"Good luck with that. I've asked him three times to fix my hot water issue, and I'm still having problems."

He tensed. "What?"

"Yeah. The first time, he couldn't even be bothered coming to check. The second time, he did, but it was working fine then, and he thought I was making things up."

And he'd made several insinuations about why he thought she was making up lies to get him into her apartment.

Gross.

The third time, she'd waited for weeks to contact him. But she'd been desperate.

And still, nothing was fixed.

Maxim had gone kind of quiet. She opened her mouth to ask him if he was all right just as the lights came back on and the elevator lurched, dropping about a foot before stilling.

She screamed, wrapping her arms around his neck. "Eek!"

"Hey, it's all right. You're all right. Seems like they're fixing it."

"Then why did it start to drop?"

Had she peed herself? Darn it. It felt like she'd peed herself. Fear had her heart racing.

"It's all right. Everything is going to be just fine."

She could barely hear his voice trying to soothe her over her own heartbeat. But then the elevator started gliding smoothly down.

"Oh, fudge. Thank God."

It stilled and she let out a sigh of relief. They hadn't plummeted to their death. She lurched off Maxim's lap, standing. She turned toward Maxim before freezing in shock.

"Who the heck hit you?"

3

Maxim winced. Shit. He'd forgotten about his bruised face. Luckily, his eye hadn't swollen shut. Although it was still irritating.

To save himself some strange looks, he'd put his sunglasses on after leaving his car. But he'd pulled them up onto his head when the lights had gone out in the elevator.

And forgotten to put them back on.

Dumbass.

"No one."

Yeah, that was a smart answer, idiot.

He stood and stretched. Fuck, his body wasn't used to fighting anymore. Maybe he needed to practice more in the ring. Although he was sick of Victor beating him every time.

Rainbow rolled her eyes at him. God, he loved how much shit she gave him. Everyone else in this city was either scared of him because of his brothers' reputations, or they were trying to get into his pants. Mostly so they could get close to Regent, his oldest brother.

Everyone wanted something from him.

Except for her. In fact, not only did she not want something from him, but he was only fifty percent sure she'd douse him with water if he was on fire.

The doors to the elevator opened before she could call him on his shit.

"You two getting out of there or what? I need to put shut the elevator down so it can get checked out," a disgruntled voice grumbled.

Maxim turned and gave Brian, the building manager, a sharp look.

The older man gulped and took a step back. "Mr. Malone, sorry. I didn't realize it was you."

He could sense Aston stiffening beside him and knew what she was likely thinking. He waited for her to rip this asshole a new one.

Instead, she said nothing. He shot her a confused look. She looked cool and collected, as though nothing had happened.

"What happened?" Maxim asked as he placed his hand on her back. He could feel her trembling and frowned.

He knew the sort of control it took to pretend to be calm when you were falling apart on the inside.

And he didn't like that she knew how to do that.

Who had taught her that she had to hide her fears like that?

"Power outage," Brian said, scratching his head.

Aston grimaced, but still didn't say a word as Maxim gently pushed her out of the elevator.

He could feel her let out a deep breath, but her facial expression didn't change.

"Took a while for the elevator to get back on board."

"I trust you have someone coming to check it out today," Maxim said.

"Ah, yeah, sure. Fuck. Look at this mess," Brian grumbled. "I'm not a fucking cleaning service."

Aston tensed, turning back to stare into the elevator.

Maxim spotted a lipstick, a pack of gum, and a box of tampons. The lid was open, and several tampons lay around the floor.

Her tension grew. He knew she didn't want to get back into that elevator and he didn't blame her. So he walked in and picked up all of her stuff.

"I didn't mean you had to pick it up, Mr. Malone," Brian muttered. "She could have picked up her own shit."

God, he was a dick. Maxim had always known it, but he'd never seen the way he treated other tenants.

Maxim might have to do something about that.

Aston was staring at her feet, ignoring them both. He was so confused by this Aston.

He wanted grouchy, snarky Aston back. But instead of saying anything, he put his hand on the small of her back again, guiding her over to the stairs. When they were through the fire door, she stepped away from him and grabbed her things with a mumbled thanks.

"What was that?" he asked, holding his hand to his ear. "I couldn't quite hear you."

"Going deaf in your old age?" she snarked.

"Yep, because thirty-three is so ancient," he countered as they moved up the stairs.

Fuck, it was going to be annoying climbing fifteen flights of stairs, especially with his ribs aching like a son of a bitch. But he didn't complain, just stuck close to Aston's side as she moved up the stairs at a quick pace.

"Thirty-three? Wow, I could have sworn you were like forty-five. Age isn't being kind to you, is it?"

He threw back his head and laughed, sore ribs be damned. God, she was funny. Stilling, she stared at him in shock.

"What is it?"

"Nothing. I just ... nothing."

"Come on, what? You've never bothered to hold back. Why do it now? And what was that with Brian back there?"

"What was what?" she asked, clearly trying to move out in front of him. However, her legs were shorter than his and he wasn't letting her get away from him.

"You didn't rip him a new one. Didn't even give him one of those cold, haughty looks."

"I don't have a cold, haughty look."

"Sure, you do. You're giving it to me right now."

She groaned and turned around. "You're impossible. I'm going to be late. I don't have time for this."

"What time do you start work?"

"Eight."

"Eight? Babe, it's only just past eight now. How far do you have to travel?"

"It takes me about fifteen minutes on the bus."

There it was again. The b-word.

"You don't seriously take the bus."

"What's wrong with the bus?" she asked, looking confused.

"It's not safe."

She snorted. "Neither is riding the elevator in this building apparently. Do you think he's even going to get someone to check it?"

"He will," he said in a cold voice.

She stilled and glanced over at him, studying him as though trying to determine whether he was speaking the truth.

"Are you going to tell me what happened to your face?"

He gave her an irreverent grin. "That's nothing for you to worry about, sweetness."

He expected her to roll her eyes. To huff at him impatiently. But for some reason, there was a hint of hurt in her gaze.

She quickly stifled it, but he knew what he'd seen.

Why was she hurt?

He studied her, his own smile fading. "Rainbow? What's wrong?"

"Nothing's wrong. Just . . . tired."

"You should take the day off."

She started up the stairs again, shaking her head. "There's no need."

"There is when you've had a fright. You need to rest." She looked exhausted. Why wouldn't she listen to him?

Maybe because she's not yours, dickhead. Why should she listen to you? It's not like you've ever really taken care of someone before. Not really.

He glanced down at his hands, surprised to see they were clenched into fists. What was that about?

They reached the seventh floor and she veered off through the fire door. He followed her.

She paused. "This isn't your floor."

"I know."

"Then where are you going?" she asked.

"I'm seeing you to your door."

She eyed him suspiciously. "Why?"

"So I can come back in the middle of the night and murder you. Why else?" he asked.

"Be serious."

He heaved out a sigh. Fuck, he was tired and his head was thumping. He'd been awake all night. He didn't need this.

"Aren't you running late?" he asked.

She let out a tiny noise of horror and he had to grin. Who got this upset about being late? Besides, if she hurried, she'd still get there close to on time. Who went to their job earlier than they needed to?

That was just crazy.

She hurried off down the corridor. He didn't know why he

was following her. It wasn't like she didn't walk through the building on her own all the time.

But something inside him said that he had to make sure she was all right. Maybe it was because he'd seen a side of her that he bet few people ever saw. And it roused his protective instincts which wasn't something he was used to feeling about anyone other than his sister.

So, yeah, this was weird for him too. But he was just going to roll with it because he knew he'd regret it if he didn't.

And Maxim Malone refused to live with regrets. He'd spent most of his childhood trying to be someone his father would notice, would be proud of. And he'd never managed it.

So screw him and screw the rest of the world.

Maxim was who he was and he wasn't apologizing for it.

She stopped in front of a door and side-eyed him. Damn, that look was a killer. If he had less self-confidence, he might be hurt by it.

Instead, he grinned.

"This is my apartment."

"Is it?" he asked.

"Yep. So you can leave now."

"Can I?"

She groaned, looking up at the ceiling.

"Praying?" he asked.

"Yep."

"What for?" He leaned against the wall by the door, crossing his arms over his chest.

"Patience."

He nodded slowly. "Yeah, you're kind of lacking in that department."

"What . . . you . . . I . . . urgh! Are you this annoying with everyone, or is it just me?"

"Never had any complaints."

"So, just me. Awesome. Look, we got through *that* . . . and now I'm fine. So you can leave."

He barked out a laugh. "Is that you saying thank you?"

She threw her hands into the air. "Yes! That's me saying thank you."

"Hmm, I think you can do better."

She pointed a finger at his face. "You're a pain in the ass. That's all you're getting. Take it or leave it."

"I think I'll leave it."

She narrowed her gaze at him as he handed over her basket of stuff. She looked down at it in confusion as if she hadn't realized he'd been carrying it for her.

He walked backward, away from her as she watched.

"I'll wait until you're ready to give me a proper thank you, babe."

"Urgh! Don't call me babe! And you shouldn't hold your breath as I'm never saying thank you!"

A woman with a toddler and baby exited their apartment just as she yelled that.

He grinned as her face went red and then he winked at the woman, who gave him a flustered look back.

With a whistle, he turned and left. Suddenly, the day was looking up.

4

Aston studied the invoices in front of her.

What was she missing?

Things just weren't adding up. Why were they paying so much for cement mix? And for so much of it? Where the hell was all that cement?

Should she take inventory? But with over thirty building sites throughout the state of Louisiana, that was kind of impossible. Stuff came and went very quickly.

Maybe you should just let this go.

She knew better than to stick her nose into things that weren't her business.

The last thing she wanted was for anyone to pay her too much attention.

She kept nose to the grindstone and her opinions to herself. But what if she said nothing and this company was ripping her boss off?

Mr. Leeds had always been good to her. He'd given her a job when she was desperate, with next to no references. He'd even given her a pay raise last month. She couldn't just ignore this.

So even though her head was thumping and her brain was telling her this was a stupid idea, she got up, strode over to his office, knocking on the door.

"Oh, Aston, come in." He turned from his computer to smile at her.

"Sorry for bothering you, Mr Leeds."

"Not a bother, dear. What is it?"

"There's something wrong with the invoice for cement," she told him.

He frowned. "What is it?"

"Here, see?" She showed him the invoice. "They seem to be overcharging, and see this? It's a lot of cement. Do we really need this much?"

"Oh, that's my fault, my dear. I have a new, big project coming up. Very hush-hush, though. Don't worry about the cost. Just pay it and then I'll sort it out."

That was an odd thing to do. She stared at him in confusion.

"Really, don't worry. I'll sort it all out."

"But I'd be happy to help—"

"Leave it, Aston," he said firmly, looking annoyed. "Thank you."

She closed her mouth. Right. She got it. This wasn't any of her business. And this is what she got for sticking her head out.

Should have just minded her own business.

She knew there wouldn't be a hint of hurt on her face. She'd learned a long time ago not to show any pain.

All that did was enable someone to use your pain against you.

Instead of arguing, she turned on her heel and headed back to her desk.

All she had to do was let this go.

Easy-peasy.

When she reached her desk, she groaned inwardly to find

Gretchen leaning against it. Gretchen was Dayton's spoilt, slightly selfish daughter. She was a real estate agent who worked for her dad, marketing and selling his residential construction projects.

Why was Gretchen here? It wasn't like they were friends. Aston couldn't have friends. They could make you vulnerable.

And it put them at risk. She couldn't put other people at risk.

She was trying to be a better person.

However, Gretchen just didn't like to hear the word, no. Her dad doted on her, so she was used to getting her own way.

What would it be like to have a parent who actually cared about you?

"Hi, Gretchen."

"Aston, where have you been? I've been waiting ages."

Gretchen tended to exaggerate.

"Sorry, just checking something with your dad."

Gretchen waved her hand in the air. "Whatever. I need you to come out with me this weekend."

"Um, what?"

"Come on, it will be fun. We'll go to Glory."

Glory?

"Isn't that the nightclub that Maxim Malone owns?" Aston asked as if she didn't know the answer. Because once she'd known his name, she'd looked him up online.

"Yep. It's the hottest club in the city. And Maxim Malone is the most eligible bachelor in the state. LadyB did a whole article on him last month."

Yeah, she'd seen that too.

LadyB was a gossip website that Gretchen loved. Last time Aston had looked at it, she'd thought it seemed kind of bitchy and rude.

"I'd love to be on her gossip column," Gretchen said with a

strange light in her eyes. "I'll see if I can get us some passes. No way am I lining up to get in"

"I'm sure you'll be able to get some, you know so many people. But I'm not sure that I—"

"You're right. I'll figure it out and be in touch. Bye!"

She walked off before Aston had the chance to tell her that she didn't actually want to go.

Drat.

So much for that backbone.

∼

Gracen's gasp of horror made him wince.

Awesome. Now Maxim was going to be in trouble with Victor for upsetting his girl.

"What happened?" she asked as she moved toward him, her hand rising as though to touch his face before she seemed to think better of it.

Victor's girl was a sweetheart. Kind and caring, she was almost the opposite of his largest brother. Victor was enormous. He used to get into the boxing ring regularly and win. Most people were terrified of him, either due to his size or the reputation he'd earned as Regent's enforcer.

But when it came to Gracen, he was a complete marshmallow.

"Would it help if I said you should see the other guy?" he asked with a grin.

She glared at him. "No, it would not. Did you get into a fight? Who hit you?"

"You gonna beat them up for me, little sister?" he teased. "Defend my honor?"

"You think I won't?" She scowled up at him, her hands on her hips as she tapped her foot. "Explain."

"What's going on out here?" Victor walked into the foyer from the kitchen. His gaze went to his girl first, taking in her agitation. Then he moved his gaze to Maxim. "Why are you upsetting Gracen?"

"I'm not upsetting Gracen," he said as he stepped into the house. The house he'd grown up in.

Fuck, he'd hated this place when his father was alive. It had been cold and terrifying.

It hadn't gotten much better if he was honest. The only reason he came here was because of his family.

He didn't know how Regent could stand living here. But he knew that part of it was tradition.

The head of the Malone family had always lived here.

"He is!" Gracen countered.

Maxim gaped at her. "Are you trying to get me killed? I thought you liked me."

Victor strode toward him, a scowl on his face. "What did you do?"

Fuck!

"Nothing! I didn't do anything!"

Gracen stepped between them, and Victor glanced down at her, his whole body softening.

"Baby, out of the way. I need to give him a beating for upsetting you."

"No, you don't. I'm upset because someone hit him and he won't tell me who!" Gracen said.

"What happened?" Regent walked into the foyer and Maxim sighed.

"I knew I should tell you all that I was sick," he muttered. Only, then he would have missed out on Gerald's cooking and Gracen's dessert. He knew she would have made him his favorite.

She always took care of them all.

Hmm. Maxim wondered what kind of sweets Rainbow liked? She probably didn't let herself indulge.

That was a shame. Everyone should spoil themselves now and then.

If she was yours, then you could spoil her.

Fuck. Where had that thought come from? Aston Symonds wasn't his type. Not that he had a type, really. He loved all women. But she was so serious and driven. She wore these long dresses with buttons up the front, covering every bit of skin she could.

Her hair was always back in a bun. Never a hair out of place.

Except for today. When she'd stepped out of the elevator, her hair had fallen from its bun, cascading down her back.

She'd looked younger. Sweeter. Like the first time he'd met her at the swimming pool and she'd given him a mild concussion.

Gracen turned to him, digging her finger into his chest. "Who?"

"No one for you to worry about, sweetheart. Just some problems at the Glory with a couple of drunk assholes touching things they shouldn't have been."

Glory was his baby. His first nightclub. He now owned several across the state, but Glory was his first love.

"Don't you have bouncers to take care of those sorts of things?" Regent asked dryly.

He shrugged. "Sometimes, I like to get my hands dirty." He'd spotted a couple of drunk assholes cornering one of his bar staff by the break room door, so he'd taken care of it.

Gracen was still looking worried. He knew if he didn't wipe that frown off her face, Victor would be in a vicious mood all night. And would likely blame him.

"Please tell me that you've made some mocha brownies?" he asked.

"Promise that you're not badly hurt."

"Cross my heart and hope to die."

She sucked in a breath at those words and he instantly regretted them.

"I'm fine, little sister. Promise."

"All right, then. And yes, I made you some mocha brownies, some of my sticky buns for Victor, and Regent some Regent's Rum Delight." She threw a wink at Victor before smiling at his oldest brother.

Regent's gaze softened. There wasn't much that made him smile these days. He seemed to be growing more distant and colder, something that Maxim hated, even as he didn't know what to do about it.

However, the women and children in their family were always treated to a different Regent. One who was kinder and softer. He was especially like that with their sister, Lottie, who he'd always doted on.

It had been especially hard on him when she'd moved to New York with her husbands.

Yep, husbands. Plural.

Maxim didn't intend to settle down for a long time, but when he did, he couldn't imagine sharing his girl with someone. Although they all shared each other.

He wasn't into that either. Nothing wrong with it, he just wasn't into dick.

No, you'd much prefer Rainbow's round ass pressed against your cock, wouldn't you?

Yeah, he hadn't minded that at all. He'd been lucky that she'd been too scared to notice how his cock had gotten hard as she'd squirmed around on his lap.

"Yum, thanks, sweetheart. You know I live for your brownies. If I don't get a weekly fix, I start to go into withdrawals."

Gracen shook her head. "I wish I had your metabolism. If I ate as much as you did, I'd be as big as a house."

Victor reached over and drew her to him, whispering something in her ear that had her going red.

"Victor, Maxim, can I see you in my office before dinner?" Regent asked. It was worded as a question, but they all knew it was an order.

"Sure," Maxim replied.

"I'll go check how Gerald is getting on with dinner," Gracen said, turning away.

Victor slapped her ass and she glared at him over her shoulder.

Maxim and Victor followed Regent into his office.

Another room he hated. Although at least Regent had replaced all the furniture in it from when their father used it. There were several photos on one wall. A lot of them were of Lottie. But there were some of him, Victor, and Jardin. As well as some of Gracen, Thea, and Carrick.

And, of course, there were also several of Ace and Keir. They were Thea's brothers, but she had custody of them.

"Jardin coming tonight?" he asked as he helped himself to a glass of expensive Scotch.

Regent frowned at him. "No, Thea and the boys all have some sort of vomiting bug."

He shuddered, imagining how much fun that would be.

"Gracen made them soup," Victor said. "We dropped it off earlier along with some medicine. She wasn't happy because I wouldn't let her go in."

"I'll also get some ready-made meals sent over to them," Regent said. "But we don't need Jardin for this conversation."

"What's going on?" Maxim asked.

"Someone is smuggling in and distributing a new drug."

"What kind of drug?" Maxim asked. And who the fuck

would dare to sell drugs in their town? The Malones had always run the drug trade in New Orleans.

"Did you hear about those tourists found dead in their hotel room about three weeks ago?" Regent asked.

"Uh, yeah, I guess." Maxim tried to recall what he'd read. "Don't remember hearing about the cause of death."

"Cops finally figured out they'd taken this new drug called Mixology."

"I've heard of it," Maxim said grimly.

"We've kept it out of our city until now," Victor said. "But someone has found a way of bringing it in. With the Ventura Gang gone, there was a hole in the city that someone thinks they get to plug."

The Ventura Gang had been basically destroyed a few months ago after they'd joined forces with Carlos Santiago to try to get rid of them. But they'd wiped them out because they'd dared to go after Gracen. No one went after their family and survived.

"You haven't heard of anyone taking it at your clubs?" Regent asked.

"You know I would have told you if I had," Maxim replied. "But I'll have everyone keep an ear out at all the clubs. We don't want that shit being distributed. Hadn't heard of it killing anyone before now though."

"Rumor is that it was a bad batch," Regent said.

Great. That's just what they needed.

"Just let me know if you see or hear anything," Regent commanded. "I want to get my hands on some to have it tested myself."

"What about whoever is smuggling it in?" he asked.

"Don't worry, we'll find them," Victor said grimly.

And when his brothers found them, they were toast.

5

Aston scowled as she stomped her way down the hallway to her apartment. She'd thought yesterday was bad enough. Getting stuck in an elevator was surely the worst thing that could've happened, right?

But nooo. Then she had to go and try to help her boss. Only for her boss to make her feel like a school child who'd spoken out to turn.

Yep, yesterday had sucked monkey balls.

Yet, somehow, today was awful too. Her boss had asked her to run a million errands. Which wouldn't be so bad if she had her own car. But instead, she had to take the bus or walk. And while walking, she'd tripped over an uneven bit of pavement and twisted her ankle.

So not only did she have to walk up seven flights of stairs to her apartment, but she had to do it with a limp.

Awesome.

Even though the elevator had apparently been checked and was now working, she wasn't going to risk using it.

No. Way.

As she approached her apartment, she noticed something sitting in front of the door.

She picked the item up and stared down at the brand-new, still in its packaging travel mug.

With a rainbow on the front.

Couldn't be a coincidence.

But why would Maxim Malone buy her this?

Something that felt like happiness filled her.

This made no sense. She didn't think he even liked her.

"Oh, Aston, there you are. You're late."

She glanced over at her neighbor, Eva, with a sigh. She wanted to argue that she couldn't be late when she wasn't actually supposed to be anywhere.

But that would sound bitchy. And she was trying to be nice. As hard as it was some days.

So she plastered on a smile and turned to her neighbor. "Hi, Eva. How are you?"

"Tired. Felix was awake all night."

Felix was sitting in a front pack, currently sticking his fist into his mouth. Aston liked kids. It was hard not to like them. But she really, really wasn't in the mood for what she knew Eva was about to ask.

"Can you look after the kids for a few hours? I just want to meet Dan downtown for a couple of drinks. We'll be back by ten."

Sure they would. Last time they'd told her that, they'd stumbled in the door at one in the morning.

She didn't want to sound like a prude, but it had been a weekday. While Aston hardly slept, there was a difference between sitting awake at home, and waiting for her neighbors to stumble home so she could leave.

When she was with the kids she always had this low-level anxiety humming under her skin, stressed that something would happen to them and she wouldn't know what to do. That they'd get hurt or fall ill.

The stress usually made her stomach ache to the point that she vowed every time that she'd say no the next time they'd ask.

Well, this time she wasn't doing it. She was going to grow a backbone and tell her no.

"I'm sorry, I really—"

"I knew you'd say yes," Eva spoke over her, as though she couldn't even conceive that Aston would say no. "Thanks so much. Fletcher has a bit of a cold, so there's some medicine on the table for him. Just follow the directions and give it to him before he goes to bed. I just need to go finish getting ready. You can come over now, right?"

Say no.

"Sure," she grumbled.

Great. That backbone growth was going so well.

~

Thank God today was Friday and she could spend the entire weekend doing nothing.

Which was pretty much what she did every weekend.

Of course, she'd spent half the week avoiding Gretchen, which had made her feel terrible. But she really didn't want to go out to some club this weekend. That wasn't her scene.

But you love dancing.

Yeah, by herself, where no one else could see her. Then yeah, she'd bust some moves. But in a nightclub with people watching?

Nope. Not happening.

However, first, she actually had to get home. Her bus had broken down about ten blocks back. And instead of waiting for a replacement bus, what had she decided to do?

Yep, she'd decided to walk home.

With a sky that was darkening by the minute. There was a definite feel of a storm in the air.

But she was going to make it before it rained. She would make it. Tightening her hold on the bag of groceries she was carrying, Aston sped up.

You can do it. You can do it.

A crack of thunder made her jump and she nearly lost her hold on the bag.

No!

No, that was not a spot of rain. She was imagining it.

The wind whipped through her, making her shiver.

She had this.

More rain.

Shoot.

She really didn't have this. Those first few spits soon became a downpour, and her teeth chattered as she battled the elements to get home.

The paper bag of groceries in her hand was getting saturated.

Why had she gone to the shop by work instead of the one closer to home?

Oh yeah, right. Because the last time she'd stopped at that store, one of her neighbors had cornered her to ask her if she could feed her cat while she was away.

Which normally wouldn't be an issue, except that this particular cat hated Aston. Every time she entered the apartment, the cat laid in wait, pouncing on her and biting her ankles.

That cat was pure evil.

She didn't mind helping out. It was just that . . . was anyone ever going to do the same for her?

Sometimes, she wondered . . .

You just need to learn how to say no to people.

Yeah, but then she'd feel like a terrible person.

She'd promised herself that she was going to be better. Someone who did good things for others.

But why did it feel like the universe kept crapping on her all the time?

She cleared her throat, wincing. Damn it. She was not getting a sore throat.

She. Was. Not.

Six blocks out. She could do this.

Then it happened.

The bag started giving way. She grabbed the bottom, but it was too wet and weakened.

It went to pieces and she stared in horror as her groceries exploded across the sidewalk.

That was it.

It was too much. Aston could feel the tears forming.

She didn't cry.

She would not cry. Crying never solved anything. It had never done anything but draw attention to her. The wrong sort.

So she would not do it.

But God . . . she wished she could. She wished she could just sit on the sidewalk and cry. A few people stared at her as they hurried past, trying to get out of the storm.

She didn't blame them for not stopping. No one wanted to be out in this weather.

After gathering up what she could find and putting as much into her handbag as it could hold, she was soaked, shivering, and miserable.

And of course . . . of course that was when he showed up.

Because why not?

The car horn was her first warning, although she didn't look over. She had a carton of milk precariously balanced on top of three microwave meals and two packets of muesli bars. The only thing holding it in place was her chin and a prayer. And since no one had ever listened to her prayers, she just knew she wasn't going to make it.

So nope, she didn't look. She didn't think that beep was aimed at her anyway.

Crap. The rain was coming down hard. Aston thought about sheltering, but at this stage, she wasn't really going to save herself from getting any wetter.

Another blast of a horn. Then a voice.

"Rainbow! Come here."

This time she turned to look at him. There he was, driving slowly along the road beside her, his passenger seat window down as he peered out at her.

"No!"

"Rainbow, you're soaking wet."

"Yep."

"Get into my car."

"If you offer me candy right now, I will scream."

"Hate to tell you, babe, but you're already screaming."

"Don't call me babe. And you need to move along, you're blocking traffic." Someone was driving up behind him.

"Get in the car, Aston." This time, his voice was firmer.

It sent a strange shiver down her spine. One that had nothing to do with the storm raging around her and the wet clothes clinging to her.

She should not like that firm tone of voice. She should want to fight against it. She'd been around controlling men for most of her life and they'd never once looked out for her. Never taken care of her.

Stop feeling sorry for yourself, Aston. That's as useless as crying.

There was a loud beeping before the car behind him drove around him.

Maxim didn't even flinch or spare them a glance.

"You need to watch where you're going." Not that she cared if he crashed or anything.

Actually, yes, she did. She didn't want him to die or get hurt. Maybe a paper cut. They really hurt.

Oh, crap. She didn't even want him to get a paper cut. Things would be so much easier if he was an actual jerk and she could pray for him to fall down the nearest sink-hole.

"Come here, Aston," he ordered.

Shoot.

"No," she told him. "Watch the road!"

"I'll watch it if you get into my car."

She let out a loud groan. He was insufferable.

"Fine!" She stomped toward him, giving the person driving the car behind him an apologetic smile.

She was fairly certain they gave her a middle finger back. But it was hard to see properly in the rain. So she was going to pretend that they'd waved.

When she got to the door, Maxim leaned across to open it. She hopped in and put her stuff down before leaning over to close it.

A beep sounded from behind them.

"Maxim, go," she urged.

"Put your belt on."

"Maxim!"

"Aston. Belt. Now."

Urgh, he could be so annoying sometimes. How could he go from carefree to all bossy and commanding? She never knew where she stood with him.

She quickly belted up as another car shot around him.

"You're making friends."

"I always do, Rainbow. I always do," he said cheerfully.

See? It was like he had some sort of personality disorder. She couldn't keep up.

"There were only a few more blocks to go," she muttered.

"Safety first. Won't have you getting hurt on my watch."

That shouldn't fill her warmth. It shouldn't. This was just stuff that people said to each other. It didn't mean he actually cared about her.

"Or did you mean that you wanted to keep walking in the rain? Carrying a pile of microwave meals?"

Urgh. So what if she ate microwave meals? She couldn't be bothered cooking for one person because it just made her feel sad.

She shivered and he directed the heater vent so the warm air all went onto her. She glanced over at him, taking in how perfect he looked. Today he was wearing a dark blue shirt that went perfectly with his complexion. He also had on jeans that she bet cost more than she made in a week.

And his car . . . his car was divine. Heated seat and leather interior. That she was likely ruining with her wet clothes and hair.

"You suck."

He laughed. "Why? Because I'm dry, and you're not?"

"Yes."

Really mature, Aston.

Why're you walking around in a storm, Rainbow?" he asked as he drove toward their apartment building.

"I figured it meant that I wouldn't have t-to wash my c-clothes if I walked in the r-rain."

"Ahh, smart thinking. Very environmentally friendly of you."

"I thought so." She sneezed.

"Aston," he said warningly. "What were you thinking?"

"I was thinking that my bus broke down and I just wanted to get home rather than wait for a replacement."

"The bus again," he said in a dark voice. "You need to stop taking it."

"Sure, I'll just walk everywhere instead." Was he nuts? She couldn't walk to work. Not to mention that her ankle was still a bit sore from the slight sprain the other day.

"It's not safe."

"It's fine." She rolled her eyes.

"Don't roll your eyes at me, Rainbow," he told her sternly as he found a parking spot right outside their building.

Seriously. How did he manage to find a spot so close?

"How'd you know I was rolling my eyes?" As far as she could tell, he'd been looking at the road the entire time.

"I know you that well. And you just confirmed it."

Lord, he was hard work.

"Thanks for the ride." She reached for the door handle, but her hand didn't seem to want to work. Shoot. She was freezing, even with the warmth of the car.

"Wait there, Rainbow. I'll come around for you."

"But then you'll get wet."

"Gonna get wet anyway."

"But you could make a run for it. Then you won't get too wet."

He sighed. "You really do have a poor opinion of me, don't you?"

There was a comeback on her lips, but it froze there as she stared at him. Because there was something about the way he'd said it that made her think he was serious. That it wasn't a joke.

"I don't . . . I just don't want you to get wet and sick."

"And what about you?" he asked.

"Well, I'm already wet."

A smile teased the edges of his lips and she groaned. "Do. Not. You're better than making that sort of joke."

"Am I, though?" he asked thoughtfully. "I'm not sure I am."

She shook her head. But there was a smile teasing her lips as well when she grabbed the handle of the car door to try again. Why wouldn't it open?

"It's locked," he explained.

"Could you unlock it?"

"Nope." Then he reached into the back of his car to grab an umbrella. He jumped out of the car and rushed around to her, holding the umbrella above him.

He really shouldn't have bothered, but she didn't argue as he unlocked then opened the door and helped her out, grabbing the carton of milk and the muesli bars out of her hands.

After closing the door, he held the umbrella above them both as they rushed into the foyer.

"T-thanks," she said, her teeth chattering.

So. Cold.

"No thanks needed," he said as he left his umbrella by the door.

"No? And you sh-shouldn't leave that there, someone will s-steal it."

"They wouldn't dare. And no. You just owe me. Big time."

She rolled her eyes at him. "What do you want? My first-born child?"

"Hmm. Now, that's a thought. With your looks and smarts and my charm, that baby could rule the world."

Now she knew he was teasing. Her looks? She was plain. Ordinary.

Where he was . . . a god.

Not that she'd tell him. Lord, no. The man had an ego the size of Australia.

And wait . . . he thought they'd have the baby together?

Ha. Right. Not happening.

Except in her dirtiest thoughts, but she wasn't going there.

Suddenly, she realized he was pressing the elevator button.

"Th-thanks f-for the r-ride," she managed to get out as she tried to grab her things from him.

"What are you doing?" He used his free hand to lightly slap hers away.

The elevator doors opened and he gently prodded her forward. But she dug her heels in. She was freezing cold, dripping water everywhere, and she knew the quickest way to get to her apartment would be to just get in the elevator.

However, she wasn't getting into that death box.

And he couldn't make her.

"What's wrong?" he asked.

"I'm n-not getting in there."

She waited for him to give her an impatient look. To sigh. Or to just hand her stuff to her and get in, leaving her behind. Lord knew he'd done more than enough. But instead, he used his foot to make sure that the doors didn't close and looked at her with sympathy.

"You're scared to get in the elevator?"

"I'm not s-scared," she countered, out of habit more than anything else.

Because, yep, she was totally scared. A hundred percent wimping out.

But she had been taught to never let anyone see when she was afraid.

"Yeah? Then how come you don't want to take the elevator?" he asked in a voice that was way too gentle.

She couldn't handle him being gentle right now. She was too close to breaking, so she needed him to be mean to her in order to keep herself from falling to pieces.

"Maybe I just don't want to take it with you."

He gave her a knowing look. Shoot. How did he know her so well? They hadn't spent that much time together.

Forty minutes in a broken elevator is probably like four weeks in normal time.

Shoot.

"Come on, Rainbow. In you come."

"I don't w-want to."

"I know, baby," he said in that same voice. The one that she could not let seduce her. "But you have to."

"D-don't have to. I'm in charge of m-me."

"Normally, yes. But right now, you're freezing, you're scared, and you're not thinking properly."

"I'll take the s-stairs."

"Baby, your lips are going blue. You need to get warm asap. And I'm not going to stand here and argue with you anymore."

"Then o-off you go!" She was fooling herself. And she knew it.

He reached for her, wrapping an arm around her back.

"You're going t-to get w-wet," she warned.

"Don't care."

"I'm not d-doing it. I'm not."

He drew her into him, his hand resting on the back of her head as he pressed her face against his chest.

"You don't have to," he lied.

"G-good. Because I'm n-not."

"I know. Of course you're not. You're going to put your health at risk by climbing seven flights of stairs in wet clothes, carrying a pile of groceries."

"Y-yep."

"Starting to rethink my stance on acquiring your first-born, Rainbow. Your self-preservation is pretty crap."

She shuddered as she heard a ding and then the sensation of moving hit her. She tried to stifle the cry of fear against Maxim's chest, but she knew he heard her when he started hushing her.

He rocked her back and forth in his arms. Had anyone ever rocked her before? If they had, she couldn't remember it.

"I d-don't want to d-do this."

"You're not doing anything, baby. Just keep your face in my chest and pretend we're somewhere else. Like a tropical island. Hawaii. We're in Hawaii. I'm going to get you one of those lava drinks, all right?"

"O-okay." She had no idea what a lava drink was, but him in his swimming trunks on a sandy beach . . . yeah, she could be down with that.

The elevator stopped with a ding and then she was being shepherded backward.

"Good girl. See, you did it."

She drew back to see they were standing in the hallway, just in front of the closed elevator doors. Then she formed her hands into fists to whack his chest.

"You suck."

"Hmm, I wouldn't object if you sucked." He winked at her.

Her mouth dropped open.

This. Guy.

"That was beneath you," she told him.

He slowly shook his head. "You know, as soon as I said it, I realized how bad it was. I can do better than that."

"You really can."

He started directing her down toward her apartment and it was a sign of how exhausted she was that she didn't resist.

They stopped outside her apartment door.

"Where are your keys?" he asked as she stood there, staring at the door.

"Just wait a moment. I'm hoping it will open using the power of my mind."

"While I'd generally be all for experimentation of the mind, your body is about to give in. Keys, baby."

"Stop calling me baby," she protested without any real conviction as she searched through her handbag for her keys. Where were those damn things?

"You don't like it?"

That was just the problem. She liked it way too much.

"Did you lose your keys?"

"I never lose anything. They're in here. I know they are." She found them as the apartment door next to hers opened.

"Oh, Aston, I thought I heard you." Eva smiled as she looked out at them both, her gaze eating Maxim up.

She tried not to tense. Not to push her way between them both to stop Eva from staring at him.

What right did she have to be jealous?

"Hello, Mr. Malone."

"Call me Maxim. Mr. Malone is my father," Maxim said with an easy smile.

"Hi, Maxim," Eva purred.

Good Lord. Had Eva forgotten that she had a husband? What was she doing talking to Maxim like that?

Eva shot her a look that she didn't understand, or maybe she just didn't want to. Couldn't the other woman see that she was wet and freezing?

Aston stuck the key in the lock, but she didn't push it in far enough, and it fell to the floor.

Motherfudger.

"I'm Eva." Eva smiled at Maxim.

"Here, let me get that." Maxim bent and grabbed the keys at the same time she did.

Both of them banged their heads together. She groaned.

Ouch.

"Well, there's some déjà vu," Maxim muttered with a laugh, rubbing his forehead.

"Your head is still made of concrete," she complained.

"Oh no, are you all right, Maxim?" Eva asked.

"Nope. Pretty sure I've got a concussion."

"Oh dear! Do you want to come and sit down? Aston, you need to get him an ice pack!"

Aston gaped at Eva. Was she for real right now? What about Aston? She'd hit her head too. And even though she was standing there, doing a good impersonation of a popsicle, Eva only cared about Maxim?

Fudge it.

"Get him an ice pack if you want. I'm going inside for a hot shower."

Maxim had gotten her key and had put it in the lock on his first try.

Show off.

He unlocked it and she hastily opened the door.

"Oh, but, Aston, I wanted to ask you a favor—"

Aston moved quickly through the doorway and turned to slam the door shut.

In Eva's face.

She'd feel bad about that later. When she was dry and warm.

"Whoa, is she always like that?"

Crap. How had she not noticed that Maxim had landed on the wrong side of the door?

"Why are you here?" she asked.

"You know, short-term memory loss at your age is worrying." He looked around her apartment.

"You d-don't know how old I a-am."

He tilted his head. "You're right, I don't. But I'm guessing you're under seventy, so it's worrying."

She heaved out a breath. He guessed she was under seventy? Ouch. He could have said under forty.

"Take your clothes off."

She gaped at him. Um. She couldn't have heard him correctly, right?

"Take your clothes off, Aston," he repeated firmly. "You're freezing and you're going to get sick."

She was already worried that it was too late. That tickle in her throat was becoming more like a razor blade.

But she wasn't going to let it take hold. Aston didn't get sick. She didn't allow herself to get ill.

So she would just fight it back the way she did everything.

On her own and with sheer stubbornness.

"Clothes off. Hot shower. Now." He took the items from her arms and put them on the table at the entrance. Then he turned her around. All the apartments she'd seen in this building had the same layout. Small entrance leading to an open-plan kitchen and living area. Beyond that was a hallway that led down to the bedrooms and bathroom. This apartment had just one bedroom, the one next door, where Eva lived, had two.

Shoot. She was going to have to apologize for being rude.

Something slapped her on the ass. "Get moving."

He didn't . . . he couldn't have, right?

Spinning back, she gaped at him. "You did not just smack my ass."

He grinned, rocking back on his heels. "Totally did. And I'll do it some more if you don't get moving."

"You can't just slap my ass."

"Can if you're not doing as you're told. Now, you can stand here and continue to backchat me, and I'll get to see what that pert ass looks like naked right before I turn it red. Or you can do as you're told, and go strip off and shower. Then put on some warm clothes. I'll make you a hot drink."

"I . . . you . . . who . . . what?"

He shook his head. "Are both your hearing and your short-term memory going?"

"You cannot threaten to spank me! You shouldn't even be in here!"

"Relax, baby. I'm not going to do anything to hurt you. I'm here to help."

"You just threatened to spank me! You don't think that would hurt?"

"Oh, it would hurt. A punishment spanking should always hurt. Unlike one for fun."

For fun? Spankings could be fun?

Not in her experience.

Although she couldn't deny that she felt a rush of pleasure at the idea of him touching her.

No. Bad Aston.

Not happening.

"You should leave," she told him.

"Not until I'm sure you've warmed up."

"I can look after myself."

"See . . . that's where we disagree. If you could take good care of yourself, then you wouldn't have been walking around during a storm."

As he spoke, he moved closer to her and she found herself backing up. Not because she was truly scared of him . . . but well, what happened if he caught up to her?

Suddenly, she had visions of him looking at more than just her bottom naked. Images of him stripping her and helping her wash herself . . . no, nope.

You are not doing this.

But her body hadn't quite caught up to her mind because even though she was freezing on the outside, her insides were all warm and gooey.

She wanted Maxim Malone.

It wasn't a huge revelation or anything. Her body had known since that first meeting. But her mind kept trying to deny it.

"And if you could take care of yourself, then you wouldn't have been swimming on your own at close to eleven at night where anyone could attack you."

Um. Okay. Why was he bringing up stuff from five months ago?

"So I'm not going to leave you to take care of yourself. I'm going to stay here until I'm sure you're warm and dry. You hear me?"

"I could call the cops on you."

"And tell them what? That some guy is standing in your apartment wanting you to look after yourself? Yeah, Rainbow. They'll come running."

Well, he didn't have to point out the flaws in her plan.

"You can really be a jerk sometimes."

He just smirked. "Admit it, you like me."

Holy. Crap.

Did he really know that she liked him?

"Admit it, you want to be friends with me."

Friends. Right. Of course he meant friends. What else would he want?

Silly Aston.

Dumb. So dumb.

"I need to have a shower. You can really leave. I'll be fine now."

"Nope. Friends make sure that their friends don't catch pneumonia and die. Looks bad on our friend card."

"Friend card?" she asked.

"Yep. Now, go."

Motherfudger slapped her on the ass again!

Jerk.

6

As soon as he heard the shower go on, Maxim closed his eyes and took a deep breath, trying to calm his raging hard-on.

He wanted her.

His prickly, somewhat uptight, gorgeous neighbor who wouldn't accept help until you held her down and whacked her over the face with it. Who seemed to have no idea of just how beautiful she was.

He didn't know the moment it'd all changed. When he'd gone from enjoying their banter and her sass, to wanting to pull her against him and kiss her.

He really needed to know what she tasted like.

Fuck.

This was a stupid idea. Aston wasn't some hook-up. She wouldn't just want sex. And the truth was . . . he wasn't sure that was all he'd want from her either.

But what did he want?

Fuck. This was a dumb idea. He needed to keep his distance from her. He wasn't looking for anything serious at the moment.

However, that didn't mean he'd just walk out of there without ensuring she was all right.

They were friends.

Just friends.

Following his vow of being just friends, he decided to put away her meager groceries. He frowned as he took in how little food was in her cupboards. He heated her up one of those instant cups of soup.

The water was still running in the shower, so he thought it was safe for him to snoop.

Not that there was much to snoop at. As he'd suspected, her apartment was painfully tidy. It was like no one lived here. No leftover dishes from breakfast in the sink. No crumbs on the counter. Heck, there wasn't even any dust.

In fact, there was nothing much of anything. These apartments came furnished with the basics, and it seemed like that was all she had.

Two pots. Four mugs. Four glasses. Four forks.

A couch. But no throw pillows.

A television, but no pictures on the wall.

No photos anywhere.

This was . . . it was hurting him. Where was her personality? Photos of family? Friends?

He might live in what his sister called a bachelor pad, but even he had things. Photos of his family. A few throw pillows that Lottie bought him. A dead plant that Gracen had given him.

Shit, he needed to replace that in case she ever came over. Victor would kill him if he hurt her feelings by not taking care of the plant.

When Aston finally stepped out of the shower, he was sitting on the couch, watching some animal documentary.

"Ow, damn," he commented. "That gazelle is gonna be dinner."

She walked into the room, rubbing her wet hair with a towel. She was wearing a tracksuit in a soft pink color.

And she looked freaking adorable.

Fuck. Adorable wasn't sexy. He should not want to lie her down and strip that damn tracksuit off her.

"Feeling better?" he asked.

"Yep," she said in a low, husky voice that he thought was probably due to embarrassment. She had some slashes of red on her cheeks as well. She winced as she watched the lion bring down the gazelle.

"Oh no. The poor gazelle."

"Just life, baby," he said. Fuck. He needed to stop calling her baby. What was wrong with him?

"But why does it have to be? Why does the predator always have to win?"

He eyed her curiously. "There some predator in your life I should know about?"

"What? No. Just making an observation."

Hmm. Was that the truth?

He wanted to press her. But he also knew that he had to get out of there before he lost control. So he jumped to his feet, startling her.

"I've got to go. Work stuff."

"Oh. Right. Of course. Um, thanks for the ride and getting me up in the elevator and stuff."

"You're welcome. I made you soup."

"Thanks."

"There wasn't much in your cupboards." And he was worried it was because she couldn't afford much food. Why had he never looked into what she did?

Because it's not your business.

She's not your business.

"I don't buy much at a time."

Because she had to take the bus? Although there was a grocery store not that far from here.

"You look better, anyway." At least she wasn't blue.

She looked flustered and unsure with him there. He didn't think she was the type to have men over.

She better fucking not. Because he'd take every one of those bastards out.

Jesus. Calm. Down.

"See you, Rainbow. Take care."

He left.

Seriously. Take care. What was he thinking?

~

GOD, she felt awful.

She was so cold her teeth were chattering. Yet, her face felt burning hot.

When she tried to swallow, it felt like there were razorblades in her throat.

Crap. She was sick.

And not just a little sick.

Really, really sick.

Her phone buzzed. Was that what had woken her up? Who the heck would be texting her at . . . ten in the morning. Really? How was it ten in the morning?

Sheesh.

Last night, after Maxim left, she'd lay on the couch to watch some mindless TV while sipping on the soup he'd made her.

Someone had banged on the door at one stage, but by the time she'd found the energy to get up, they'd been gone.

Probably a good thing. She didn't want to be spreading this around anyway.

Maybe it's Maxim texting you?

That spurred her into picking up her phone. Urgh, this was so ridiculous. She shouldn't want this guy. He was so far out of her league, it wasn't funny.

And why would he text her anyway?

He'd walked out of here pretty quickly last night, almost as though he couldn't wait to leave.

As though she was an inconvenience. Which, let's face it, she was.

Grabbing her phone, she squinted at it.

It wasn't him.

And that wasn't disappointment she felt.

Liar.

Instead, she had a message from Eva asking her to babysit today. Actually, she wasn't even really asking, she was demanding.

God.

There was no way she could handle looking after kids today. She wasn't even sure that she could get out of bed.

Aston: *No.*

Guilt filled her at her short answer. So she added another text.

Aston: *Sick.*
Eva: *I don't mind if you're sick. So are the kids.*

Yeah, she knew that. Because they'd given her their germs.

. . .

ASTON: *Can't. Too sick.*

THERE WAS NO REPLY. Well, hopefully, she'd gotten the message. Another text came through.

Damn, why was she popular all of a sudden?

GRETCHEN: *Glory tonight. At ten.*

SHE GROANED. This is what she got for being friendly. She should just stick to being grumpy and cold to people. It was easier.

ASTON: *Can't. Sick.*
Gretchen: *Come on, you can't be that sick. I can't go on my own.*
Aston: *Sorry.*

THAT WAS IT. She was done. She was sure that Gretchen had to have other friends she could take. Or maybe she didn't.

Rolling over, she snuggled under the blankets. She didn't care what else was going on today. There was no way she was getting out of this bed.

7

"Maxim! Fuck, Maxim!"

Maxim glanced up as Stephanie, one of the younger servers, burst into his office. Her eyes were wide and filled with tears. He immediately jumped to his feet. There was one thing he'd never be okay with and that was people messing with his staff. Male or female.

He wasn't the most protective guy in his family . . . that award probably went to Victor.

No, wait, definitely Regent.

But Maxim looked after the people that belonged to him.

"What is it? What's going on?" He rounded the desk. "Did someone hurt you?"

"N-not me."

His phone buzzed with a call as she tugged at his sleeve. He followed her out of his office and down the hallway.

"Jones? What is it?" he said into his phone.

"Come out back," Glory's manager replied. "It's not fucking good. Keep anyone from looking. We've done our best, but we can't be too careful."

Fuck.

Dread filled him as he exited the back entrance, following the young server.

She let out a small, distressed cry at the sight of a body on the ground of the back alley.

"Fuck. What happened?" he asked.

Jones, and Will, one of the bouncers, were there. Will was bent over, searching the body.

"He was found out here?" Maxim asked, looking up and down the alley.

"No," Jones said. "A guy flagged down Steph and told her that someone had been in the toilet for a while. She got Will and he kicked everyone out so he could check. Found this guy dead in the stall. That's when they called me. We cleared the bathroom and the hallway and brought him out here."

It might seem callous and wrong to move a dead body. But if anyone had seen him, they'd have called the cops.

And that was the last thing Maxim needed.

The police would just love a reason to raid one of the Malones businesses.

And Will and Jones knew that.

"You guys did good. Overdose then?"

Jones nodded. "Yep."

"And here it is." Will held up a small baggie with a bit of white stuff left in it.

Shit.

There was a familiar logo on the front. The image of a beaker.

Fuck.

"Mixology," he muttered.

"Yep. This shit has is making its way through the city and it's not good," Jones said. "They found a couple of homeless people dead early this morning and there's a rumor these baggies were found on them."

"What the fuck? How would a homeless person get their hands on this?" he asked.

"Apparently, some of the distributors are handing out free samples," Jones said grimly.

Jones had a network of people he knew across the city. If there was anything you needed to know, you went to Jones.

"Free samples? Fucking great."

"Good for business," Will muttered. "Get them hooked and they'll be back for more."

"Only problem is that this shit is killing people and on my fucking territory." This wasn't acceptable.

"Why are only some people dying, though?" Jones wondered. "Bad batch?"

"That's my guess. I need to call Regent. He'll want to get this tested, and get a clean-up crew here."

"We're not calling the police?" a small voice asked.

Shit. He'd forgotten about Stephanie. Turning, he took in her trembling form, the way she bit her lip. She looked scared out of her mind, which didn't sit right with him.

"Steph, sweetie, we can't have the cops here, okay?" Jones said in a surprisingly soft voice.

Maxim's eyebrows rose. Jones was usually a hard ass. He didn't suffer fools and he had a slight temper. He'd been in trouble with the law when he was younger, but had kept clean for years now.

However, he disliked law enforcement even more than Maxim did.

"It wouldn't be good for business," Jones continued. "They'd shut us down. No one would get paid. This is better and he doesn't care. He's dead."

"What about t-the drugs? Where did he get them from?" she asked.

Good question.

"Can you send me all the camera footage?" Maxim asked Will, who nodded.

Seems that was how he was going to spend the rest of his night.

Fuck.

∼

She still had no hot water.

With a groan, Aston leaned her forehead against the shower wall. This sucked.

It sucked even worse because it was late Sunday evening and she still felt like utter crap.

But she'd forced herself out of bed and into the bathroom, determined to shower.

She was sweaty and gross. Her head was thumping and she couldn't breathe out of her nose.

So sick.

But she had work tomorrow and was hoping she'd sleep better after a steaming hot shower.

Or at least breathe a bit easier.

However, she'd forgotten about the lack of hot water situation.

Brian had a lot to answer for. How hard was it to get someone in to check what was going on?

Moving to the bedroom, she grabbed her phone to call him.

No answer.

Yeah, it was a Sunday night, so she kind of understood why he wasn't answering.

But screw it. She'd put in several requests during workday hours. Enough was enough.

Slowly, because she had to rest every few minutes, she got her clothes on.

Crap.

That took way too much energy.

That should have clued her into how sick she was. However, sheer stubbornness kept her moving forward. Without grabbing anything, she made her way to the stairs.

Take the elevator.

She wanted to.

She really, really wanted to.

"Motherfudger," she muttered. "I hope he fudging finds his way down a fudging long drop and stinks of manure for a year."

Holding on to the rail, she slowly and painfully made her way downstairs. By the time she got to the ground level where Brian's apartment was, her head was spinning and she could barely breathe.

She had no idea how she was going to make it back up. Sitting on a small bench in the foyer, she rested momentarily before forcing herself to stand. She walked down the corridor to his apartment. There, she hit the doorbell.

Nothing.

Again, she pressed it.

Nothing.

After the fifth time, the door opened suddenly. Brian was wearing a white sleeveless see-through vest and loose gray pants with stains on them that she didn't even want to think about.

"You're outside office hours." He attempted to close the door in her face, but she stuck her foot out, wincing as the door swung into it.

"Building emergency."

"Unless it's a fire or flood, I don't wanna know."

"You ignored all my complaints about the hot water during office hours. I had no choice but to come down here."

"What's wrong with you? You look like shit."

Wow. Like he could talk. He looked like he hadn't washed his hair in the last decade and the smell wafting out of his apartment was truly disgusting and.

"I'm sick."

"Jesus, what are you doing coming down here if you're sick?"

"I want hot water," she snarled. She closed her eyes.

Be nice.

Don't be rude.

"Well then, come back tomorrow. As long as you're not sick. Don't nobody want your germs."

And just like that, she snapped. Reaching out, she took hold of his shirt and wrapped her hand around it, shaking him back and forth.

It was probably only because he was shocked that he let her shake him like that. But she was going to take it.

"Get me some hot water now!"

Fury filled his face. "Listen, bitch. Maybe if you'd been a bit nicer, fucking did something for me once in a while, then I would have fixed your fucking hot water."

"Are you saying if I'd sucked your scrawny, cheese-crusted dick, you'd have fixed my hot water?" That was it. She was going to vomit.

"Yes!" Spittle formed on the corner of his lips. "And it's not cheese-crusted. I'll show you!"

She started gagging. Yeah, no. That was definitely something she didn't need to see.

Not today, not ever.

"Fuck you, bitch. Have fun with your cold shower." He shoved her back and she fell onto her bottom with a wince.

Ouch.

The door slammed shut.

Great. It seemed she was stuck having cold showers for the rest of her stay here.

Maybe it was a sign that it was time to move. But she liked it here. Or at least she had. Now . . . with how things had been at work lately, she wasn't so sure.

Rolling onto her hands and knees, she used the wall to pull herself up onto her feet. Then she leaned against it for a moment, trying to catch her breath.

Being sick sucked. Aston made her way out to the foyer and rested on a bench. There was no way she was making it back up the stairs. She was just going to lie here and sleep.

That worked, right?

She lay on her side and curled her legs up on the bench before closing her eyes.

Perfect.

8

Well, that wasn't a sight he expected to see.

Maxim wiped at his eyes. He'd barely gotten any sleep in the last twenty-four hours, so perhaps he was having delusions.

But, nope. Aston was still lying there.

Why was she lying on a bench in the foyer . . . asleep?

Anger filled him, surprising him. He had to breathe through it for a moment. But hell . . . it was so stupidly reckless of her.

She better have a damn good reason for falling asleep in a public area where anyone could hurt her, or he was tanning her hide good and proper.

Okay. Didn't you just recently decide that you needed to stay away from her because you were developing this weird attachment?

Spanking her ass was *not* staying away from her.

Still, his hand itched as he moved forward and crouched in front of her. Wait. What if she'd hurt herself? Or was ill?

He shook her urgently.

"What? No, go away, Benny, you dick. I'm not playing games with you tonight."

Who was Benny? That was the second time she'd mentioned him.

Jealousy surged.

What sort of games did he want to play with her? And at night?

"Wake up, Rainbow. Come on, what's going on with you?"

She rolled onto her back. She was remarkably pale except for two red blotches on her cheeks.

What the hell?

A bad feeling filled him and he put his hand over her forehead. God, she felt so hot.

"Shit. You're ill. Wake up, baby. Come on, wake up and look at me."

Worry filled him. What the hell did he do? Did he call an ambulance?

Then her eyes opened and she glared up at him. "Go away."

"Can't do that, Rainbow." At least she was awake, even if she was looking at him like he'd kicked her puppy.

"Shoo, bug, shoo." Her hand fluttered through the air as though she was actually trying to shoo him.

Was she serious right now? He would have laughed if he wasn't so worried about her.

"I'm not going to shoo, baby. What are you doing walking around the building when you're so sick, huh?" He took her pulse. It seemed a tad fast to him.

"Stupid Brian. Crusty dick. Hot water," she complained miserably.

He stiffened. "What? What did you say about Brian's dick?" And how would she know anything about his dick?

"It's crusty, and he wanted me to suck it. But I said no! I am in charge of my body now and I'm not sucking anyone's dick ever again."

"Well, now, that's a shame," he muttered without any humor. "Did someone make you suck dick before?"

He really didn't know anything about her. He was now thinking that might have been a mistake.

"Not literalably... litteraty... what am I trying to say?"

"Literally?" he suggested.

"I dunno. I wanna sleep now."

"You can't sleep out here, Rainbow."

"Why not? Why are you hating on the place I want to sleep?"

His lips twitched. "I'm not hating on the place you want to sleep."

"Yeah, you're being a real downer. Just shoo, little fly, shoo."

"I'm going to forgive you for telling me to shoo like a fly because you are obviously sick. But you won't be shooing me again."

She cracked an eye open, looked straight at him, and said, "shoo."

This brat.

She was definitely headed toward a spanking.

"Right, come on, time you were in bed. Before your mouth gets you into trouble."

"I can't."

"Why not?"

She opened both her eyes. "Isn't it obvious? My legs have stopped working."

He shook his head at her dramatics. He bet she'd be horrified if she remembered any of this tomorrow.

"It's good that I'm going to help you then, isn't it?" he said.

"Why would you help me? Why do you care about me?" she asked pitifully.

"Well, why wouldn't I? We're friends, aren't we?" But that sounded wrong. Because he didn't want to be just friends, did he?

Which is why he'd decided to keep his distance. And yet, here she was again. Seemed like the universe kept pushing them together.

"Are we friends?" she asked.

"We're friends." If he said it enough, then he might begin to believe it. He put an arm under her legs and the other around her back, then lifted her against his chest.

"Friends. I don't really have any friends."

"You don't?" Yeah, Aston was going to be really pissed off if she realized what she'd told him while she was mostly out of it.

"Nope. Tooooo risky. Risky. Risky. Have you ever noticed that if you say a word too much that it sounds weird? Maxim. Maxim. Maxim."

"You're right, baby. That does sound weird. Why is it risky to have friends?"

"Who said that?" She stared up at him as he shuffled her weight onto his raised leg so he could hit the elevator button. "You're so handsome."

"Am I?" He stepped into the elevator and it worried him that she didn't even notice.

"Yep. Really sexy. Of course, you're a bit of a dick, too."

He couldn't help but laugh. She always came out with shit that he wasn't expecting. Was there anyone else in the city who would call him a dick?

Well, not to his face. He was certain they did it behind his back. But this slip of a girl . . . she just told him exactly what she thought and be damned the consequences.

"Are we in the elevator?" she asked in a small voice.

"No," he lied.

"We're not?"

"No, baby. We're not."

"Good. I don't like the elevator. If we were in the elevator, I'd have to get mad."

He smiled. "And what happens when you get mad?"

"I cut off ears."

That was ... random.

"Do you?"

"Yeah. Just ask my brother. I cut off a piece of his ear."

"You did?" he asked in shock. Was she having hallucinations?

"Yeah. But he was being a dick."

He shook his head, still smiling, as he stepped out of the elevator onto her floor. She was obviously making stuff up.

It was pretty cute.

Cut off part of her brother's ear because she was mad. Right.

She was like a kitten when she was mad. All hiss, no bite.

When he got to her door, he set her down on her feet, holding her to him.

"Where are your keys, Rainbow?"

"I don't know. Maxim?"

"Yeah?"

"I don't feel so good. I don't like it." She sounded so pitiful.

"I know. I'm going to help you."

"Nobody ever helps me," she said sadly. "Nobody."

"Well, I am, baby." And she was breaking his fucking heart right now. He was so used to her sharp words and cutting looks. That sass that didn't stop. And those secret smiles that could bring him to his knees.

But this sadness ... he couldn't take it.

"Keys, Rainbow. Where are your keys?"

"I don't know. Where are your keys?"

"In my pocket." He started patting her down. No keys.

She wouldn't have . . . reaching out, he turned the door handle.

Fuck.

She hadn't even locked up.

"Rainbow, you forgot to lock your door," he scolded, picking her back up and carrying her into the apartment. He shut the door behind him.

"I locked it."

"No, you didn't."

"But I always lock it. Safety first. Is there someone in here? Is it him?" she whispered.

"Is it who?" he asked.

"That asshole, Brian."

"Why would you think Brian was in here? Aston?" he pressed as she didn't say anything else.

He walked her into her bedroom and, noticing the unmade bed, he set her down on the armchair. Then he kneeled in front of her, grasping her chin.

Shit. Too hot. He needed to get some fever reducer into her and get her back into bed.

"Rainbow?"

"Why do you call me that?"

"That doesn't matter right now. Listen to me. Why would Brian be in your apartment?"

She gasped. "He's in my apartment? Is he here to fix my hot water? I don't have any. And I really want a hot shower. I should have kneed him in the balls. Ew, but I don't want to touch his balls."

"You still don't have any hot water? That fucking bastard."

"Crusty dick."

"What? Rainbow?" he pressed. Why was she talking about his dick? "Did Brian do something to you?"

"Said if I wanted him to do anything, I had to do something for him. But I am not touching his crusty dick."

Fury filled him. "You certainly won't be. Don't worry about Brian. I'll take care of him." He wouldn't even breathe the same air as Aston anymore.

She gasped. "Will you cut it off?"

"What?" he asked, distracted. He'd been thinking of all the ways he could make that bastard's life miserable.

"His dick."

"What! No." Mainly because he didn't want to go near that appendage. "But you won't have to deal with him again, I promise you that."

"You're so good to me, Maxy-Moo." She patted his cheek.

Good Lord. "You're welcome. But don't call me that." His brothers would just love that nickname.

"Okie-dokie, Maxy-Moo."

She wouldn't remember this tomorrow. He hoped.

"Do you have other sheets, Rainbow?"

"Yeah."

That was all she said. Yeah.

Shaking his head, he glanced at her as she slumped in the chair.

Fuck. How sick was she?

"I should call the doctor."

"Why?" she asked tiredly.

"Because you're sick."

She snorted. "Been worse than this, Maxy-Moo, never been to the doctor."

He didn't like the sound of that. Who was taking care of her before? And why hadn't they done a better job?

"Do you have some medicine? A First-Aid kit? Thermometer?"

"Uh-huh."

He sighed. She was being extra helpful today. Instead of prodding her for more information, he gave her a stern look. "Stay there."

She sent him a half-hearted salute. Damn, she was a brat.

But a cute one at that. Her hair was a tangled mess and she had to be running a fever.

Walking away, he entered her bathroom and searched through the cabinets until he found everything he needed.

Then he grabbed some clean sheets from the linen cupboard.

Only when he got back to the bedroom . . . she wasn't fucking there.

"You have got to be kidding me," he muttered.

She couldn't have gone far, right? He searched the living area and kitchen, then returned to the bathroom and bedroom.

She wasn't anywhere.

How hard was it to keep track of one small person?

"Rainbow? Aston, where are you?" Alarm started to fill him. So he moved toward the front door and opened it, looking up and down the hallway, where he spotted her near the stairs. She was slumped against the wall.

Fucking hell.

He ran toward her, worry flooding him. "What the hell do you think you're doing?"

Right. That could have come out in a softer tone.

She looked up at him, tears filling her eyes, and he felt like a complete ass. He hadn't meant to snap at her. He'd just been worried.

"I'm sorry."

"Hey, it's all right. Although I did tell you to stay put."

"I don't want to be a hassle."

"You aren't a hassle," he soothed, cursing himself as she sniffled. What the fuck was he supposed to do now?

Maxim had to admit that most things came easily to him. He might have lived in his brothers' shadows when he was younger and might have been ignored by his father. But in a way that had been easier than having his father's full attention.

Nothing good had ever come from that bastard paying attention to you.

However, he'd always been able to charm his way into and out of trouble. Women always approached him, he didn't have to pursue them. And he'd never had any issues getting people to do what he wanted.

Except for her.

He'd never felt the need to protect and care for someone like he did her . . . and frankly, that scared the shit out of him. His feelings for her were far more intense than anything he'd ever felt before.

And you need to just keep it friendly, remember?

You aren't looking for anything more.

However this stubborn brat needed to learn that when he told her to do something, she should do it.

"You aren't a fucking hassle," he told her as he swept her up into his arms. "And I ought to spank your ass for calling yourself one."

"That's not very nice."

"Never claimed to be nice."

"That's good. Because you aren't."

He had to grin. "You're always sassing me."

"I am not."

"Yeah, baby. You are. And you need to learn to stay where you're put."

She huffed a breath as he carried her into her apartment. "I do not."

"Yeah. You do. I told you to wait for me, and then I found you wandering off down the hallway. What did you think you were doing?" He set her down on the chair again, waiting a moment to see if she'd try to move. But she just laid her head back, closing her eyes.

"Thirsty."

"I'll get you a drink. You will not move, understand me?" He made his voice as stern as he could.

"You got it, Maxy-Moo."

Crap.

This time, she only got as far as the bed before he was back.

He sighed. "What am I going to do with you, Aston?"

"I dunno. You can yell at me if you want. I'm used to that."

What the fuck?

"Who the fuck yells at you?"

She winced. "You just did."

Crap. Fuck. "I'm sorry, baby. I didn't mean to yell." He directed her gently back to the chair.

"I wanna lie down again. Please."

The begging tone in her voice actually hurt him. He didn't like to hear her begging.

Well, not unless she wanted to beg him to kiss her or touch her or fuck her.

Mind off that.

She's your friend.

But what if he wanted more than that? Otherwise, why was he still here? Why could he not stop thinking about her?

Fuck.

He had to think about this. She wasn't the type of girl who should get mixed up with him and his family.

But Victor shielded Gracen from their world. However, Victor was built like a tank and a scary fucker. How could Maxim keep her safe?

"I know you do, Rainbow. But I need to change the sheets. They're dirty."

"It's okay. I've slept in worse places."

What the fuck? What worse places? What the hell had she been through in her life?

"Like where?"

She waved a hand in the air and let out a dismissive noise. "Don't matter. I just wanna sleep. Please."

"Soon," he promised. "I need you to take these pills."

She wrinkled her nose. "I don't do drugs."

"That's good to know," he soothed. "But these are just fever reducers. They'll help you feel better."

"Promise?"

The vulnerability in her voice was killing him.

"I promise. I wouldn't lie to you." He winced at those words. "Not about that anyway. And I'll try not to lie about anything else."

"It's okay. I know all about lies. Lies and secrets."

"Do you?" Should he push her to tell him?

She'd hate you if you did. And telling yourself it's because you're worried won't make her less mad.

"Everyone lies and has secrets, right? You do too. I know you do."

She wasn't wrong.

"Take these, Rainbow. I'm not trying to drug you."

She swallowed them, sipping on the water as he held the glass up for her.

"Pills are yuck. Can I tell you a secret?"

"I guess," he said as he took her temperature. 102. Crap.

Hopefully, the medicine kicked in quickly. Turning, Maxim started to strip her bed.

"I buy gummy vitamins."

After a pause, he looked over at her. Huh? What did that have to do with anything?

Wait . . . was that her big secret? He bit his lip as he shook his head.

"Gummy vitamins, huh?"

"Yeah. I like them. It's the only way I remember to take my vitamins. Do you take big boy vitamins?"

His mouth dropped open. Big boy vitamins? Was she for real right now?

"I don't take vitamins," he said in a choked voice. "But if I did, I'd definitely take big boy vitamins." Fuck. Had he really just said that?

She flicked a finger through the air. "You should take vitamins, Maxy-Moo. Make you big and strong. Keep the bugs from getting you."

He wasn't going to point out the obvious. That they hadn't helped stop her from getting ill.

He finished making her bed and then came back over to her. Lord, she looked miserable.

His poor girl.

No. Not yours, you idiot.

Kneeling, he removed her shoes. "Need to get you out of your clothes."

"I think you're supposed to buy me a drink first or something," she muttered.

He paused and stared up at her incredulously. "Did you just make a joke?"

"Rude. I know how to joke. Some people think I'm very funny."

"Who are these people? Your mom and dad?"

She tensed, and he wasn't sure why.

"No. Not them. You're right. No one thinks I'm funny."

Fuck. He really was an asshole. Now, he'd made her feel bad when he'd just been teasing.

"Rainbow? I think you're funny."

She wrinkled her nose. "Funny looking, I bet." She attempted to smile, but there was this wary look oh her face, as though she was used to people making fun of her.

"Baby, no. You're beautiful."

She huffed out a breath. "Not even on a good day. Certainly not today. Maxim?"

"Yeah?"

"I don't feel so good."

He got her to the bathroom just in time before she started vomiting. Then shivering.

Yeah, he was definitely getting a doctor here.

9

She felt like crap.

Complete and utter crap.

"Shoot," she muttered as she rolled over in bed. Her head was thumping and her body felt as though she'd slid down a hill and hit every rock along the way.

Ouch. Everything was ouch.

What day was it? What time was it?

She reached for her phone on the nightstand. It looked to be evening outside. But her memories were kind of fuzzy.

An image of Maxim Malone stripping her off and putting her to bed filled her head.

Now she knew she was losing her mind. Because there was no way that would ever happen.

Thankfully, her phone was on her nightstand. And it was plugged in. She must have done that before she started having delusions about Maxim.

Then she squinted at the time . . . and the date.

Holy crap.

Monday evening. How could it be Monday evening?

She had two missed calls from her boss. Crap. Shoot.

She called him back. It went to voicemail so she left a message explaining what had happened and that she'd be back at work tomorrow.

Slumping back on the pillows, she tried to get her brain to work. She remembered feeling horrid and getting in the shower only to find there was no hot water. Fuck. Had she gone to talk to the apartment building manager?

Great. She was never getting a hot shower again.

And then . . . her next memory was of Maxim carrying her to her bedroom. There had been another man here too, she was pretty sure.

Why?

All she got was a calm voice and cool hands. Someone saying that she needed to keep hydrated and to rest.

And . . . oh fudge.

Had she vomited? Had Maxim held back her hair while she'd vomited?

No, no, no.

That hadn't happened.

She smothered the whimper that wanted to escape and sat up. The drink bottle by her bed was empty, so she decided to refill it and get some painkillers for her head.

As she walked through the living area to get to the kitchen, she came to a stop.

A man was lying on the sofa in her living room.

Not just any man . . . Maxim Malone.

Dressed in a wrinkled white shirt and dark pants, he looked tired and delicious. How could someone still look so sexy when they were so wrinkled and exhausted?

"Maxim?" she asked before thinking better of it.

He shot up and she let out a squeal, unable to stop herself. The water bottle dropped to the floor as she turned around.

What was she thinking? She looked terrible! What if her hair was a giant mess? Or she had stains on her . . . on her T-shirt. Was she really just wearing a T-shirt? That barely covered her panties.

Oh crap.

Had he seen her panties?

Damn it. Double damn it.

She couldn't remember the last time anyone had seen her panties. Okay, it seemed a silly thing to focus on . . . but most of the time, she tried to keep herself covered up. She wore conservative clothes and tried to make herself seem invisible.

Nothing to look at here. Glance away. Forget me.

But underneath that armor that she needed . . . well, she might show more of herself. Because all of her panties were sexy in one way or another. Satin and lace. Silky. They had either bows or cut-outs, and all of them were in bright colors.

They were only for her . . . but they made her feel happy.

They made her feel like she hadn't lost all of herself, even when she felt like she didn't know who she was anymore.

"Rainbow? What are you doing up?" he asked in a sleep-roughened voice. It wasn't that late at night. How come he was so tired?

Maybe because he's been taking care of you for over twenty-four hours?

Shoot.

"I, um, I just . . . I didn't realize you were here!" she managed to get out. "I will, uh . . . fudge!"

"What's wrong? Are you feeling ill again? What do you need?"

"I need to get dressed! I'm not really dressed to receive visitors!"

There were a few beats of silence before he let out a low bark of laughter. "Dressed to receive visitors?"

She felt something hot and solid at her back and knew he was standing there. It took everything in her not to melt back into him. To let him take her weight. She was already feeling worn out just from standing there for a few moments.

This was ridiculous.

"Uh-huh."

"That's cute, Rainbow. And you're right, you're not. You shouldn't ever wear just this around visitors. But I'm not a visitor." He was talking close to her ear, and she had to work hard to control a shiver.

"What are you then?"

"I'm a friend."

A friend. Right. That was . . . good. That should be what she wanted. Nothing more.

Just friends.

Then why did a stab of disappointment hit her?

Perhaps because you're an idiot. You can't have anything more. Hell, having him as a friend is risky enough.

Get your head on straight.

"I just need to go find my, uh, robe."

"All right. You do that. And I'll heat you up some soup."

"I'm not hungry," she protested.

"Tough."

Aston turned toward him, raising her eyebrows at his statement, but he was already moving away from her toward the kitchen. She thought about arguing . . . but why?

Why get upset at someone heating her up some soup? It wasn't like she'd had anyone in her life look after her.

Ever.

And even if he was just here as a friend . . . even if he never did anything else like this again, well, he'd done more to help her than anyone else in her life.

And wasn't that depressing?

"Go put your robe on, Aston. And use the bathroom."

Her mouth gaped open. Use the bathroom? Was he serious? Who was he to tell her to use the bathroom? She didn't need to pee ... actually, wait a minute.

She really did.

Darn it. She stomped away ... okay, let's face it, she stumbled away. After grabbing her old, worn robe, she made her way to the bathroom.

A squeak of fright left her mouth as she stared at herself in the mirror.

Holy. Crap. Balls.

She looked terrible. Her hair was a mess around her face. A very pale face with sunken eyes. Drat.

And now that she thought about it, she really needed to brush her teeth.

After peeing, she cleaned herself up as well as she could.

She really needed a shower.

Was it too much to ask to have some hot water?

A knock on the door made her jump. "Yes?"

"Come out and eat your soup, Rainbow."

He was being even bossier than before.

But she didn't keep him waiting. She owed him more than she could express. And she wasn't sure how to pay him back. It didn't feel right to owe him.

Opening the door, she kept her gaze down as she shuffled out of the bathroom. Embarrassed, she headed into the living room. There, she saw a bowl of chicken noodle soup along with some dry crackers and a Gatorade sitting on the coffee table.

"Whose robe is that?" he asked.

Huh? That wasn't a question she was expecting?

"Um, mine. Did you think I stole it?"

"If you stole a robe, I'd hope you'd steal a better one," he countered, sitting on an armchair across from her.

"Hey! I like this robe. It's soft."

"It's a man's robe."

She shrugged. Yeah, it was. It was too big, but it was nice and soft and she liked it. She sent a glare his way before she remembered she was trying not to look at him. "I like it."

"I'm going to get you something better."

"You are not!" Another glare, then she glanced away. Fuck. This was ridiculous. "I like this one."

"I don't."

"What is wrong with you?" she asked.

He ran his hand over his face with a tired sigh.

Stupid question, Aston. What's wrong with him is that he had to stay here and take care of you because you couldn't take care of yourself. And he probably got no sleep.

He was tired and grumpy, and he had every right to feel that way.

Had she taken advantage of him? She had to right the scales.

"Your couch is fucking uncomfortable."

She winced, drawing in on herself as she stirred the soup.

Yeah, she knew the couch sucked. She'd slept on it a few times when she'd nodded off while watching television. There was this spring that seemed to dig right into the middle of your back.

"I know, sorry."

She hadn't asked him to stay . . . but it was really decent of him to look after her.

"Nothing to be sorry about. I just . . . didn't get much sleep. So I might be slightly grouchy."

"I thought you didn't sleep much anyway."

"I'm getting older, baby girl. Got to sleep sometimes."

She looked up at him as he winked, then away again. Only this time, her face grew hot. A wink from Maxim Malone . . . hell, it was like someone running a thumb along her lips or kissing her neck.

It made a hot rush of pleasure fill her.

"What's wrong?" he asked.

"Nothing. I just . . . I really appreciate you staying. You didn't have to. I would have been okay. You didn't have to try to sleep on my uncomfortable couch or change my sheets or make me food."

"I wasn't going to leave you while you were sick, Rainbow." He sounded affronted.

"Well, thank you. I appreciate it. I owe you big time."

He sighed. "Aston, look at me."

She flicked her gaze up and away.

"Aston," he said in a firmer voice that made her shiver in reaction. Crap. What was it about that voice that just did it for her? That made her want to do whatever he told her?

She'd promised herself when she left *them* that she would never have to do anything she didn't want to.

Only . . . that was the difference, wasn't it? With Maxim, she wanted to do whatever he asked of her.

Anything. Everything.

Which was more than a little terrifying.

"Baby, why aren't you looking at me?"

"You held my hair back while I puked. And helped me change my clothes. And carried me into bed."

He made a strangled noise. "I went too far? I made you uncomfortable?"

Her head snapped up so fast that the room around her spun. She held a hand to her temple. "No, that's not what I meant!"

He stood and she dropped her head again.

Great. Now, he was leaving. She got it. Really, she did.

Didn't mean it didn't hurt less.

But then he suddenly returned, moving the food aside to sit on the coffee table in front of her. He held his hand out, showing her the painkillers in his palm.

"Take them. Your head hurts."

"That obvious, huh?"

"Only a little bit. Drink now." He held up the electrolyte drink. "You need to drink all of this and eat some food, understand?"

"I'll try." She swallowed the pills down.

Reaching out, he lightly grasped her chin, tilting it back. She attempted to keep her eyes down, but he held her chin there until she raised her eyes up to look at him.

"That's better. Are you upset with me for helping you?"

"I can't . . . no. You helped me. Why would I be upset about that?"

"Because I stayed in your apartment. Got you undressed. Called a doctor. Saw you while you were vulnerable and weak."

Shoot. Yeah. There was all that. But still . . .

"It would be unfair of me to be upset at you when you were looking after me."

"So if you're not mad at me and I didn't upset you, then why are you so against looking at me?"

"I just . . . don't know how to repay you. And I feel bad that you stayed the night on that horrible couch and felt obligated to take care of me—"

"Whoa, I'm going to stop you right there. I know you don't know me that well, but there is something you should know. I never do anything that I don't want to do. *Ever.* Understand me? I didn't feel obliged. I also didn't feel sorry for you or whatever shit is going through your head. Got me?"

She felt lighter.

But she still didn't understand.

"Then why? Why help me?"

"Because we're friends, silly girl. And you're worth helping. You deserve someone to help you. You don't have to do it all alone, Aston."

What was he talking about? He didn't know about her life before now, so it wasn't that.

"I know that."

"Do you?" he pressed. "Because someone else would just say thank you. They'd expect some decency from a friend who saw them in need. They wouldn't expect me to have just walked away. Would you have done that? Left me sick and sleeping on a bench in the foyer? Or walking in the rain, sopping wet and hunched over some groceries? Or let me freak out in an elevator without helping me?"

Would she?

Of course not.

"No."

"So why are you so shocked that I would? Have I made that bad of an impression on you?"

Well . . . crap, no. She couldn't even lie. Maybe she used to think of him as a playboy who spent his time partying and fucking. But she knew better. And she really shouldn't ever judge a book by its cover.

"No. You've been nothing but, well, I won't say kind . . ."

He grinned. "I'm your knight in shining armor. Admit it."

"What?"

"Yep. I'm totally a hero. Your hero. This might be where you swoon in my arms. But you already did that."

"I did not!" This guy.

"You sure did. You swooned. I'm your hero. Admit it."

"You've got an ego the size of my ass. That's all I'll admit."

Instead of firing back with a grin, he looked serious. "The size of your ass?"

Crap. She shouldn't have said that. Or what came next. "Yep, it needs a sign saying 'wide load' so people can get out of the way."

"Is that what you think about your ass?" he asked in a low voice.

Uh-oh. Warning. Stop.

But she couldn't exactly deny thinking it. She was trying so hard not to lie. At least not about anything trivial. The big things in her life . . . those things she couldn't tell anyone about, so yeah, she had to lie about them.

However, this wasn't one of those things.

"I don't like that."

She stared at him in surprise.

He gave her a stern look. "Don't do it."

"Tease you about your ego?"

"Refer to your bottom as a wide load."

Why would he care what she said about her ass? It was her bottom.

"Do you understand me?" he pressed.

"You're right. You do get cranky when you're tired."

"I didn't say cranky, Rainbow. I said, grouchy. And I'm upset that you're saying bad things about yourself."

Why would that upset him? She still didn't understand.

"Christ," he muttered. "You're killing me here."

"What did I do?"

"You're looking at me like you have no clue why I'm saying this."

Because she didn't. Then again, she wasn't exactly thinking with a fully functioning brain. It was still muddled from her fever. Her tummy chose that moment to rumble as she slumped back on the sofa.

"Okay, this isn't the time for this sort of conversation. You need to eat and go back to bed."

She couldn't believe he was still here. That he hadn't run the moment she'd woken up. There was no way that he actually wanted to be here with her. Especially not when she was sick.

"I'll reheat the soup," he said.

"No, it's fine."

He frowned at her. "You can't eat cold soup, Aston."

She shrugged. "Eh, I've eaten worse."

He stared at her for a long moment. It was just the truth.

"You should have stayed away from me."

"What?" His head reared back. "What do you mean?"

"I might be contagious. What if I gave you my flu?" The flu that she was certain had come from looking after the kids next door.

When was she going to learn to say no?

But she was trying to be a better person. She had things she needed to atone for. So perhaps being sick was just part of that atonement.

That sounded kind of stupid to her, though.

Lord, she didn't know. She really just wanted to have some soup and go back to bed. She hadn't slept this much in a long time. Maybe her body was trying to play catch up.

"I don't care if you make me sick, Rainbow," he said tiredly. "I just want you to be okay."

His words warmed her, even as she told herself not to let them fill her with crazy thoughts.

She sucked in a breath. "You know what?"

"What?"

"You don't suck."

He grinned at her. "I don't?"

"Nope."

"That's high praise indeed."

"I'd tell you not to let it go to your head . . . but I already feel like you have."

He let out a low chuckle. And she was glad she'd broken the moment. If this was all she'd ever have with this man . . . well, it would be enough.

It had to be.

10

Maxim longed to take her into his arms.

To tell her that she wasn't a bother, that it was his privilege to take care of her.

But that would be too intense.

So he was grateful that she'd managed to break the strange mood between them since she'd woken up.

"I'm going to reheat your soup and you'll eat it."

"Aye-aye, Captain." She gave him a sassy salute. A bit more co-ordinated than she had been last night.

Fuck, was it only just over twenty-four hours ago that he'd been carrying her to bed?

It had been a long twenty-four hours, filled with him worrying over her. While he'd waited for the doctor to arrive, he'd sat in her bedroom and watched over her, concerned that she might vomit and choke on it.

He wasn't used to taking care of someone else. And that kind of shamed him. All his life, he'd been taken care of. Even when he was older, someone else had always taken responsibility. Usually Regent.

While Maxim had worried over his younger sister and would have done anything for her, he hadn't really looked after her. But she'd always seemed to prefer Regent anyway.

And why wouldn't she? Regent was the biggest caretaker of them all. Just really overprotective with it. To the point where Maxim knew if he hadn't moved out, they would have had issues. He could appreciate his brother, but he was his own man and didn't need to be smothered.

However, last night, Aston had needed him. Really needed him. Just him. And yeah, it was a boost to his ego. Maybe she believed his ego didn't need it. But he couldn't deny it had made him feel a hundred feet tall.

Apparently, he enjoyed being needed.

He liked being a hero.

And he'd had no idea before now.

As he was waiting for the soup to heat, he glanced over at her. She looked a lot better. Still, he should take her temperature and get her back into bed.

Fuck. He really didn't want another night on that couch, though. It was a nightmare. The armchair was more comfortable.

Was she well enough to be on her own?

Did he want to leave her?

No. Not really.

His phone buzzed and he drew it out. Victor.

VICTOR: *We found who delivered those packages. At the warehouse.*

FUCK. He frowned. He'd received enough of these messages to understand the hidden message.

They'd found the person who'd been supplying Mixology at

Glory the other night and had him at one of the warehouses. He'd need to call Victor and find out where.

But could he leave Aston?

You have to. This is about business. Your business.

And you could probably do with some space.

Yeah. He couldn't deny that.

Maxim: *One hour.*

There was no reply. But he wasn't expecting one. Victor wasn't big on talking. Nope, he was more a man of action.

Pouring out some soup, he walked over with the bowl.

"Aston?"

She startled, then gave him a small smile. Fuck. He realized then that she didn't smile a lot . . . but when she did, well, it was like the sun coming out after a storm.

It made him feel lighter and brighter.

Like he was a thousand feet tall and could do anything.

And that feeling was addictive.

"Sorry, I was daydreaming, I guess. Thank you so much for the soup. It was really nice of you." She was staring at the soup like he was bringing her a bowl of gold.

"You don't have to thank me again."

She raised her eyebrows, probably wondering why he sounded so grumpy.

"It's just soup, Rainbow. It was barely any bother at all."

Fuck, he felt like shit as her shoulders deflated. "Oh, well, I still thought it was nice. Can't remember the last time anyone made me food other than when you made me soup the other night."

Fuck. She was definitely killing him.

"I have to go," he said abruptly.

She gave him a surprised look before her face went blank in that way that he hated.

He could admit to himself that he often riled her up just to get her to lose that blank look.

Maybe not exactly mature of him . . . but he preferred her fiery to closed off.

"Of course. I've held you up long enough. Did you have to take time off work?" She winced.

He shook his head. "No. The club is closed Sundays and Mondays. It's all good. But I have a few things I need to do." However, he still didn't move. He couldn't seem to leave her.

This was ridiculous.

Friend. She was a friend.

"Of course. Thank you so much. I owe you big time."

"You don't owe me shit, baby girl." Fuck. Stop calling her that. "All I want is for you to rest and get better. All right?"

"I'll be spending the rest of the night laying around."

"And tomorrow."

"Tomorrow?" she asked innocently.

"Yes. Stay home tomorrow. No work."

She sighed. "You let a man make you soup and suddenly he thinks he's the boss."

He smirked. "Baby, I am the boss. All the time. And you're staying home tomorrow. You're not well enough to go to work."

She rolled her eyes. "So you think."

"So I know. I find you went to work and you'll be in trouble." He didn't make threats he didn't mean. But even he knew he didn't have much right to punish her.

You could . . . if you claimed her.

Fuck. Someone like Aston wouldn't be right for him. She was too sweet and innocent. She deserved her normal life.

Not to get messed up in his shit.

It wouldn't be fair to her.

"What are you going to do?" she challenged.

"I'll think of something. You've been warned. Now, give me your phone number so I can put it in my phone."

He deliberately didn't ask. He'd learned a long time ago that you didn't get what you wanted in life by asking. Maybe that made him an asshole in some people's eyes, but he didn't care.

She eyed him.

"Friends share their phone numbers, don't they? And that's what we are, right?"

"Are we? Because I'm pretty sure that friends don't threaten their friends."

"Course they do. If their friend is being an idiot, they'll do what they need to in order to put them on the right path."

She opened her mouth, then closed it.

"No comeback, Rainbow?"

"There are so many things wrong with that statement. I don't even know where to start. Right path." She snorted.

"Phone number, Aston. I'm not leaving without it." And he'd be checking that she gave him the correct number. She was a tricky little thing.

She reluctantly gave him her number. He texted her a message and heard her phone beep. Good.

"I'm going to call you tomorrow. You text me if you need anything, understand?"

"I will."

No, she wouldn't, and they both knew that. He'd had some groceries delivered today, so at least she wouldn't starve if she was sick for a few days.

Still, he lingered over her.

Fuck. He had to leave.

Her face softened as she stared up at him. No doubt he looked fucking confused.

"Maxim, you've done your time. Now go."

He rolled his eyes. "I haven't been in prison."

"Some people would say that spending time with me feels like being in jail."

She grinned up at him, but he didn't like that. Not at all.

"No talking about yourself like that."

"It's called making a joke."

"I don't find it funny when you say bad things about yourself, Aston." He made certain that his voice was stern.

She bit her lip, looking unsure.

Without thought, he moved forward and removed her lip from between her teeth. "Don't be upset. Just don't do that, all right? As your friend, it's up to me to make sure that you treat yourself well."

Then he realized he was still touching her, his fingers on her chin, and he moved his hand away.

"I have to go. Lock the door behind me. Be a good girl."

Once he was on the other side of the door, he waited until he heard the lock engage.

Then he slumped against the wall.

Be a good girl? Friends didn't say that to each other, did they?

Friends didn't notice that their friends wore sexy as fuck panties. And had smooth, firm thighs.

Or soft, warm lips.

Or the sweetest little dimple when they smiled.

Nope. Friends didn't do that.

Lord. He was so fucked.

~

OVER AN HOUR LATER, he pulled up to the warehouse that Victor had directed him to. One of Regent's men was outside, waiting for him.

"Inside," Logan said. "Down below."

Maxim nodded. After dragging himself away from Aston, he'd quickly showered and changed, putting on some old dark clothing.

He walked into the warehouse, over to where he knew the secret trap-door that led down to the basement was.

That was where he found Victor and Regent. That surprised him, as he hadn't expected his oldest brother to be here.

"You only left one guy on the door?" he asked.

Regent raised his eyebrows. "There are more out there."

Good. He nodded.

Victor turned to give him a surprised look. "You've never worried about Regent's protection before."

No, that was Victor's job and Jose's, Regent's bodyguard, who was standing off to the side.

"Just making sure he's safe. There a problem with that?"

"No problem," Regent drawled. "Glad you could make it, brother."

"I came as quickly as I could."

They were all looking at him like he'd grown a second head. Was it so strange that he was worried about Regent's protection? There were plenty of people who would love to take out Regent Malone.

And he wasn't late because he'd been fucking around.

He turned away from their curious glances and looked at the guy hanging by his wrists from a chain attached to a hook on the ceiling.

The guy groaned. He was in a bad shape.

"You started without me?" he asked.

"I didn't realize you wanted a piece of interrogating him," Victor replied.

Because he never had before. But this was personal.

"He sold this shit at Glory. I have the right to interrogate him."

Regent nodded slowly. "That you do. He hasn't given us anything concrete yet. Feel free to take a turn though."

With a nod, he stepped toward the guy. He was young, and while Maxim didn't exactly want to look at him, he forced himself to study his face. It took him a moment to recognize him, mainly because his face was swollen and bruised.

"It's Jeremy."

"You know him?" Regent asked.

"Yeah, he used to work for me. Fired him when he stopped turning up." He pulled his fist back and slammed it into his stomach.

He smacked his fist into the other man's balls. Jeremy let out a choked cry that would have had Maxim's own balls shriveling in sympathy. If he wasn't so mad at himself for banning him from Glory.

Then he wouldn't have been selling that shit in his club.

And perhaps that poor guy, whose Regent's cleaning crew had dumped across the other side of town, would still be alive.

And Maxim wouldn't be worrying that Stephanie would crack and go to the cops on him. It wasn't like they didn't have cops on their payroll to take care of shit like that, but he didn't want to fire the girl or run her out of town.

Which is what would happen if she blabbed.

Fucking Jeremy.

He landed another jab to his dick.

Jeremy started gagging, and Maxim backed up quickly before he puked. As soon as he was finished throwing up, Maxim stepped back in until Victor pulled him away.

He was heaving for breath, angry at everything this asshole had done.

"Let me finish, brother," Victor said in a calm voice.

He glanced around, surprised to see that Jose had left. Regent gestured to him.

Fine. Fuck.

He headed over to his oldest brother. The one that had been more of a father to him than their father ever had.

"Everything all right?" Regent asked, pulling out a cigarette. He'd quit a long time ago, around the time that Lottie had been found. They all knew he'd stopped for her. Because he didn't want to chance her taking in his secondhand smoke. But sometime after she left, he'd started up again.

Was the stress getting to him?

"Want one?"

Maxim shook his head. Cigarettes had never been his vice. Sometimes, he was surprised that Regent let himself have a weakness.

"What's going on?"

"Nothing. I'm just pissed that guy died in one of my clubs," he explained. "From drugs, this asshat was selling."

Regent nodded. "I get it. But if we don't find out who is supplying this shit, then it's likely to happen again. And there's no way of stopping it until we get to the source."

"I know."

"So there's no use blaming yourself for shit you can't control."

Maxim eyed him incredulously. "Do you ever take your own advice?" Because his brother was the epitome of a control freak. If you looked that term up in the dictionary there would be a picture of Regent Malone.

Regent shook his head. "I don't blame myself for things that are out of my control. I just make sure that I control as much as I can in my life."

Yep. Total control freak.

"Tell us who supplied you with the drugs." Victor was doing

something to Jeremy that had him making pained, guttural groans.

Fuck.

He didn't have a weak stomach, but those noises weren't something he ever wanted to hear again.

Victor was whispering something in Jeremy's ear. Then Jeremy said something back. Something he couldn't hear. He moved closer.

"Did he give you a name?"

"Yeah," Victor said with a sigh. "It's another middleman."

Disappointment filled him. He'd hoped they'd have a name tonight.

"It's a lead," Regent said, patting his back. "The supplier is using layers to protect himself. But we'll work our way back. We have to be careful, though. Those low down the chain won't be missed, but someone higher up might be."

"Yeah, I need to send men to scope this guy out," Victor said. "Then bring him in. I have this."

Maxim felt helpless. "What can I do?"

"Keep your staff watching for this stuff being distributed," Regent said.

That was it? He wanted to do more. But he got that he had little experience in this side of the business.

"You're helping," Regent told him. "We'll get the bastard pushing these drugs in our town. And then we'll make him wish he'd never been born."

11

I wish you'd never been born.

Those words sang through her brain. Like a Ping-Pong ball firing around her head, they wouldn't stop.

I wish you'd never been born.

You were a mistake.

Should have smothered you as a baby.

Stop! Just stop.

Aston paused and took a deep breath in, letting it out slowly. She probably shouldn't be back at work. Exhaustion had her moving slowly and her brain didn't want to function.

Plus, she was pretty sure she still had a slight fever. She felt her forehead.

Darn it.

Yeah, she probably should have stayed at home. But the walls had felt like they were closing in on her, especially after her nightmare.

You are my greatest regret.

Stop it! Stop it!

This was ridiculous. She'd gotten away from them. They couldn't hurt her anymore.

Only you can let them affect you. So just push it aside and get on with living your life the way you want to.

"Wow, you look like shit."

She glanced up at Gretchen as she pulled a face, staring down at her. "Tell me what you really think."

"I just did."

She sighed. Maxim would have understood the sarcasm. He might have fired back at her.

Darn it. Was she missing him? Why would she be missing him?

Because you like him. He was nice to you.

She was not going to fall for the first man who was nice to her.

"You're not contagious, are you?"

Shoot. She hoped not. She hadn't thought about that. How irresponsible was that?

"I don't think so." But now, the guilt was overloading her.

Her phone buzzed and she drew it out of her handbag, wondering who it could be. Maxim had somehow managed to get Brian to fix the hot water in her apartment so she could shower this morning.

It had felt like the best shower of her life.

PITB: *Where are you? I'm outside your apartment and you're not coming to the door.*

PITB: *You better be in the shower or on the toilet and not at work.*

PITB: *Aston . . . answer me. Now.*

. . .

Shoot. She'd somehow missed the first two messages. What was he doing outside her apartment?

And yes, she'd entered him in her phone as PITB: Pain-in-the-butt.

"Aston? Are you paying attention to me?" Gretchen whined.

She winced, that noise was not doing her head any favors.

Aston: *I'm in the bathroom.*
PITB: *No, you're not.*
Aston: *How do you know? I could be on the toilet.*

Why did she say that? Giant dork.

"Aston! Are we going to the club this weekend?" Gretchen demanded.

"Huh?" She glanced up at Gretchen, whose face was growing red. Uh-oh. Gretchen didn't like to be ignored. And when she lost her temper . . . well, Aston didn't want to be on the receiving end.

"Of course we're going," she said quickly.

What the heck had she just agreed to? Was she really going to go to a club with Gretchen?

But the other woman's face lost that reddish-purple tinge and Aston started breathing easier.

"Good. I'll pick you up at ten on Friday night. Make sure you're club appropriate."

Ten? Jeez, that was late. And what was club-appropriate? She stared down at her long-sleeved shirt with its high neck and at her long skirt that went down to her ankles.

She didn't think she owned anything club appropriate. Crap. Gretchen walked past with a swish, her perfume clinging to the air. Aston's nose twitched, her headache growing.

Yeah. Coming to work hadn't been her brightest idea. Aston glanced down at her messages, seeing that she'd missed several more from Maxim.

PITB: *I know because I'm in your apartment.*
PITB: *Newsflash, you're not in your bathroom.*
PITB: *You're also in big trouble, Rainbow.*

She was not turned on by that. In fact, she was outraged. He had no right to dictate what she did. Or scold her.

Except . . . he was doing it because he was worried about her. She couldn't think of any other reason why he might care.

So it wouldn't be very nice of her to get angry over him caring.

Shoot.

She went to write back an apology when the rest of what he'd said hit her.

He was in her apartment?

She hit the call number and he answered immediately, his voice silky smooth.

Aston should have realized that was a dangerous sign. But she was used to men who yelled and got violent when they were angry.

"Where are you, Rainbow?" he asked.

"Where am I? Where are you?"

"I told you, I'm in your apartment. Where you should be. Only, you're not here. So where are you?"

"But how are you in my apartment? Oh my God! Did you break the door down? I'm not paying for that. Or dealing with Brian."

"Brian is no longer the building manager. He's been fired."

"What? How?"

"It was a condition the new buyer of this building had. There will be a new building manager in place by tomorrow. But I didn't break in, so you don't have to worry. Are you at work?"

"That still doesn't explain how you got into my apartment," she pointed out, her mind spinning.

A new buyer? She hadn't even known that the building was for sale.

This all sounded rather . . . strange.

"You don't need to worry about that right now," he told her in that oh-so-quiet voice. "What you need to worry about is the trouble you're going to be in once I find you."

Um. Gulp.

"Why am I in trouble?" And why did her butt cheeks tingle? Was it because she was thinking about how he might punish her?

"What did I tell you last night?"

"You mean before you left me?" Shoot. She hadn't meant to sound like she was accusing him. "Look, that doesn't matter—"

"It matters."

"It doesn't matter because I am an adult who makes her own decisions." That would have sounded better if she hadn't had to pause to cough.

"Where. Are. You?"

"Maxim Malone, you're not the boss of me!" Okay, she'd tried to be patient and nice. But she was tired and her head hurt.

"No?"

"No!" She took a calming breath and reminded herself that he was concerned about her.

Remember all those times you would have killed for someone to care about you? To look out for you?

Well, now she had that. Even if he was demanding and thought he was in charge.

"I appreciate all that you've done for me—"

"No."

"No?"

"You're not blowing me off, Rainbow. I don't want your thanks. You can thank me by getting your butt home and into bed where it should be."

"I'm feeling much better."

Liar.

"You think you can lie to me just because I'm not in front of you?"

Drat. She had kind of thought that.

"You can't. I know you feel like shit. I can hear it in your voice. My bet is that you've got a headache and you're exhausted. Plus, you're going to make yourself even sicker if you keep pushing yourself into doing things you're not ready to do yet."

Shoot.

She hated how he made sense.

"You really suck sometimes."

Really mature, Aston.

"Because you know I'm right," he said with amusement. "It's all right, Rainbow. You can rage at me, get upset, and tell me I'm a bossy jerk. I can take it. But you will let me take care of you. Now, are you at work?"

"Yes."

"Where do you work?" he asked.

"You mean you don't know?" That surprised her.

He grunted. "I could find out, but it would be quicker for you to tell me."

Or maybe she just wouldn't tell him.

Except, he had a point. She'd been foolish to come here. But other than yesterday, she'd never missed a day of work and she felt terrible about it.

"I work at Dayton Leeds Construction," she admitted.

"Okay, I know it," he replied. "I'm going to come and pick you up. Tell your boss that you're going home ill."

"I'm here now, though. I should really stay."

"How are you feeling?"

Terrible. However, she didn't want to tell him that.

"Aston."

Crap. She'd promised herself that she wouldn't lie anymore. At least, not if she could help it. And hadn't she already lied when she'd told him she was in her apartment when she wasn't?

Her tummy already felt sick with guilt over that.

"Not so good, I guess."

"Which I'm guessing means you feel terrible. Baby, why'd you go to work?"

"I just don't like to let anyone down."

"You're not letting anyone down by taking time to look after yourself. I'm sure your boss doesn't want you to get ill. Or spread your germs among everyone else."

"I guess you're right." Although he'd seemed slightly annoyed that she hadn't come to work yesterday. However, he had the right to be since she hadn't called in.

"I'm going to come and get you."

"No, you don't have to do that. I know you have better things to do. I'll get myself home."

"How?" he asked.

"Uh, I don't know. The bus?"

"Nope."

"An Uber, then." She didn't really feel like going on the bus anyway. This morning, all the stopping and starting had made her feel nauseous.

"Not happening," he growled. "Just go tell your boss that you're leaving, gather your stuff and wait there for me."

"Maxim," she protested.

"Do as you're told, Rainbow. I'm not very happy with you right now, and you don't want to upset me more, do you?"

No. She guessed not.

And hearing that he wasn't happy with her . . . well, it made her stomach churn even more.

"I'm sorry," she whispered.

"For what?"

"For being a nuisance."

He sighed. "Rainbow, you're not a nuisance. But you have to learn when to accept some help. You don't have to do it all yourself."

But that was the thing . . . she did.

Because no one else was going to help her.

Except Maxim is right now, isn't he?

Shoot.

Fifteen minutes later, she was waiting outside the front of the building. Her hair was in its usual bun, but it felt so tight and her head was aching.

All she wanted was to go home and sleep.

Finally, she saw his car pull up. It was a Mustang and probably cost more than she made in a year. She stepped out toward it, waving her hand so he'd see her. He stopped in front of her.

She couldn't believe she was letting him take her home. Dayton hadn't been all that pleased about her leaving, but Gretchen had sided with her. Which was kind of shocking. She'd convinced her dad that it would be better for Aston to keep her germs out of the office.

So here she was, about to get into the car of the sexiest man she knew.

To her surprise, he exited the car and rounded the hood.

"You don't have to get out," she protested.

He just frowned at her. Then he walked straight to her.

"What are you doing, waiting outside? I would have come inside and gotten you."

"I thought this would be easier for you."

"Damn it, Aston. You're allowed to be selfish sometimes. You're allowed to have other people take care of you."

She stared up at him in surprise. "It's not a big deal."

"It is when you're standing out here, swaying in place and looking half dead."

"Thanks, that was the look I was going for."

"Congrats, you achieved it."

"You're a jerk sometimes."

"Only sometimes? Seems I'm slipping."

She rolled her eyes at him. He opened the passenger door and held her arm as she climbed inside. As though he was worried she wouldn't make it on her own.

She didn't look that bad, did she?

Reaching up, she drew down the visor and checked herself in the mirror. She gulped.

Okay, maybe she really was rocking the half dead look. Putting the visor up, she glanced up at the building and spotted Gretchen staring down at her. She waved, but the other woman didn't wave back.

Perhaps she didn't see her.

That was likely it.

Maxim climbed into the driver's side, looking as gorgeous as always.

He started the car. "Seatbelt." He clicked his into place.

"Huh?"

"Put your seatbelt on, Rainbow."

"Oh, right. Yes."

He waited until she was belted in to take off.

"Your car is so nice. So pretty."

"Pretty? My car isn't pretty, Rainbow," he grumbled.

They stopped at the lights and he put his hand on her forehead. "Fuck. You're fucking hot."

"Thanks. That's better than being half dead."

"I meant that your skin is hot."

"Oh." Motherfudger. She could feel her cheeks heating.

"But you're also hot in looks."

Right. Because he had to say that now. Awkward. Why couldn't there be a giant sinkhole ahead of them? Something that would swallow her whole.

What could she say to distract him? "How did you get into my apartment?"

"I have my ways."

So he wasn't going to tell her.

"Anyone ever tell you that you're irritating?"

"Other than you?" He sent her a sexy grin.

"Yeah."

"Nope," he replied. "Most people find me charming."

"They were lying to you."

He laughed. "Were they?"

"Yep. Bet they told you that you are so lovely."

"And those were lies?" he asked with amusement in his voice.

"All lies. You're a pain in the behind. Total irritation. Bossy. And you don't like to hear the word no."

"You're right. I don't. So you should probably lose that word from your vocabulary when you talk to me."

"Ha."

"You're being awfully rude to the person who went out of his way to pick you up."

Crap.

Guilt flooded her stomach, knotting it tight. "Sorry, you're right. I don't know why, but stuff just comes out of my mouth when I'm around you. I apologize. Thank you for coming to get me. It's really nice that you care. Just ignore me. Maybe it's the fever talking ... urgh, no, that's a cop-out."

"Whoa, hey. I was just teasing you, Rainbow," he told her softly. Reaching over, he placed his hand on hers where it rested on her thigh.

A zing of heat ran through her body, which she knew had nothing to do with her fever.

And everything to do with him.

"You don't need to apologize, all right?"

She nodded. But she still felt terrible.

"Can I tell you something?"

"Sure," she said, unsure of what he was going to say.

"I like when you give me shit. Nobody else in my life would do that except my siblings. It makes me laugh. And I know you're not bullshitting me."

"Oh." That made sense. "So you like when I tell you the truth about your ego getting so big that it will need its own postcode?"

"I have a feeling I'm going to regret telling you that."

She had to grin. She wouldn't give him a hard time. Well, not too much.

And she did feel better. Lighter.

Her eyes drifted closed and she forced herself to open them. Sleeping right now would be rude.

"It's all right, Rainbow. You can go off to sleep. I'll wake you when we get home."

Home.

She wished it really felt like a home. But then, she had never really had one of those so how did she know what she was missing out on?

"I don't want to be rude ..."

"Stop worrying about silly shit," he scolded. "We're friends, aren't we? Friends don't worry about stuff like that. They take care of one another."

"So far, you seem to be doing all the taking care of . . . while I create all the trouble."

"Well, some of us are destined to be troublemakers, while others are angels."

She grinned as her eyes closed. "You're an angel?"

"I am. Thanks for noticing."

A snort escaped her. "More like the devil."

"Well, I am devilishly handsome. Wickedly smart."

"Sinfully self-confident."

"Good one."

She yawned. "That wasn't supposed to be a compliment."

"Wasn't it?"

Aston fought against falling asleep. She should really keep him company since he'd gone out of his way to come and pick her up.

"Go to sleep, baby," he murmured.

Her breathing deepened. And she was sure she imagined the following words.

"Everything is all right. I'll keep you safe."

12

Aston studied at the line outside the nightclub as they approached. They'd had to park two blocks away, which hadn't made Gretchen happy. Although Aston could empathize with her reluctance to walk given the five-inch heel stilettos the other woman was wearing.

"Perhaps we should have come earlier," she suggested as she took in the line that went halfway down the block. Would they even be able to get in?

"Oh, we're not waiting in line. That's for common people."

Aston shot her a look. "That's not very nice." And in case Gretchen wasn't aware, Aston wasn't rolling in money.

"Screw being nice. Aston, you can't be a pushover all your life." Gretchen strode toward the front of the line as Aston stood there, staring after her.

Ouch.

It wasn't that Aston wanted to be a pushover. She was trying to do what was right.

But was Gretchen correct? Did she let people walk all over her? Today, after work, she'd had to tell Eva she couldn't babysit because she was going out. Eva hadn't believed her and accused her of lying to get out of looking after her kids.

But it wasn't Aston's job to take care of her children. Besides, it wouldn't hurt Eva to say thanks every once in a while. Then, they day before yesterday, Mr. Logan had asked for fifty dollars to help cover his rent. She'd given it to him, but she knew she'd never see it again.

Had her endeavor to help people turned her into a pushover? Or had she always been like this? Her brothers and father had taught her that it was better to give in, to let them have whatever they wanted.

Fighting only meant more pain before the inevitable.

But she wasn't under their thumb anymore. They didn't rule her life. And maybe she was letting people take advantage of her.

"Aston, come on!" Gretchen called back from where she was talking to the bouncer at the door.

Aston strode forward, giving everyone in the line a sympathetic smile as they groaned or glared.

She got it. She'd be annoyed too.

There was an audible grumble as the bouncer let them in.

"How did you get us in?" Aston asked, looking around the foyer. Wow, this place was gorgeous. It wasn't done up like a sleazy nightclub but rather a nineteen-twenties club. There was a black and white checked floor and off to the right was a bar with tables and booths done in red velvet set around the room.

"This is the nightclub?"

"No, the club is upstairs," Gretchen said with a scoff. "We need to check our coats." They moved to the coat-checking area, where Gretchen removed hers.

Aston gaped at her.

"Like it?" the other woman asked with a sly grin.

"Oh, um, yep. Sure. It's cute." What there was of it. The

dress was a deep red and silky, so it clung to Gretchen's curves. It stopped just below her ass cheeks and the back had a big dip.

It was pure sex.

Wow. Aston wished she was brave enough to wear something like that. But she wasn't.

She drew off her own coat and handed it over.

Gretchen groaned. "Aston, is that the best you had in your wardrobe?"

Well, no. She'd had to go out after work yesterday to buy this dress. She hadn't had much time to look, so this was the best she could do. It was black, which wasn't her best color since it washed her out even further. But the tiers hid the softness of her tummy and helped lessen the impact of her huge ass. It stopped just below her knees.

"It will do, I guess. Let's go." Gretchen latched onto her arm and dragged her past another bouncer, then up the stairs to the nightclub above.

Holy crap. She was dressed like a nun.

Well, not really. But compared to everyone else in the club, she was the odd one out, not Gretchen.

Great. Her first time in a club and she was going to make a complete dork of herself. Feeling awkward and unsure, she followed Gretchen toward the bar that was in the middle of the room. This one was circular, and the bartenders behind it were busy fielding orders.

The whole place was packed and the vibe was good.

But she felt out of place.

Maybe she should have pretended that she was still ill. She'd ended up going back to work on Wednesday and worked a long day catching up on her work. Then, yesterday after work, she'd gone shopping for this nun's dress.

Which meant she hadn't really seen Maxim much the rest of

the week. But he'd been texting to check in on her. He'd told her he was busy with work stuff.

Would he be here tonight? Even if he was, she wasn't likely to see him.

Gretchen handed her two shots, keeping two for herself. Aston watched as the other woman downed them both quickly.

So . . . it seemed they'd be catching an Uber home.

"Come on! Drink them down! They taste like jam donuts."

Shoot. She wanted to refuse, but what could it hurt? She gulped the first one.

That actually was pretty delicious. After the second one, she set the glass down. Her head was buzzing slightly. She rarely drank alcohol so she was basically a lightweight.

"Come on, let's dance!"

Well, all right. Aston loved dancing. And at least no one would be watching her in this crush of people.

∽

MAXIM WATCHED HER DANCE.

God she was . . . she was . . . so fucking bad at it.

How could anyone be that terrible? It boggled his mind. It was like she couldn't hear the beat of the music at all. The dance floor was crammed and yet people managed to give her space. Probably worried that if they got too close, she'd take them out with a flying arm or leg.

It was how he'd spotted her. What was she doing here? Had she come to this club because she knew it was his? He hadn't told her that he owned Glory, but it wasn't a secret, either. She could easily have figured it out . . . if she'd been looking into him.

Satisfaction filled him.

Had she been researching him? Was she as interested in him as he was in her? All week, he'd wanted to pop into her apartment to check on her. But he'd restricted himself to several text messages. And the one time he'd stopped by and knocked, she hadn't been home. But her neighbor had basically pounced on him the minute he'd appeared, eating him up with her gaze.

He didn't know what that woman's problem was, but she needed to keep that hungry look under wraps. That should be for her husband only.

Maxim winced as Aston bent her knees, trying to dip, then rise. She seemed to trip over nothing and fell onto her ass.

Fucking hell.

She was going to injure herself if she kept going like that. Then he spotted something that made his blood boil.

Sharks were circling.

They could see what he saw. Fuck, it wasn't hard to see it.

That she was special. She might be wearing a dress that was meant to disguise rather than reveal, but that made her all the more appealing.

One of those assholes held out a hand to her as she lay on the floor. Maxim wrapped his hands around the balustrade, fury striking him hard and fast.

She shook her head and he started breathing easier.

But the asshole didn't move. Kept his hand out. And then she did it . . . she took hold of his hand.

No. Just fucking no.

He was moving before he even realized it. Walking down the stairs and rushing toward her. The top level of the nightclub had high ceilings, and his private area was on a mezzanine floor above the club.

He strode through the dancers. They might not all know who he was, but enough of them did to have them stepping out of his way. And then he was close to her. So close, he swore he could almost smell her scent. And she was smiling up at the idiot who'd helped her up.

He had two seconds to stop touching Maxim's girl before he removed his hand from his body.

Moving closer, Maxim wrapped his arm around her from behind, drawing her back into his body. She tensed and he dropped a kiss on her neck. Even out clubbing, she still had her hair in a bun.

Fuck, he was going to make it his mission to get her hair out of that ridiculous bun every chance he got. Although, right now, it was enabling him to kiss the soft skin of her neck, which suited him just fine.

"Who . . . Maxim?" She turned her head to stare up at him in shock.

"Hey, baby. Sorry I'm late." Before she could say something to deny his statement, he dropped his mouth to hers and kissed her.

She grew even more tense in his arms. Drawing back, he looked over at the guy who'd helped her, pleased to note he appeared rather ill.

Maybe it wasn't nice of him to take pleasure in the other guy's discomfort. But he needed to know that Aston didn't belong to him.

She belonged to Maxim Malone.

"Hey, man, saw what happened. My girl gets a bit enthusiastic when she's dancing. I appreciate you helping her up." Maxim held out his free hand, the one that wasn't wrapped around Aston's ribs, pinning her to him.

Could she feel how hard he was?

Fuck, he couldn't hide it. Didn't know if he wanted to. Because he wanted her to realize what she meant to him.

The other man flicked his gaze to Maxim, then down to his hand. He gave it a limp handshake before mumbling something and running off.

Good. He got the picture. He obviously knew who he was

and even though he wasn't the scariest Malone, the last name was enough to have most people treading carefully.

"What did you do that for?"

He raised his eyebrows at her pissed-off tone. Turning, she glared up at him.

"Why did I do what?" He practically had to yell over the music. Just then, he glanced around to see that they had gathered an audience. This wasn't the place for this conversation.

"Oh, don't you start with me, mister." She pressed her finger into his chest. "You know very well what I'm talking about."

Capturing that hand, he brought it up to kiss her palm. Her mouth dropped open, her whole face softening as a glazed look filled her eyes.

Oh, his girl liked his touch. Good, because he loved touching her. And he liked that he could distract her from her temper by kissing her. He had a feeling that was a trick he would use often.

Another kiss and then he reeled her in close, his arm going around her shoulders to pin her against him. He led her through the crowd of people toward the stairs. She dug her heels in as they got to the private stairs.

Was she worried about going with him alone? He gazed down at her, but she was looking around.

"What is it?" he asked.

"Gretchen. I can't just leave her on her own. I came here with her. She said she was just going to the toilet, then she'd be back."

"Rainbow, I've been watching you for the last fifteen minutes and didn't see your friend once. Seems like she's not as worried about you as you are her."

"But there could've been a line at the toilets."

"Not that big. So unless she's constipated as heck, she's found something else to do. Which means that you are free to do what you like."

She didn't look at all convinced, but she let him tug her up the stairs. When they got to the top, she looked around the small area in interest. A plush sofa as well as some chairs scattered around, and a private wet bar made up the entire area. It wasn't large, but it didn't need to be. Truthfully, he didn't spend a huge amount of time up here. Often, he was downstairs in his office, taking care of work.

But he was glad he'd been up here tonight.

"What's going on? Why bring me up here? And why did you do *that* downstairs?" she asked.

That?

"Why did I do what, Rainbow?" he asked, moving closer to her.

She backed away, giving him a cautious look. "That."

"You're going to have to be more specific. Why did I hold my hand out to that guy? Why did I thank him for helping you? Is that what you want to know?"

By now, he had her against the back wall. It was quieter back here. Secluded.

Perfect.

He placed his hands on the wall on either side of her head and leaned into her.

"You know that's not what I was talking about," she told him.

"Well, now, Rainbow, I'm not sure I do."

Was that a flash of fear on her face? He frowned, even as it disappeared quickly behind a blank, haughty mask.

Uh-uh. He didn't like that look on her face. He didn't like her hiding stuff from him.

"Baby, look at me." He bent his head, trying to capture her gaze, but she'd shifted it to his chest.

"Don't call me that."

"Look. At. Me." He put plenty of force into his words.

Her gaze shot up. She glared at him. He didn't care. She

could get mad all she liked. He'd take her angry over her withdrawing.

He didn't like her hiding from him and he wasn't going to allow it.

In the back of his head there was a voice telling him to slow down. That friends didn't treat their friends like this. That he was stepping over a line with a girl who didn't necessarily know how to play by the same rules.

But he ignored that voice. Because he wanted to taste her again. To kiss her. To feel her melt in his arms.

Screw just being her friend.

"You are being deliberately obtuse."

"Now, that's mean. Maybe I'm just simply obtuse."

"You are not, Maxim Malone. We both know how smart you are, so don't try to pull that with me."

Yeah, she had him pegged.

"Or perhaps I want you to say the words. Why did I do what down there?"

"Kiss me!" she practically yelled. Then she took a deep breath. "Why did you act like we were together? Like I was your girl? Why the pretense?"

"Who said it was a pretense?"

13

Aston stared at him in shock.

"Um, newsflash, I am not your girl."

Yeah, he didn't like hearing those words.

"And if I want you to be?" he asked in a low voice.

She glanced away. Was that a flash of fear again? Yeah, he definitely didn't like whatever was going on in her head.

"Doesn't matter if you want it, I don't."

He frowned. Now, Maxim could admit that he'd never had to chase a woman before. They came to him. And if one of them wasn't interested, of course, he'd back off. Even if they faked disinterest, thinking to play it cool . . . well, he wasn't interested in those sorts of games.

But he was certain that wasn't what was going on here. Aston wasn't pushing him away because she wasn't interested or because she was playing a game.

There was a reason. And it stirred an instinct he didn't realize he'd had.

To hunt. To protect.

"Why're you lying to me, baby?" he whispered as he moved one hand to cup her cheek.

Her gaze shot up to his in shock. Clearly, she'd been expecting him to either back off or get upset. But he couldn't do either when he didn't know the full story.

"I . . . I'm not."

"You're going to want to stop," he warned. "Because I don't like you lying to me."

"I try never to lie."

"Yeah? You're not doing a very good job of that."

With a groan, she rested her head back against the wall. "Why are you doing this to me?"

"What am I doing? Making you face the truth of how you feel about me?"

"I don't want to feel anything for you."

"Why? Because it would be easier? Do you wish we could just go back to sniping at each other? To seeing each other for brief moments? Moments that I did my best to make happen?"

Her mouth dropped open in surprise.

"Because let me tell you, now that I've had your smiles, your laughter, and just now, your lips, I want more than just moments. Which means I can't go back to the way things were, Rainbow. I looked forward to seeing you because you made me smile. Because you were funny. Because no one else would speak to me the way you did. And because it's become clearer that during those brief moments, I started to feel more for you."

"M-more?"

"More," he said firmly. "So now there's no going back, there's only going forward. Which is why I couldn't let you sleep on a bench in the foyer, or leave you alone when you were sick, or let your foolish ass try to work while you were sick."

"I'm not a foolish ass."

"Baby, try to concentrate and listen to me."

"How can I when you're . . . when you're . . ." she trailed off.

"When I'm what?" he asked in a low voice.

"When you're touching me!"

Touching her?

"You mean my hand touching your cheek?"

"Yes, I mean your hand touching my cheek!"

"Because I could do so much more touching . . . I want to do so much more," he told her with a smile.

"But . . . but . . . why?" The bewilderment on her face floored him, wiping away his smile.

Didn't she know?

Didn't she look in the mirror? Or realize the way that men noticed her?

Then again, she made disappearing an artform, didn't she? Always trying to hide the light that shone out of her.

A light that had taken him a while to see. But now . . .

"Rainbow, are you fishing for compliments?" he asked.

"What? No! You know I'm not."

"And how would I know that when you're the most beautiful, sexy woman I've ever seen in my life?"

Something like shame filled her face and her shoulders hunched.

Oh no. He didn't like that.

Not. At. All.

"Aston Symonds, you look at me right the fuck now."

Her gaze snapped to him.

"What was that look about?"

He waited to see if she'd snap back at him. That was their game. But she bit her lip, still looking unsure. And he really didn't like that either.

She clearly didn't know her own worth. He'd gotten hints of that in the five months or so since they'd first met. But now it was undeniable.

"You know, if I'm not allowed to lie to you, then you should do me the same in return."

"How am I lying to you?" he asked.

"I'm not beautiful, Maxim! Anyone can see that. I'm not sexy. Or sensual or gorgeous. I know you've been with plenty of women. I've seen them on your arm in the gossip columns."

So she had looked him up. Too bad, she'd seen things he wished she hadn't.

"And I've seen those women. They're gorgeous and sexy. I. Am. Not."

"Then what are you?" he whispered.

He wanted all this poisonous shit laid out on the table. He wanted it out of her head. Because he was going to have to lay a few truths on his girl.

"Wow, are you enjoying torturing me?" she asked.

"Not at all. Tell me. What are you if you're not beautiful?"

"I'm plain, all right? I'm not going to turn anyone's head. Look at me! I stick out like a sore thumb here. Boring, forgettable, and chubby. The only reason anyone would notice me is because of my awesome dance moves."

Was she being sarcastic? He studied her face. Hell. She really thought she had awesome dance moves.

He filed that away to remember later.

"Have you had your eyes tested lately?"

"No." She looked confused.

"You should. You're obviously going blind."

"Maxim—" she protested.

"And together with those short-term memory issues, I'm starting to get concerned."

She huffed and rolled her eyes. "I am not blind, you daft man. I know what I see when I look in the mirror. Someone chubby, plain, and forgettable."

"Then your eyes are lying or your mirror is. Because that isn't what I see and it isn't what anyone else sees."

"You don't have to try so hard to get into my pants. I bet any woman out there would want you."

"That so?"

"Uh-huh."

"Well, that doesn't really matter to me much when the only woman I want is standing right in front of me, giving me sass."

"Giving you sass?"

"Yep, giving me sass, putting herself down and earning herself a punishment."

She gulped heavily.

"You are not punishing me."

"Oh, I am." Drawing back, he grabbed her hips and spun her. "Hands on the wall, baby."

"Maxim."

He waited to see if she'd try to move away, would protest more. He'd let her move if it was what she really wanted. This was only sexy if they both consented to it. But he knew she wanted him.

She just had a problem with self-worth.

And that was something he could help her with. Because he'd been there. And he'd conquered that asshole.

Sort of.

"Hands on the wall, Rainbow." He made his voice go low and stern.

"You suck."

He grinned, knowing he had her. Particularly when her hands slammed down on the wall.

"Happy?"

"Not yet. I won't be truly happy until my girl knows her own self-worth. Until she looks in the mirror and sees staring back at her the sexy goddess that I see."

"Maybe you're the one that needs glasses."

"My eyesight is perfect."

"Then you need your head examined."

"I know what I'm doing, Rainbow."

"Do you?" she murmured. "I don't think you do. You and me . . . we aren't made for each other."

"Says who?" he murmured, pressing his lips along the back of her neck. Fuck, she was far too covered up. He liked that when she was out there, among all those assholes who wanted to look at his girl.

But when it was just the two of them . . . yeah, he wanted all that delicious skin accessible.

"Says everyone."

"Baby, why do you care what other people say? You should only care about what I want."

"Oh, I should only care about what you want?" she said with fire in her voice.

He smiled. That's what he wanted. Some anger rather than despondency.

"Yep. You should only care what I want."

"Your ego is going to need two postcodes. Ohhh."

He'd kissed that spot beneath her ear. A spot where she obviously liked being kissed.

"All that matters is you and me. I don't care whatever anyone else says or thinks unless it hurts you. So if anyone says anything that hurts you, tell me, and I'll take care of it."

"Maxim." Her whole body softened. "You can't do that."

"Course I can." And he would.

He'd do anything to take care of her.

14

"I'm not yours." This time, it was said quietly, with regret.

"Maybe you don't realize it yet, but you are."

"Darn it, Maxim!" She stomped her foot.

Oh, that was cute. He was determined to make her do it again.

"I am not!"

"I took care of you while you were sick, let you sit on my lap while you had a panic attack, made you soup, carried you in my arms, picked you up from work, stopped to help you in the rain, and rescued you from that asshole down there."

"That doesn't make me your girl."

"It does if I want you as my girl. And if you want it too."

"Glad you added on that second part. Stalker."

He laughed. "I'm not a stalker. But I could be if you wanted."

"Maxim!" She tried to move away, her hands slipping from where they rested against the wall.

"Uh-uh, you can't move your hands, remember? Now you've just added to your punishment."

"You're not going to punish me."

"Course I am. You were naughty."

"How was I naughty?"

"You said bad things about yourself. That's not allowed. My girl doesn't say those sorts of things about herself."

"It's like talking to a brick wall. I talk, and I talk, and nothing changes."

"It's good you're learning that now, baby."

"Are you like this with all the women you try to coax into bed with you?" she asked dryly.

He stiffened. "Is that what you think this is? Just sex?"

"Well . . . I mean, why would it be anything else? That's what . . . I mean . . . you've been with a lot of different women on those gossip sites, Maxim."

He closed his eyes. Yep, this is what he deserved. He finally found a woman who he wanted to spend time with and she was fighting him. Something was holding her back . . . and part of that was his past. His reputation.

"I don't . . . I can't be another notch on your bedpost. I'm sorry. It's just . . . I know I should fall on my knees in gratitude that someone like you wants someone like me, but I don't have it in me to do that."

Oh, fuck no.

He turned her and pressed her to the wall, being as careful with her as he could when he was in this state.

"You should get down on your knees and thank me for being interested in you?" he repeated in a low voice.

She winced. "Well, yeah."

"Baby, there's something you need to get into your head really quickly before I lose my mind."

"What is it?"

"I am the one who would be on my knees if you agreed to be mine. Thanking you."

Her mouth dropped open. "What? No!"

"Yeah, and you know how I'd show you my fucking gratitude?"

She shook her head, struck mute for once.

"By spreading your legs and eating you out until you came on my tongue at least three times."

"Maxim."

"I could do that right now."

"Maxim."

"But I want to wait so I can show you just how lucky I would be to get a gorgeous, sweet, smart, sassy girl like you."

"Maxim." A tear dripped down her cheek.

"Don't break, baby." He wiped that tear away.

"I will, though. If I let you close and then I have to leave you, or you leave me . . . I'll break."

"So it's better not to try?" Was that it? Was she scared of being hurt?

She looked away. "Yeah, I guess so."

"I don't think so. I believe you should live every moment to the fullest because you never know when you will breathe your last breath."

She sucked in her breath, moving her gaze back to his. Those brown eyes were filled with pain, hunger, and loneliness.

"Rainbow, this is not about sex." He ran a finger down her soft, smooth cheek.

"So you don't want sex with me?" she asked in a confused voice.

"Oh, I want that. Trust me, I do. But you're not a notch on my bedpost. Not that I do that. I'm not a complete asshole you know. The women I've slept with . . . they've always known the deal."

"The deal?"

"Yeah, that it doesn't mean anything beyond having a night of really great sex. Maybe two. Nothing more. They all know that, so no feelings are hurt."

"You don't think any of them ever caught feelings for you?"

He frowned. Had they? He'd never thought so. But could he be wrong?

"Not that I know of, Rainbow," he murmured.

"I bet they did," she replied. "A guy as nice as you. Kind and thoughtful. I mean, you're obviously a bit of a dick at times with an enormous ego too. But still, you can be kind."

"You forgot hot," he mumbled, mostly because now he was wondering if any of those women had caught feelings for him. And if he'd been a complete dick in disregarding those feelings.

Fuck. What was this girl doing to him? She was making him rethink his life, and everything that had happened in it.

"Nobody can forget that you're hot. That's why we're a ridiculous mismatch."

"You need to stop with that. And I know how to stop you."

He turned her again.

"You're giving me whiplash."

"Hands back on the wall."

She huffed but did as she was told. He liked that. Seemed he also had a need for control. At least when it came to her.

He lifted the back of her skirt.

"Maxim?"

"Shh, baby. I'm not going to hurt you or even touch you much. I just need to get this out of the way so I can spank your ass."

"Oh, that's all right then . . . no, it isn't! Wait. You're going to spank me? You are not going to spank me."

"If you're naughty, then you get punished. It's the rules. I don't make them."

"You don't make them?"

"Yeah, that wasn't the truth. I totally make them. For you. And your first rule is that you won't talk badly about yourself."

He revealed the tiny scrap of underwear that lay beneath her dress.

Holy fuck.

His girl had great taste in lingerie. And he had to say he loved the juxtaposition of her prim and proper outer layer to the sexy kitten that lay underneath. Because this layer underneath?

It was going to be just for him.

"Maxim, you can't do this."

"If you really want me to stop, just say red and I'll stop."

"And you'll back off?" she asked.

He couldn't tell if she was sad at the idea or relieved.

"Nope. I'll back off this, for now. But from you, no way."

"Why?"

"Because you're my girl, even if you don't believe it yet. That makes it my job to show you. Just like it's my job to show you how I see you. And I'm going to do that by wooing you."

"You . . . you what?"

"I'm going to court you. Some old-fashioned dating with some heavy petting and kissing. Holding hands. Late nights talking on the phone. Sneaky groping in my car or a dark movie theatre. If you're a good girl, you'll even get to come. But if you're naughty, then you get punished. If you don't like being spanked, we can come up with something else. You ever been edged?"

"What? No!"

"That would be an interesting punishment for you, then. Once you're more comfortable. If you break the rules, you get punished, Rainbow."

"And if I don't want that?"

"You don't want that? And before you answer, I'll know if you're lying and I won't be happy about it. No lies between us."

"I never lie," she said.

He scoffed. "Surprised you can say that with a straight face."

"Rude. All right, maybe I lie sometimes."

"Uh-huh."

"I try not to, though."

He ran his hand over her buttocks, feeling them clench. "Sure you do. Tell me, if I was to dip my finger under these pretty pink, lacy panties, which are sexy as fuck, by the way, would I find you wet?"

"Maxim!"

"What? Is that a no?"

"No! I mean, yes. I mean, you can't check!"

"Baby," he pressed.

She groaned. "I want the spanking."

He chuckled against her skin. "I take it that's a yes. You want me."

"It still can't work."

"It will. And I'll show you."

"By not having sex with me?" she asked.

"Yep," he replied.

"You're nuts, you know that, right?"

"I think you can handle my crazy."

"And you have an answer for everything. That's. So. Annoying."

He laughed. Then he ran his finger between her cheeks, over her lacy panties.

"Maxim . . ." There was more worry than threat in her voice this time, and he paused.

"Don't worry, baby. I won't hurt you or push for more than you're willing to give."

"Then you're not spanking me."

"Oh, I'm spanking you. You broke the rules."

"I don't have rules!"

"You do now. So listen up. What's your safeword?"

"Safeword?"

"The word I gave you so you could stop everything if you got scared or were in genuine pain."

"Genuine pain? The spanking will be painful!"

"Yeah, but it's something you've earned," he muttered.

"You suck."

"Nah, eventually that will be your job."

"Maxim! That was terrible!"

He chuckled. "Don't worry, baby. More than happy to return the favor."

"You are not doing that to me!"

"Has anyone ever eaten you out, Rainbow?"

The way she stiffened told him his answer. Interesting. He'd often wondered if she wasn't very experienced. But now might not be the time to press her. She was about to bolt, and he hadn't yet given her the spanking she was owed.

"That's all right . . . I like being the first. Now, onto your rules and your spanking. Press your ass out a bit. And widen your legs."

"Maxim, I don't know."

"You trust me?"

"I barely know you!"

"You've known me for over five months, baby. And that wasn't an answer to my question. You trust me. You let me into your apartment. Let me look after you. Got into my car of your own free will. You trust me."

"You bullied me into your car the first time. I got in to stop you from getting punched in the face by an irate driver."

"Aww, and you care about preserving my good looks."

"I can't breathe."

"What's wrong?" he asked in alarm. Fuck. Was she that upset about all of this? Maybe he really should back off.

"From your ego taking up all the space in here," she added dryly.

"Jesus, baby. You scared me. I thought you were serious."

"I was!"

"You just added two more spanks for scaring a year off my life."

"I did not!"

"You definitely gave me a new gray hair."

She snorted. "You don't have any gray hairs. And even if you did, you know they'd only make you look sexier."

"They would. Can't deny it. Doesn't mean you're not in trouble, Rainbow. Well, even more trouble than you were in."

"Maxim!"

15

Damn, if his brothers could see him now, they'd fucking laugh. Well, Jardin would. Victor and Regent would just be dumbfounded.

And then they'd all be blind.

Because he'd have to cut out their eyes for looking at his girl's pert ass. And it wasn't even bare—she wasn't ready for that yet.

And yeah, that's why they'd be looking at him like he had a second head. Because, apparently, he had a whole lot of possessiveness and protectiveness inside him. It had just been buried deep.

"What's your safeword?" he asked.

"Red," she said quietly.

"You say it if you need to. I want you to trust me. I won't do anything to destroy that."

"You promise?"

"Promise, baby." His hand smacked down on her right ass cheek. Once. Twice.

Then her left ass cheek. Once. Twice.

He paused to rub the heat into her skin through the lacy panties. "You good?"

He heard her moan. Oh yeah, she was good. But he wanted to hear a verbal reply.

"Rainbow, you doing all right?"

"Yes," she said breathily.

"Good. Because this ass is better than all right. It. Is. Fine."

"Maxim," she groaned. "You can't say that."

"Sure I can. And I am loving these pretty panties. Are all of your panties this pretty?"

"I think so. Except when I'm on my . . . ugh, never mind."

"When you're on your period? That's all right. You can tell me. I have a sister, you know. And periods are nothing to be embarrassed about."

"If I ever mentioned the word period around my brothers, they'd make vomiting noises."

"When they were younger?" Teenage boys could be dicks.

"They did it last year. They're thirty and thirty-four."

Wow. Dicks.

He didn't say that, though. Because they were her brothers and it was likely she was close to them. With a sister like Aston, they'd be protective of her . . . although where were they? Why'd they let her live on her own? And take the fucking bus?

Hmm. He needed to know more about her past and her family.

But not right now.

Slap! Slap!

Rub.

Slap! Slap!

Rub.

As he rubbed her bottom this time, he saw the way she tried pressing her thighs together.

Yep. His girl definitely liked a spanking. Too bad they wouldn't always be as fun as this one.

He was taking it easy on her, not wanting to scare her away. But she was in for a rude awakening if she broke the rules again. Because he'd tip her over his knee and spank her hard and fast. Without any rubbing or kisses in between.

Yeah, he was kissing her shoulder again. Her skin was smooth and he liked the noises that came from her mouth when he did that. Also, she smelled amazing.

He turned her to face him, cupping her face between his hands before leaning in to nip at her lips. Those same moans escaped her mouth.

Oh yeah, he liked that a lot.

Fuck, his dick was already hard and aching. Dating her was going to be a delicious sort of torture.

If something is worth having, it's worth working for it.

Right.

He deepened the kiss. She was hesitant at first. Shy. Almost nervous. And that wasn't like his girl. She usually met every challenge head-on. Again, like her sex kitten panties, this side of her was only for him.

And fuck if that didn't make him feel a thousand feet tall.

But he finally drew back, because he knew she likely needed a breather.

Lord knew, he did. He hadn't been this close to coming in his pants since he was a horny teenager.

"Come here, Rainbow."

"Huh?"

He had to grin as he took her hand and led her to the sofa. He sat and tugged on her hand. She tried to sit next to him.

But he wasn't having that.

He drew her onto his lap, trapping her against his chest. She held herself stiffly.

"What are you doing?" she asked.

"Holding you to give you a moment to calm."

"Calm? I'm calm."

"Nah, you're not. Your heart is racing and your skin is flushed."

She tried to get out of his hold. But he worked out daily and he could hold her easily.

"Baby, you might want to stop wriggling around on me," he said with a groan.

She froze. And then she obviously caught on as to why he wanted to get her to be still.

Her eyes widened and she glared down at him. "That's your dick."

He burst into laughter. "Ah, yep. I know. It's been attached to me for thirty-three years."

"Your dick is . . . hard, and it's pressing into me. Maxim!"

"I love it when you say my name. Much better than when you say your nickname for me."

"I don't have a nickname for you."

He grinned. "You do. You just don't remember."

"I don't remember . . . dude, I think you're the one with memory issues. I'd know if I had a nickname for you."

"Would you? Because you have a nickname for me, you just don't remember. So I'm thinking that you don't know."

"Can you please let me up?"

"We're dating now."

She gave him a bewildered look. "I don't think we are. And even if we were, what does that have to do with anything?"

"While we're together, you sit on my lap. If you can't be on my lap, then you're tucked into my side. If that's not possible, like when we're in the car, then I've got my hand on you. Do you understand?"

"I understand that you're bonkers."

"I like you, Aston," he said, deciding to lay it out straight to her. When she stiffened, he knew she understood that he was speaking the truth. "I want to get to know you. And I don't intend for this to be a quick fuck. I know you're worried that I'll hurt you, but guarding yourself against getting hurt by never getting involved with someone in the first place sounds really lonely."

"It is."

"I can't promise that I won't ever hurt you," he told her slowly. "Because I can't predict the future. But I do promise to try really hard not to."

"I don't want to hurt you either."

And yep . . . he was falling for this girl. Fast.

"I know you'll try not to hurt me, okay?" he said.

She nodded shakily. "This is probably a really stupid idea."

"Sometimes you just have to take a leap of faith and trust that the other person will catch you. I'm here to catch you, baby."

"I hope so. I really do." Turning, she buried her face in his neck. He held her tight.

Fuck. Had someone let her down before? Someone she trusted?

He ran his hand up and down her back, feeling her shake slightly. She shifted around again and he hissed. She stilled then drew back to give him a guilty look. "Sorry."

"Baby, that ass of yours is a lethal weapon."

"Are you in pain?"

"Yes."

"Well, good. You spanked my bottom and it hurts. That wasn't nice."

"Yeah, and now your ass is definitely getting its revenge."

She surprised him by grinning.

"I like when you smile." He ran a finger along her lower lip, and to his shock, she bit it.

Damn, he also liked this playful side of her. Reaching behind her, he drew out the ugly scrunchie holding her hair in a bun.

"What are you doing?"

"I wanted to see your hair down. It's beautiful." Although there was something off about it. The color. "Do you dye it?"

She stiffened. Why was she upset? Lots of women dyed their hair. Men too. It wasn't something to worry about.

"I . . . I . . ."

"Rainbow, if you're about to lie to me, you should know that your second rule is no lying. I'm sure I've made it clear that I don't like lies. Not sure why you'd lie about this, though. I don't give a shit if you dye your hair."

She heaved out a breath. "Yeah, I do. And I don't see why I need rules."

"Because you're trouble."

"I most certainly am not trouble," she replied haughtily. "If anyone is trouble in this relationship, it's you."

"Ahh, you finally admitted we're in a relationship. About time, I waited a long time to hear that."

"You waited no time at all," she protested. "And I didn't mean it like that! Maybe I should give you rules."

"Not the way this relationship works, baby. But if it eases your mind, I won't be lying to you. There might be times that I can't tell you something, but I won't ever lie."

She nodded. "Same."

Okay, he didn't like that. Maybe it made him a hypocrite, but he wanted to know everything in her life.

"What would you be keeping from me?"

She just eyed him, lifting one eyebrow. Hmm, going to remain tight-lipped, was she? He'd get it out from her.

Eventually.

"Next rules. If you get into trouble, you're to call me. Straight away. Not an hour after it happens, not half an hour. Straight. Away."

"Why would I get into trouble?" she asked in a voice so quiet he could barely hear her over the blasting music. Thank fuck, it was quieter up here.

"Because you *are* trouble. And you attract it."

"I most certainly do not. I live a boring life. Nothing ever happens."

Yeah, he didn't believe that.

"If you want to go somewhere, you're not taking a bus."

"Whoa, buddy. That's a step too far." She tried to turn around so he helped her straddle his lap. No doubt she hadn't factored in her skirt rising up her thighs. But damn, those were some gorgeous legs she had.

"No bus, Rainbow."

"And how do you expect me to get around? I haven't quite mastered teleportation yet," she said dryly.

He narrowed his gaze. All right, so he hadn't thought this through.

"We'll get you a car."

"I don't have the money for a car, plus I don't drive."

"You don't drive?" He gaped at her. She had to be in her early twenties. So why didn't she drive?

"No."

"Why not?"

She shrugged. "I was never taught how to drive."

"I'll teach you how to drive, and then we'll buy you a car."

She shook her head. "Even if that was an option, which it is not, how do you expect me to get around in the meantime?"

"I'll take you."

She sighed. "Right. Like that will work."

"An Uber, then?"

"Okay, sure." She nodded in agreement, but he had a feeling that she didn't actually agree with him.

She was tricky like that.

"I know I could lose a few pounds, however I'm not exactly fond of starving myself."

Nope.

Not happening.

Before she could take her next breath, he had her lying over his lap and was pulling her skirt up over her ass.

"What are you doing?"

"I didn't think you'd be a slow learner, Rainbow." He smacked his hand down on her ass three times, and this time when he paused, he didn't rub the heat in. Because he wasn't going easy on her.

"Stop! Maxim!"

She tried to reach back, but he just captured her hands in his and held them in the small of her back as his hand landed several more times.

"It sucks that I have to do this again so soon—for you, not for me. I like the sight of your gorgeous ass. Especially when I can see it turning pink through your pretty panties. But it does mean that you're going to struggle to sit tomorrow. Just as well it's not a work-day, yeah?"

"Maxim, stop!"

"That's not your safeword, baby. And you know you earned this spanking."

"What? How? Stop it, crazy man!"

"You said something bad about yourself. And you said this about fifteen minutes after you last said something bad about yourself. Which is why this spanking is harder than the first one. Because you didn't really learn your lesson the first time, did you, baby?"

"Who are you?"

He frowned. "What do you mean?"

"You are not the guy I met that day at the swimming pool. I'm pretty sure he wouldn't have cared if I'd said something bad about myself. He probably would have just laughed it off."

"Maybe." He wasn't sure. What he did know was that things had changed. And it seemed that the Malone blood was pretty strong in him too.

And Malones took care of their women. They didn't let other men touch their women or look at them with hunger, and they definitely didn't let anyone put their women down.

"What I do know is that you're my girl. And my girl doesn't speak about herself like that, or she gets her hide tanned." He followed that up with several hard spanks on her ass that had her crying out and kicking her feet.

Damn. That was adorable.

"Maxim! Please, stop."

"Just as soon as I make enough of an impression on your ass, that you'll think twice about calling it fat or wide or saying you need to lose weight. Which, by the way, you do not. And I would never, ever suggest you starve. Understand me? I'm guessing you were trying to tell me that by taking an Uber, you wouldn't have enough money to buy food?"

"Yes!"

"So I'll pay for your Ubers before I teach you to drive and buy you a car."

"Not happening."

Slap! Slap!

Eventually, it would happen. But he understood it was too soon. Maybe after a week or two of dating, she'd begin to understand how serious he was.

When a Malone fell . . . they fell hard.

And they dug in deep.

16

The man was nuts!

Completely and utterly crazy.

And the thing was . . . she had to be equally as insane. Because all she wanted was more of him. His touches, his smiles, his comebacks. The way he never backed down, how he didn't let her put up barriers between them.

No matter how much she tried.

Although she'd stopped trying to push him away a while ago.

Now, though, as he smacked her ass until she knew she wouldn't sit comfortably tomorrow, she wondered how smart that had been.

Because the man could spank.

Holy. Fudge. Balls.

A sob broke free from her mouth and that was when he finally stopped. He hadn't pulled down her panties, but they also hadn't provided much protection.

Maxim didn't try to soothe the pain this time. When she tried to move, he just held her there.

"Let me up," she demanded.

"We need to continue our chat."

"And I have to be lying over your lap while we do that?" she asked.

"I think it'd be easier."

"Easier, how?"

"Well, if you say anything naughty, I won't have to move you. Easy access." He patted her ass lightly.

Grr.

"Maxim Malone, you are not spanking my ass anymore. It hurts."

"Then stop saying bad things about *my* girl. I'm going to pay for your Ubers."

She glared at him over her shoulder. "Hard no."

He raised his eyebrows.

"And do you really think it's safer for me to be in a stranger's car on my own than on a bus filled with people?"

There was silence and she knew he'd gotten her point.

"Fine. I can see that. You can take the bus during the day, but not at night. If you need to go somewhere at night, you call me. If it breaks down, you call me. You get a bad feeling. Call. Me. Agreed?"

"Agreed," she said quietly.

"And we'll start driving lessons."

She sighed. "I can't afford a car and you're not buying me one."

"We'll tackle that hurdle when we get to it. Lessons are happening."

"All right." She agreed to that as well because it would be helpful to know how to drive.

"If you need anything, I want you to tell me. I don't want you holding things back."

She huffed. "And if I tell you, what will you do?"

"Get you whatever you need."

Yeah, that's what she'd thought.

"You can't get me whatever I need, Maxim. Life doesn't work that way."

To her surprise, he helped her sit up so she was straddling his lap and facing him again. Then he cupped her chin in his hand. "Sure it does."

"Maybe when you're Maxim Malone. But when you're Aston Symonds, you don't get whatever you need or want."

"Ahh, but Aston is now Maxim's girl. So her life is going to change."

And then he kissed her.

And that kiss . . . it was everything.

～

The knock at her door had her jumping, even though she was expecting it. She got to her feet and quickly walked over to the door.

Taking a deep breath, she opened it.

Before she could even greet him, her breath caught in her throat.

Maxim was half-hidden behind the hugest bunch of red roses she'd ever seen. There had to be at least three dozen, which must have cost a fortune.

He peeked at her around the flowers. "You going to let me in, Rainbow?"

"What? Oh! Yes, of course." She stepped back. Yesterday, he'd taken her out for brunch and a walk around the French Quarter. Tonight, he was here to take her to dinner.

She hadn't really known what to wear, as she'd been worried he might be taking her to a fancy place. So she'd quickly gone shopping at lunch today and bought this simple black dress.

The sleeves were sheer, which was about as daring as she got. It was tiered with little sequins sewn into the bottom of each tier and ended mid-calf.

It wasn't super fancy, but she'd added a lot of pretty silver bangles, a delicate necklace, and dainty earrings. Still, she was always going to pale next to him anyway.

"Are those for me?" she asked in amazement.

"Yeah, baby, these are for you," he said softly. He was nice enough not to point out what a silly question that was.

"I don't think I have a vase. I should get a vase."

"Why don't you find something to put them in now, and we can get you a vase tomorrow?"

"Right, right," she said, flustered.

She ended up filling the sink and putting them in. It was the only thing big enough to hold them.

"Maxim, they're beautiful."

"Not as beautiful as you." He drew her away from where she was admiring the roses and pulled her against him. He cupped her cheek with his hand. "Hello, baby."

"Hello." She could feel herself blushing.

"You've forgotten to do something."

She had? What? She tried to think. Had she forgotten to put something on? Oh my God.

"I'm so sorry! I forgot to say thank you!"

"Thank you?"

"For the flowers." How rude. "No one has ever bought me flowers before."

His gaze narrowed. "Never?"

"No. And those are so beautiful and I didn't say thank you, I was just so shocked—"

Leaning down, he kissed her. It was hot. Her skin sizzled and her brain turned to mush. She leaned into him and he wrapped his hand around the back of her neck.

She had her hair up in its usual bun, and once again, he reached up to pull the tie out so it lay down her back.

Drawing back, she stared up at him, feeling dazed.

"That's what you forgot to do," he told her.

"What?"

"Kiss me. If you haven't seen your man in a while, then the first thing you do is kiss him."

"How long is a while?"

"Hmm, five minutes?" He grinned, winking at her.

She huffed out a breath, resisting the urge to grin back. Just.

"I'll try to remember in the future."

"You do that, baby. I'll be sure to remind you if you forget."

"I'm certain you will," she said dryly. "Can I have my hair tie back?"

"Why?"

"I need to fix my hair."

"No, you don't." He took her hand in his and tugged her toward the door.

"Maxim! Yes, I do!"

He picked up the handbag that was on the hall table. "Do you have your phone and keys in here?"

"Yes. But I need to do my hair and get a coat."

"No, you don't." He drew her out the door, then shut and locked it with the keys he'd pulled from her handbag.

"Maxim!"

"Yes?" He wrapped an arm around her.

"I can't go out with my hair like this." She knew it was silly. It was just a hairstyle. But it helped her feel safer.

He stopped at the elevator and turned to her. Crap. He wanted to take the elevator?

"Baby, look at me."

She stared up into his knowing gaze.

"I'll never let anything happen to you. You know that, right?"

She sucked in a breath. She'd never had anyone's protection before. It was both overwhelming and amazing. It might take some getting used to.

"I know."

"You're safe with me. I will protect all of you. Body, mind, and emotions. If anyone ever threatens you, then you tell me immediately. I will take care of it. I will look after you."

"I know you will. I'm sorry I'm like this."

"There is nothing to be sorry about."

She nodded. Although she wasn't so sure. She was filled with silly fears and habits.

"Do we have to take the elevator down?"

He pulled her close and she pressed her face against his chest. To her surprise, he suddenly lifted her with an arm under her ass.

"Maxim."

"Just hold on tight, Rainbow," he whispered as she nuzzled her head into the curve of his neck.

Then she felt him moving into the elevator and she tightened her hold on his shirt, letting his heartbeat soothe her. Strangely, it felt like they were going up rather than down. It didn't take long before he was stepping out and putting her on her feet. He lightly kissed her cheek.

She looked around the small foyer in surprise. "Where are we?"

Instead of answering straight away, he moved to a door and unlocked it before ushering her in. "Welcome to my apartment."

Aston studied his apartment in surprise. "We're having dinner here?"

"Yep."

Relief filled her and she walked farther into the penthouse. She should have realized something was up when he wouldn't let her grab her coat.

"I've ordered in. It should be here soon. I never really learned to cook. I hope you like Thai food?"

"Love it. This is . . . it's gorgeous." She wasn't sure what she'd been expecting. The rest of the building was fairly plain. It was in a good area of the city, but it was an older building.

However, the penthouse had obviously been refurbished. It had pale wooden floors and light gray walls. The living area was huge, with floor-to-ceiling windows to take in the view of the city.

She walked over there, staring out with her hands pressed to the glass like a small child. "This is magical." It wasn't dark yet, but she knew it would look even more impressive when it was.

Maxim moved in behind her, wrapping an arm around her waist and then brushing her hair to one side so he could kiss down her neck.

A shiver of arousal rushed through her.

"If you'd left my hair up, you'd have easier access."

"But I like your hair down," he replied. "And this just means I have to work for access to your skin. So pretty."

Lord. She leaned back into him as he held her tight. They didn't move until the food arrived. While he was collecting it, she turned to take in the rest of the space. A doorway led to a hallway beyond where she guessed the bedrooms and bathrooms were. There was an enormous kitchen at the back of the living area with sparkling granite counters and a long island.

She wandered over there, running her hand along the counter, then taking in the rest of the kitchen. It was kind of obvious that he didn't cook here. There wasn't even a crumb on the counter.

"It's so clean," she said as he placed the food on the counter.

He let out a laugh. "Were you expecting a mess?"

"Um, well, a man living alone, I guess I was." She grinned sheepishly.

"I have a cleaning lady, Rainbow. And it's not like I do much entertaining."

She stiffened slightly at the reminder of the women he'd been with before.

"Rainbow? What's wrong?" He walked toward her. Foolishly, she backed away until she hit the counter. He grabbed her around her waist, lifting her so she was sitting on the benchtop. Then he stepped between her legs. "What is it?"

"Nothing."

"Not nothing." He placed a finger under her chin, tilting her head back. "The only women I've had in this apartment are family."

She jolted in surprise. "What? Really?"

"Really." He kissed her lightly. "And now you."

Okay. She liked that a lot.

"I have a past, baby. I can't make it go away. But what I can tell you that the future is all you."

Darn. It. Just darn it.

"You are so sweet." She sniffled and wrapped her arms around him. "And don't apologize for your past. We all have those. I shouldn't be so sensitive."

He kissed her, then picked her up and carried her to the stool at the island. "Let's eat dinner. Then we can watch a movie and cuddle."

"That sounds perfect."

17

Aston wasn't going to let this conquer her.

She could do this.

She'd already carried this damn box from the bus stop to her apartment building. Now, she was standing outside as she tried to catch her breath.

Glancing around, a strange feeling of being watched came over her. But she shook it off as silly. Why would anyone be watching her? Or if they were, they were probably laughing at the stupid woman trying to carry a huge box around.

Now she just had to get it up seven flights of stairs.

Oh God.

There was no way she could get it up seven flights of stairs. She was utterly exhausted. She wasn't sure she had the energy to get herself up the stairs, let alone with this damn box. Already, her back was aching.

Seven flights of stairs would kill her.

Which left one option. The elevator.

She gulped.

Maybe she should have just paid to have it delivered. Would

have been worth it to save herself from wrecking her back. Not to mention her arms, which felt like spaghetti.

And now she was going to have to take the elevator. Something she hadn't done without Maxim since it had broken down.

Maxim... maybe she should call him.

But no, she didn't want to be a bother. And he'd probably already left for work. Their different schedules had made it a bit more difficult to date these last couple of weeks.

Not impossible, though.

After the brunch and dinner at his penthouse, the next date had been a movie and some really heavy petting. And this Sunday, he'd told her to leave the whole day free. If anyone had told her a few weeks ago that she'd get all giddy over a man... that seeing him would be the highlight of her week... she'd have told them they were nuts.

And if they'd told her that a guy who looked and acted like Maxim Malone would be taking things slow because he wanted her to know without a doubt how much she meant to him... yeah, she'd have peed herself laughing.

This was so far out of her comfort zone. She had no clue what she was doing.

But she wasn't telling him no.

Pretty much every man in her life had treated her badly. Up until Dayton hired her... and even then, he was acting slightly weird lately. What's more, she kept seeing more strange invoices and some of Gretchen's townhouses were selling for too much money.

She didn't know what was going on, but she'd learned her lesson the first time and hadn't mentioned anything else to Dayton.

Gretchen had been pissed at her for leaving the club two weeks ago, but she hadn't had it in her to care all that much. She knew it was rude, but as Maxim had pointed out, Gretchen had disappeared on her first.

So she refused to feel guilty.

Maybe she should see if the new building manager could help her with the box. He was younger and far nicer than Brian. But again, she didn't want to bother him.

This was her problem to solve, so she picked the box up again. Why'd it have to be so awkwardly shaped? It was too big for her to get her arms around it, so it constantly slipped and she had to use her leg to prop it back up.

"What the hell do you think you're doing?" an annoyed voice boomed.

Bang. There went the box onto the floor. She gasped.

"Oh no! Do you think it broke?"

"Aston!"

She glanced up to see Maxim storming toward her from where he'd just stepped out of the elevator.

"Oh, hi! I wasn't expecting to see you. I thought you'd already be at work."

He glowered down at her, his hands on his hips. "Is that your excuse for not calling me and telling me that you needed help?"

"Um. Perhaps?"

His eye started twitching. That didn't seem like a good thing.

"Ahh, have you had that tic for long?" she asked.

"It's suddenly just appeared. I've got a nickname for it, though."

"Yeah? What's that?"

"Trouble."

"Somehow, I think that's aimed at me," she mused.

"Somehow, I think you're right."

"Rude," she muttered.

"You look terrible."

"Thanks," she replied sarcastically. "It's a new look I'm going for. You think it will catch on?"

"Exhausted and pale. Hmm, not sure it will."

Grr.

"Well, I'd love to stay and chat, but I'm busy."

He stood over her, his arms crossed as he glared down at her. "Busy doing what?"

Uh. Could he not see what she was busy doing?

"I'm trying to get this up to my floor. I really hope it didn't break when I dropped it." She frowned up at him. "That's your fault."

"My fault?"

"Uh-huh. You yelled at me and caused me to drop it."

"I caused you to drop it?"

"Are you having some sort of issue with your hearing? You keep repeating what I say."

He rubbed at his forehead. "Maybe because I'm hoping that it might somehow start making sense."

"What's not making sense?"

"Well, let's see . . . it could be the fact that you're trying to lug a huge box around on your own. What is in this?"

"Um a flatpack bookcase."

"Don't you already own a bookcase?"

"Um, I do. This isn't for me."

He gave her an incredulous look. "It's not for you?"

"It's for Mrs. Strowan. She lives two doors down from me. She can't go get it herself. So she asked if I would."

"Why the hell didn't she just pay the fee to get it delivered?"

"I guess she couldn't afford it."

He continued to stare at her, then he started muttering to himself.

"And you both thought it would be a good idea for you to get it? You don't even own a car. How did you get this here?"

"I took it on the bus. And she asked me because I don't think she has anyone else."

"On the bus . . . she took it on the bus," he mumbled.

"You're really starting to worry me. I think there's a vein about to pop out on your forehead."

"Why didn't you call me?" he asked.

"Huh?"

"Why. Not. Call. Me?"

Okay, now he was down to one-word sentences. This definitely wasn't a good thing.

"You're busy. I didn't want to bother you."

"Bother. Me. She doesn't want to bother me."

She wasn't sure if it was a good sign or not that now he seemed to be talking to himself. By the way that tic next to his eye was carrying on, she was thinking not.

"How were you going to get it upstairs? Were you going to use the elevator?" he asked.

Hmm. He knew she had trouble with the elevator still.

"Um . . . I was thinking I'd use the stairs."

"You were going to lug a large box up seven flights of stairs."

His voice had gone quiet. Too quiet. She had learned that wasn't a good sign regarding the state of his temper.

"Yep."

"By yourself."

"Yep."

"Because you weren't going to do something sensible like call me."

"I thought you'd be at work," she said again.

"Clearly, I'm not. Which you would have known, if you had just called me."

"I'm beginning to think you wanted me to call you."

"Finally, she gets it."

Reaching down, he picked up the box.

"You don't need to carry it up."

"Unless you're willing to call Mrs. Strowan and get her to organize someone else to carry this up to her, then yeah, I do."

"But I can do it."

He paused and glared at her again. "Are you my girl, Rainbow?"

Lord. She liked it when he called her his girl. She liked it far too much for her peace of mind.

Because she just knew that nice things couldn't last in her life. That wasn't her fate. And Maxim Malone . . . he was the nicest. He was top-shelf whiskey, a designer handbag, a one-off pair of Louboutin's.

Definitely not for her beer and sneakers world.

But still, she didn't have it in her to turn him away.

"Yeah, I'm your girl."

"I thought I'd already made this clear, if my girl needs me, then she calls me."

"But I—"

"And if you say one more time that you didn't call me because you thought I would be too busy, I'll take you over my knee right here in the foyer."

She gaped at him as he moved to the elevator and hit the button, somehow without dropping the box.

Damn, he was strong.

And sexy.

And that ass . . . wowsers.

He was also bossy and demanding.

"I'll, um, I'll meet you upstairs." She turned toward the stairwell.

"Get in the elevator, Rainbow."

She shook her head as he put his foot out to stop the doors from closing.

"Baby. Elevator. Now."

"I didn't think it was possible for you to get bossier. Turns out, I was wrong."

"Elevator."

"No. I'm taking the stairs."

He sighed and put down the box. Then he stepped out of the elevator, leaving the box inside.

"What are you doing?" she asked as he walked toward her.

"Getting you into the elevator."

"But Maxim, I don't want to go. Oh shit! The doors are closing. The box!" She ran to the elevator and pressed the button, breathing a sigh of relief as the doors opened immediately and she saw it was still there. "Maxim! It could have gone to a different floor and someone could have stolen it."

"Well, it wouldn't have if you'd gotten into the elevator."

"And it wouldn't have if you hadn't left the elevator! I could have been down fifty bucks."

He frowned. "You paid for it?"

"Yeah, but Mrs. Strowan will pay me back."

She hoped.

"Let's go make a delivery and get your fifty bucks."

She shook her head.

"Baby, you're clearly exhausted," he told her gently. "I'm worried you won't make it up the stairs. Which means I'm going to have to walk up the stairs with you. With the box."

"All right, I'll take the elevator."

"Good girl," he told her.

Without warning, he picked her up in his arms and stepped into the elevator.

She wrapped herself around his torso, her legs around his waist and arms around his neck. And she clung to him like a monkey.

"Maxim." Lord, she hated what a wimp she was being. Hated that she had a weakness like this.

"I have you, Rainbow."

"Don't let me go."

"I won't." He shifted her to press the button for the seventh floor before pushing her against the wall and tugging on her hair tie. Her hair fell down around her shoulders.

"Maxim."

"Hush, baby. I'm taking care of you. All you gotta do is hold on, understand?"

She nodded and buried her face in his neck, breathing him in and letting his familiar scent comfort her. Lord, he smelled good.

All she wanted was to fall into his embrace. To ensure that he never let her go.

Because she'd never felt as safe as she did in his arms.

When the elevator dinged, he stepped forward before putting her on her feet.

"Hold the doors open for me, Rainbow."

"Sure," she replied. Her stomach still felt ill from the trip in the elevator, but she held the doors and watched him easily carry the box out. "I'm really sorry you had to take time out of your day to do this."

"We're going to have a chat in a moment, you and I."

"A chat?"

"A chat," he said firmly.

She attempted to tie her hair back, but he sent her a look. "Don't even think about it."

Uh-oh.

She left her hair down and directed him down to Mrs. Strowan's apartment. She knocked on the door. It opened immediately.

"Aston? Hi."

"Hi, Mrs. S. Delivery of one bookcase."

"Oh, thank you, dear!"

Happiness filled her at the look of pleasure on her neighbor's face.

"Oh, it isn't made up?" the other woman asked.

"Um, no. It's not. I suppose I could do that for you." What she really wanted was to go home, have a shower, eat some carbs, and watch TV. But yeah, putting a flatpack bookcase together sounded like fun too.

Not.

"That would be wonderful, dear. Come in. My, what a strapping young man you are."

Maxim just grinned at the older lady and put the box in her living room.

"Oh my, if I was twenty years younger," Mrs. Strowan murmured, watching Maxim's ass as he bent over.

Aston had to hold in a giggle.

Mrs. Strowan had to be in her midseventies. But she obviously knew perfection when she saw it.

Both of them sighed at the same time as Maxim straightened and turned. He raised his eyebrows at them, grinning wickedly. "Like what you see, ladies?"

"Goodness, yes," Mrs Strowan replied. "My Fred, God rest his soul. He never had an ass. Flat as a pancake back there. But you sure do fill out a pair of pants nicely, don't you?"

"I try my best," Maxim demurred. But she saw the wicked glint of amusement in his eyes. "Now, did you get your money, baby?"

"Oh, um." Awkward.

"Oh, money! Of course, how forgetful of me."

"That's okay. We can figure it out later."

Maxim gave her a strange look.

"I'll find it while you're making it up, dear," Mrs. Strowan said.

"Sure."

"Actually, Aston can't stay," Maxim said. "She's worked all day and then carried that home on the bus, so she's exhausted. But I'd be happy to come and do it tomorrow."

"That would . . . that would be just fine." Mrs. Strowan looked thrilled at this.

A few minutes later, Aston walked beside Maxim toward her apartment. "I could have stayed and put that together."

"You could have. But I can also see how tired you are. And you've done enough."

"But you don't need to go back there tomorrow. I'll do it."

He sighed and stopped outside her door. "You're not the only person who can help others, Aston."

"Well, of course not. It's just . . . have you ever been interested in helping your neighbors before?"

"Hmm. Just one." He winked at her, then ran a finger down her cheek.

It seemed silly to blush, but she still felt her cheeks heat.

"Open up. We need to talk before I head into work."

She sighed. "So bossy." Still, she searched through her bag and was drawing out her keys just as Eva opened the door.

Man, that was all she needed.

She'd looked after the kids last night while Eva and Dan went out drinking and Maxim was working. But tonight, she was done. Exhaustion was quicksand around her feet, ready to drag her down.

Aston never usually slept well, and every so often, that would catch up to her and she'd end up sleeping all day.

She could feel herself reaching that point.

"Oh, hi, Maxim," Eva said.

Grr. Eva really needed to stop looking at him. Aston's free hand fisted, and she had to take a deep breath to try and calm herself.

"Eva." He took the keys from Aston.

"Hey, Aston, you ready to take care of the kids now, or do you need a moment?"

"You're looking after the kids tonight?" Maxim asked her. "I thought you did that last night."

"I did."

"Oh yeah, you did." Eva nodded. "But I thought you'd do tonight too?"

"No."

Both women stared at Maxim in surprise.

"Oh, um, Aston?" Eva asked.

"I said no. Even if Aston says yes, which she's not going to, it's a no."

"Maxim," she whispered. Wow, that was rude.

"Baby, you don't want to take care of the kids. You want to go inside, shower, eat, and veg out. I know it and you know it. She knows it, too, but she doesn't want to admit it because she likes having a free babysitter so she can go out and get shit-faced with her husband."

"What the hell?" Eva screeched, making the baby in her arms cry.

Aston gaped at Maxim.

"Look, Eva, I get that being a parent must be hard. And it must be great to get a night off. But you need to find a babysitter. A paid one. Because your days of taking advantage of Aston's kind nature are over. Baby, inside. Now."

18

Maxim braced himself for her anger. He figured she would fire up at him for interfering in her life. But over the last couple of weeks, he'd learned a lot about Aston Symonds.

He'd learned that she didn't like to talk about her past. She rarely said anything about her brothers, and what she did say was never good.

He'd discovered that the people in this building took advantage of her good nature. And that didn't sit well with him.

At. All.

But lucky for Aston, she was his girl now. And he would take care of her.

Asking for help wasn't something that she seemed to know how to do. Aston was on a mission to help this entire building, but she was letting all of them to walk all over her. Yet, ask for help for herself?

Nope. She didn't seem to be able to do it.

So he was going to have to teach her how.

He stepped into the lounge and waited for her to blast him

over the way he'd treated her neighbor. She was the worst one at taking advantage. He understood it had to be hard, staying home with two little kids all day. But did she ever say thank you? Did she ever even ask? She just seemed to think that Aston would help her.

Well, he'd made clear that Aston wouldn't be pushed around anymore.

He stared down at her as she sat on the sofa.

Then he gaped at her in shock as she burst into laughter.

That was . . . not what he'd been expecting would happen. Was she all right?

"Aston?"

"I can't believe you just said that to her."

"She deserved it. She's taking advantage of you. And that's not acceptable."

"She totally is. And she really did. And I . . ." She stared up at him, looking dazed and tired. "Thank you."

He came and sat next to her. "Well, you just shocked the shit out of me. I thought you'd get mad."

Turning, she grinned at him.

A man would do a lot to see that smile every day. To wake up to it each morning. Go to sleep with it every night.

"You've got the prettiest smile, baby."

Her smile dropped away, but not because she was unhappy. It was replaced by a look of lust.

"Yeah?" she said huskily.

"Yeah. I'm sitting, Aston."

"Um, yep. You're sitting." She gave him a bewildered look.

"So, where should you be?"

Understanding filled her face and she scrambled to get onto his lap, very nearly unmanning him in the process.

"Watch the goods, baby."

"Shoot, sorry. We wouldn't want to harm those. I know you're attached to them." She gave him a wicked look.

"Just a bit. You'll be attached, too, once I show you what I can do with them."

She rolled her eyes. "You know that arrogance isn't attractive on a man, right?"

He simply grinned. "Are you sure about that? I saw the way you were staring at me when I bent over before. Baby, you're attracted to me."

Her eyes lit up. Oh yeah, she wanted him.

He reached for the little buttons that went entirely down the front of her dress. It completely covered her, with long sleeves and a high neck.

"What are you doing?" she asked, grabbing his hands.

He tugged one free and cupped the side of her neck. "I said we'd go slow, baby."

"Right."

"But slow doesn't have to mean we don't do anything at all, right?"

"I . . . I guess."

"Yeah? Because I've been dreaming about your breasts. Wondering what they'd feel like in my hands, what they'd taste like in my mouth, the noises you'd make as I sucked on your nipples."

"Oh, dear Lord, help me," she muttered.

He had to grin. She could be funny. So funny.

"If you don't want me to do any of that, you say stop, you say red and I'll back off. But if you do want me to touch you, to taste you, then take your hands off mine."

Her eyes widened as she stared at him with her mouth open.

She wanted more. He just wasn't sure if she felt brave enough to let him give her more.

"I, um, I don't have a lot there."

"Did you think I wanted or expected you to have a lot there?" he asked.

"Uh, well, no. I guess not. It's just . . . men like big breasts, right?"

"Sure. Some men do. Some don't."

"What do you like?" she asked.

He grinned, glad she'd asked. "You."

It took her a moment, but then she grinned back, the tension leaving her.

And then her hands dropped.

"That's my good girl."

A low moan escaped her. And fuck him, he felt that moan in his dick. Wrapping his hand around the back of her head, he drew her toward him and kissed her deeply.

"Fuck. You're so fucking gorgeous. And those noises you make . . . they're hell on a man's control."

"Sorry," she whispered.

"Never say sorry for showing me that you enjoy my touch," he told her.

She bit her lip, giving him that sweet smile. The one he knew she didn't offer to many people. And that made it all the more precious. He moved his hands back to the buttons of her dress, revealing a dark purple, lacy bra.

"Oh hell. I could die now and I'd die a happy, lucky man."

She giggled. Actually giggled. Had he ever heard her make such a carefree noise before?

If the shocked look on her face was anything to go by, it wasn't a noise she made often.

He tugged her arms out of the dress she was wearing.

"I now have a new goal in life."

"What's that?" she asked breathlessly as he reached around her and undid her bra.

"To make you giggle like that more often. And to ensure that you make those sexy noises every time I touch you like this."

"Ohh," she said as he removed her bra.

Damn. He stared down at her. She must have misread his silence because she reached up to cover her breasts. He removed her hands and then slapped them both lightly.

"Don't ever cover your body. Don't ever hide it from me. Fuck me, Rainbow. I can't believe that you were hiding these under all those dresses." He cupped her breasts, feeling the weight of them in his palm. And he liked that.

A lot.

"Do you . . . are they enough?"

"More than enough. And if you ever say that they aren't, I'm going to take off my belt and turn your ass red."

She rolled her eyes. "You're always threatening to spank me."

"That's because you're trouble." He ran his thumbs over her nipples and she let out a low moan.

"I am not. I still think I should be able to spank you."

"Baby, I'm a Malone."

"Um. I know."

"Malone men don't get spankings, we give them." He rolled her so she was lying on the couch and he was crouching over her. She had a stupidly small and uncomfortable couch, but he didn't care about it right then. Because her breasts were parallel to his face and he was about to get his first taste.

"Is that so?" she asked dryly.

"It is so. Just like Malone men take care of their women." He lightly scraped his teeth over her nipple.

"Oh my God. Do they?" she asked breathily as he gave her other nipple the same treatment.

"Yep."

"And how do they do that?"

"By giving them rules, then spanking them when they don't obey."

"Maxim!" She slapped her hands down on his chest. "Stop kidding around."

"I wasn't kidding around."

"You cannot tell me that every Malone man spanks his woman."

"Hmm. Why can't I?"

"Because . . . because that's nuts. Your brothers . . ."

"Yep. My brothers are all over that. Where do you think I learned it from? And my cousins. Rainbow, if you think I'm nuts, you want to meet the Texas Malones. There's not a sane one there, well, except Alec and West maybe. The rest of them still think it's the Wild West in Texas and that they should be able to shoot anyone that comes onto their land who they didn't invite."

She grinned and shook her head. "Now I know you're making things up."

"I swear that I'm not, baby. I'd take you there to show you, but then they might try to steal you from me. A couple of them still don't have their own women. I wouldn't want to tempt them with you."

"I'm not going to tempt anyone."

He glared at her. "Are you wanting to add to your punishment?"

"What? What punishment?"

"The one you're owed for not calling me to help you with that box. For carrying the box on the bus and then into the apartment building on your own."

"That's nuts! You can't punish me for that!"

"Sure I can. I was going to have you come in here and bend over, so I could pull this dress up over your ass and give you a quick, hard spanking. But then I got distracted by these. And what a distraction." He ran his tongue over the tip of one nipple. And then, he had to give the other nipple the same treatment.

"I had it handled. I've taken care of myself for a long time."

He drew up to stare down at her. "But the difference is that now you don't have to."

19

Aston stared up at Maxim in shock. "Wh-what?"

"I'm not sure why your family isn't around, but from what you've said, I gather that you aren't close for a good reason. And you don't seem to have any decent friends, so before now you've had to take care of yourself. But now you have me."

You don't seem to have any decent friends.

Ouch.

But it was true, wasn't it? And the truth was . . . she'd cultivated things that way. Because letting people close had never ended well for her.

"So you had to do it all on your own." Leaning in, he sucked one nipple into his mouth.

Holy. Fudge. Balls.

She swore she could feel that in her clit. And it felt damn good.

"And now you have me, and I'm going to look after you."

How . . . how had this happened? She had no idea that meeting him all those months ago at the swimming pool . . . that sharing snarky remarks back and forth . . . that getting into the elevator that day would lead to this.

To this gorgeous, sexy, *caring* man lying on top of her on her uncomfortable sofa, telling her that he would look after her. And meaning it.

"I've never had that," she told him hoarsely.

She waited for the barrage of questions. Things she couldn't answer. Would he get mad at her silence?

"And now you have."

Holy. Crap.

Was he trying to kill her? To turn her into a ball of mush? Because he was succeeding. She had to blink rapidly to keep the tears at bay. How had she gotten so lucky as to meet this man?

"That wasn't supposed to make you cry, baby," he said worriedly.

She shook her head. "I just . . . I'm so glad I didn't tell you that you should claim your ego as the ninth planet in our solar system and take your rightful place out in the stars."

He threw his head back and laughed. She grinned. She loved it when he laughed. He was always so darn beautiful, but when he laughed like that . . . he was the most beautiful thing she'd ever seen.

And she just hoped that she could hold on and never let go.

After he quietened, he lowered his mouth to hers. The kiss started off soft and sweet. But it soon deepened, getting hot and heavy.

Lord, the man could kiss.

"Fuck, baby, your lips are so soft and delicious." He moved his mouth down her neck and chest. "All of you is soft and delicious." He took as much of her breast in his mouth as he could and sucked.

Far. Out.

She moaned, arching up. Wanting more. Needing it.

He moved his mouth to her other breast and did the same. Her mind swum, her breath coming in fast pants.

More. She needed more.

"So soft and delicious." He took just her nipple into his mouth this time. Back and forth between her nipples until she was practically vibrating with the need to come. "Do you have any toys?"

What? Toys?

What was he trying to ask?

"Huh?"

"Toys, Rainbow? Do you have any sex toys?"

"No!" she squeaked. She knew she was going red. Why would he think she would have sex toys?

"Hey, there's nothing to be ashamed of. Although it is kind of criminal not to have any. Not even a clit tickler? Vibrator? Nothing?"

"No!" She shook her head. Holy. Heck. "Women have those?"

He grinned. "Women have them, baby. We'll have to take you shopping."

"For sex toys?"

There was that gorgeous laugh again. "You say that like I'm asking you to go to the dentist."

"I might prefer that."

He buried his face in her neck as he laughed. She took the opportunity to run her fingers through his thick, lush hair.

Yeah. She was so darn lucky.

"I promise that when we go shopping for sex toys, it will be better than going to the dentist."

Oh heck. Was he really going to take her shopping for sex toys?

"Why did you ask if I had any?"

"Because I thought you might let me finish you off with a clit tickler."

Her eyes widened. "You wouldn't."

"Course I would. Why wouldn't I?"

"I . . . I . . ." She couldn't think how to answer that without making it really obvious that she had no idea what she was doing here—with him.

"I thought you might prefer that to me using my fingers or mouth."

"No. I don't . . . I don't need . . ." Though she might need something. She was hot and wet and yeah, she needed to do something about it.

"I could just watch you using your fingers if you're not ready for mine," he suggested.

"I . . . no!"

He grinned and sat up, pulling her so she was straddling his lap. Her dress was pooled at her waist, her breasts on full display.

"No? Are you too shy for that?"

"Yes!"

He chuckled. "You know that one day you're going to come on my dick, right? You're going to explode in my mouth. And I cannot fucking wait."

She knew she was bright red.

He ran a finger over her cheek. "If I ask you something, I want you to be honest with me, understand?"

"All right." Now, she was worried. What the heck was he going to ask her?

"You don't have much experience, do you?"

She shook her head.

Something soft entered his gaze. Something that made her stomach fill with warmth.

"Baby. Have you got any experience?"

"No." She waited for him to ask more questions. Who had

ever heard of a twenty-four-year-old virgin? It was baffling, right?

Instead, he cupped her face between his hands and gave her that sweet smile that she was certain could make panties spontaneously self-combust.

"I'm going to take care of you. You know that, right?"

She sucked in a breath. Both in shock and disbelief.

"You still . . . you still want me?"

He raised his eyebrows. "You seriously thought I wouldn't? Because you're a virgin?"

"I don't know what I'm doing."

He grinned. "We've established that."

"I thought you might prefer someone with experience."

"If I was the kind of guy that turned you away because of your lack of experience, then I wouldn't be the kind of guy you should want in your life. Understand me?"

When she'd first met Maxim, it didn't seem like he had a care in the world, as though he skated through life by relying on his looks and charisma.

And then he said something like what he just had.

Something that made her heart stop. That made her sit up and really pay attention to him.

That's when you saw the real Maxim Malone. And that's when you understood that the outside might be sexy and hot. But the inside of him . . . it was beautiful.

"I understand."

"Baby, you're looking at me like you've never seen me before."

"I see you," she whispered. "I see all of you."

Instead of smiling or kissing her, something dark came over his face. Had she said something wrong? He helped her pull her dress up her arms and she clutched the front of it together, suddenly feeling chilled.

"What did I do wrong?" she asked in a quiet voice. Obviously, it was something. And she needed to fix whatever it was. Fast.

"Whoa, Rainbow. No. You didn't say anything wrong."

"Are you sure?"

"I'm sure. I'm positive. Don't look so stressed, baby."

"Me? Stressed? Never."

"Rainbow, you live in a constant state of stress. Always worrying about everyone else, trying to take care of them. Thinking. Thinking. Thinking."

She gaped at him. Wow. He really did know her. "So I don't understand what happened just now."

"You said you see me."

She nodded.

"There are things you don't know about me though. About my family."

"Oh." She frowned. "There are things you don't know about my family, either."

"Some of what I might tell you could be hard to understand, but I also know it should come from me. Or you might hear it from someone else and . . . shit. Sorry." His phone started buzzing and he drew it out of his pocket and read the text message. "It's my brother. Crap."

"Is something wrong?"

"He just needs me to go see him now. But you and I need to talk. Damn, and I haven't given you the punishment you're owed."

"We don't need to worry about that," she said hastily.

"Ah, yeah, baby. We do need to worry. Because you have trouble asking for help and that needs to change." He cupped her chin in his hand. "You don't need to do everything on your own anymore, all right?

She sucked in a breath. "Right."

"So next time you need help with something, you call me. Understand?"

"I do." He really meant every word, didn't he? Other people might say something similar, but they didn't necessarily mean it. She'd learned that lesson the hard way.

But Maxim wasn't one of those people.

"Good girl." He kissed her. Long and deep. Until her body was hot and aching. "I haven't got time to spank you, so your punishment is to make me a list."

"A list? A list of what?"

"A list of all the things that you need my help with."

"What? And what would I put on that list?" What the hell?

"Well, number one would be me helping you learn to drive."

Oh, right. Well, that would be helpful.

"Number two could be giving you an orgasm with my fingers."

"Maxim! That's not helping me!"

He grinned. "Isn't it? It might help you relax and get some sleep. That could be number three. Helping you sleep." He ran a finger under her eyes.

"How do you know I have trouble sleeping?"

"Couple of reasons. You look tired."

Urgh, she really had to learn how to put on make-up better.

"And I figure someone that goes to the gym that late at night either works strange hours or they want to exercise to the point of exhaustion so they can fall into bed and sleep. Am I wrong?"

"You're not wrong."

"So that's definitely number three."

She bit her lip. That seemed very one-sided to her. She wanted the scales to be balanced. "What about you? What can I do for you?"

The grin was wicked. It made her heart race. "Oh, baby. I could list a dozen ways you could help me."

"Maxim Malone!" She slapped his chest. "I didn't mean that!"

"What? I was just going to say that I need some help picking out... drapes."

"Drapes?"

"Uh-huh."

"Right."

He grabbed hold of her hips and lifted her off him, putting her on her feet. She hastily did up a couple of buttons, so she didn't fall out of her dress.

"Definitely need new drapes."

"I don't think we're allowed to replace the drapes. They come with the apartments, right?"

"You can when you own the building."

She paused and stared at him. "You don't own the building."

"Yes, I do."

"No. You don't."

"Baby. Yes. I. Do."

"Holy. Crap. Balls. Don't tell me you are the new owner?"

He just grinned.

He was the new owner. And... and...

"Did you do it to get rid of Brian? Because of the way he treated me? Maxim?" She followed him to the door, nearly stumbling in her haste.

Turning quickly, he grabbed her hips to steady her. Then he placed a soft kiss on her lips.

"Lock the door behind me."

"Maxim? Did you?" she asked as he opened the door.

"Of course I did, baby."

20

Maxim walked into Regent's office to find all of his brothers already in there.

Victor was leaning against the wall, Regent was sitting behind his desk and Jardin sat opposite him, staring down at something on his laptop.

"Hey, what's up?" It better be something good, since he'd had to leave his girl without giving her any pleasure or the spanking she deserved. This time, he might have actually pulled her panties down.

Fuck.

These past couple of weeks had been a definite test of his control. There was nothing he wanted more than to strip her off, spread her legs, and then feast.

But first, she needed to know that she was special;, she needed to know her worth.

And that was more important than his blue balls.

He just hoped that no permanent damage was being done.

After pouring himself a Scotch, he sat on the other chair beside Jardin.

"Just help yourself," Regent said dryly.

"Always do, brother."

Jardin looked up from his screen at him. "You seem in a good mood."

"When am I not in a good mood?" Maxim countered.

"You should be ecstatic after you learn what we've discovered," Regent said. "Jardin."

After pressing a few buttons on his computer, Jardin used the projector attached to the ceiling to project an image of a good-looking man in his fifties on the opposite wall.

"Uh, who is this?" Maxim asked.

"This is Dayton Leeds. He owns Dayton Leeds Construction," Regent explained.

"Such an original business name," Jardin muttered. "This guy thinks a lot of himself."

Maxim stiffened. This was Dayton Leeds? The same Dayton Leeds that Aston worked for? But why were his brothers interested in him?

"After working our way backward through the ranks of the assholes selling Mixology on our streets, we've discovered that Leeds appears to be behind the sudden influx of the drug."

"Him?" Maxim asked hoarsely. This guy was the one bringing in the drugs?

Fuck. This wasn't good.

"Yeah, our best guess is that he's smuggling it in with some of his construction materials," Jardin explained. "We have to do some more research into that, though, since we don't know who is supplying the drugs. There are rumors that one of the cartels in Colombia has a genius chemist creating all sorts of new designer drugs and that Dayton is the guy they're using to get it into New Orleans. But we've got nothing concrete linking him with Colombia."

"All we have is one guy's word that Leeds is behind all of this," Regent said. "And he gave us that name under duress."

So they tortured it out of him.

"To look at him, Leeds seems like an upstanding citizen," Jardin mused. "Gives money to charities. His wife died twenty years ago and he raised his daughter on his own. She now works for the company in sales." Jardin flicked to an image of a well-dressed, tanned, blonde woman. She'd probably be considered quite attractive, but there was something off about her.

"Gretchen Leeds," Jardin said.

Gretchen? Was that the same Gretchen that Aston had gone to his club with? Just how entangled was she with the Leeds family?

"So what's the next step?" he asked. "Do we try to bring in some more guys and question them? We go after Leeds?"

"No. We need a bit more proof," Regent said. "And I think the way we'll get that is by leaning on someone close to him. Jardin has been going through everyone who works for him."

Jardin flicked to another screen. "This is his brother. He works for him on paper, but apparently, he's rarely in the office. Even if he would turn on his brother, it's unlikely he knows anything. I'm going through the other people that work with him. Oh, he's got an assistant too. But her photo isn't anywhere I can find. I've only got a name at the moment. Aston Symonds. I'll look into her. She might be someone we could press. Let me find out where she lives."

"I know where she lives," Maxim said.

The others all looked at him.

"How do you know where she lives?" Regent asked slowly.

"Because she lives in the same building I do."

"The one you just bought?" Jardin asked, raising his eyebrows. "Because you didn't like the building manager."

"Yep. And you won't be pressing her to do anything. She's not a part of this."

Regent leaned forward, giving him a thoughtful look. "You want to explain that further?"

It might have been worded as a question, but he knew it wasn't.

"Aston and I are together."

Silence filled the room as all of his brothers stared at him.

"Together?" Jardin asked in a tight voice. "As in . . . a relationship?"

"Yes."

"You're in a relationship with Dayton Leeds' assistant?" Regent asked.

"Do you know how to be in a relationship?" Victor asked.

"Did you before you met Gracen?" he shot back.

Victor's face tightened, then he shook his head. "Not really."

"Aston is mine. She's under my protection. And she has nothing to do with this."

Regent looked thoughtful and Maxim tensed, knowing he wouldn't like what was about to come from his oldest brother's mouth. "Are you sure she has nothing to do with this?"

"I'm sure."

"Because one way for Dayton Leeds to get one over on us, to get ahead of the game, would be to send someone in to get close to one of us," Regent pointed out.

Yeah. That's where he thought he was going to go. Maxim's hands clenched into fists. "I'm not an idiot. I'd know if I was being played. Aston isn't a spy. Trust me."

Jardin whistled. "She must be something if you're this certain. You're exclusive?"

"Yes. This isn't . . . she's not just someone I'm fucking. I'm not fucking her at all. Yet."

Jardin's mouth dropped open. "Huh?"

"Aston has some issues with her self-worth. She was worried she didn't mean anything to me, so we're taking things slow. We've only been dating the last couple of weeks."

"You've been taking on her dates and then taking her home and not fucking her?" Jardin asked. "You?"

"Yes. I have been. Is there a problem with that?" He didn't really have much of a temper, except, apparently, when it came to her.

"There's nothing wrong with that," Regent said. "But since she seems so special to you, we would like to meet her."

He shook his head. "Not yet."

"Why not, bro? You ashamed of us?" Jardin grinned. "I can see where you'd be nervous of her meeting the big, scary one," he pointed over at Victor, "but Gracen owns his balls now, so she'll keep him on a leash."

"Two people own your balls," Victor grumbled back. "And she does not have me on a leash."

"All right, enough," Regent said, instantly making them both quieten. He didn't have to speak loudly or with anger to make everyone pay him attention to him. That was just who Regent was. "Why don't you want us to meet her?"

"Well, for one, things are new, and she's . . . shy." Hmm, not quite the word. "She's a worrier. Worries about shit constantly, and this will freak her out. Plus, she doesn't know who we are."

"She doesn't know about us?" Jardin asked. "How? Has she been living under a rock?"

"She's lived here for six months and I don't think she knows of us. Or if she does, she hasn't worked out that I'm one of those Malones. Not everyone knows about us."

But most people did.

And most people would be scared.

"So you tell her about us," Regent said. "And you do it soon before she finds that out from someone else."

"I'm going to."

"And then you bring her here to meet us," Regent ordered.

"Aston's not a spy for Leeds, Regent," he told the other man. "She's a rule follower. She helps out everyone in the building. Runs herself ragged, taking care of others. I had to work hard to get her to date me."

"Wow, that must have been a shock for you. Having to work to get a girl's attention." Jardin smirked.

"It was, asshole. But I'm up to the challenge. I know how to romance a girl."

"Hey, we both have a girl." Jardin pointed at himself, then at Victor.

"Yeah, but Carrick did all the work for you and Victor stalked Gracen."

Victor grunted, but didn't disagree.

"Plus, your girl proposed to you." Maxim smirked as Jardin's face darkened.

"Do not mention that to me. She couldn't sit for a week after pulling that stunt."

Thea had proposed to both Carrick and Jardin on a recent trip away without the boys. To say they'd both been unimpressed was an understatement. And she'd soon had a huge rock on her finger. Put there by Jardin and Carrick after *they* proposed.

About damn time, too.

"Fine, if you say she's not a spy, then we'll believe you," Regent said, garnering all of their attention. "But if you trust her, then she might be able to help us."

"No," he said firmly. "I'm not putting her in danger."

"Of course not," Jardin said. "But maybe she's seen something . . . heard something. Or if she does happen to hear something, then she could let us know."

"Is Leeds really going to be so stupid as to let something slip in front of his assistant?" he asked.

"He's stupid enough to move in on our territory," Victor said.

That *was* pretty dumb. And Maxim really didn't like that Aston worked for this guy.

"I need to get her away from him." No way could she work for this guy if he was smuggling drugs into the city. Even though he doubted that he mixed his legit and illegitimate businesses, Maxim still didn't like it.

His brothers shared a look.

"This is my girl. We protect the women of our family. If this were Lottie, Thea, or Gracen, you'd never suggest this."

"You're that serious about her?" Jardin asked.

"Yes." And he was. She was it for him. "I won't use her. And I won't put her in danger."

"You might need to back off her, then," Regent warned.

"What? What do you mean?"

"If he sees you with her, he might jump to conclusions," Victor warned. "Might think she's working for us."

"Does he know that we're onto him?"

"He shouldn't," Regent mused. "But we've worked a few people over to get his name, so there's a possibility of this getting back to him. And even if he doesn't think we know, he could be paranoid enough to worry if he sees her with you."

Fuck. That was it. He was going to have to get her to quit her job and let him protect her.

Right. That was going to be so simple.

21

It definitely felt like someone was watching her.

Which was nuts, right?

Why would anyone watch her? However, now she wished she hadn't decided to go for a late-night swim. The pool was only around the corner from her apartment building, and typically, she didn't feel unsafe.

Tonight, she did, though.

Aston slipped her hand into her bag and drew out her Mace as well as her phone as she walked to her apartment building.

Call Maxim.

But what could he do? He was working. She hadn't even seen him today, which was slightly odd. He'd texted her last night to ask her if she could help Mrs. Strowan put together her bookcase and that he would be busy all day.

It was fine.

He was a busy guy.

Nothing to get upset or worried about.

Finally, she made it to her building. After eight, you had to use a code to get into the building so she felt much safer once she was inside.

See? Silly to worry. And if she'd called Maxim, she would have felt like a complete idiot. Plus, he probably wouldn't have been happy that she'd been swimming at night alone. Once she was inside her apartment, she locked the door and walked into the bathroom.

It was the lack of sleep making her lose her mind. She really hoped she could sleep for more than a couple of hours tonight.

After showering, she got into her favorite pajamas—a short-sleeved pink top with a sloth drinking coffee on it, along with long gray pants also covered in sloths. Then she made herself something to eat and sat down to watch some television before bed. She was feeling tired.

She had a feeling tonight was going to be a good night.

∽

YOU'RE A USELESS LITTLE BITCH, *Aston.*
I wish you'd never been born.
Should have smothered you as a baby.

SHE SAT UP WITH A GASP, taking a few deep breaths.

Tonight wasn't a good night.

Glancing around, she saw that she'd fallen asleep on the sofa. The TV was still on, and a late-night news show was playing.

Getting up, she stumbled to the kitchen and grabbed a bottle of water from the fridge, chugging it down as she tried to rid herself of the bad dreams.

Stupid nightmares.

She hated them. She struggled to fall asleep, and then when

she did, she was plagued by memories of the past.

You're a mess, Aston.

Picking up her phone, she moved to the small balcony off her living room. Despite the fact that it was nearly three in the morning, the night was still quite warm.

The balcony was as simple as the rest of the apartment. Just two chairs and a small table between them.

Sitting, she took in the city. It felt like this place never slept. Not fully.

And that's when she saw him pull up. Maybe that's why she'd come out here. Her body knew that this was about the time he got home. Perhaps she was unconsciously seeking him out.

Because he made her feel safe.

He got out of his car and turned to stare across the street. And that's when they attacked. Someone grabbed him from behind while another person ran to help.

Maxim fought, but he was caught by surprise.

Someone was hurting him. She stood, her heart racing. Then, without thought, she ran back into her apartment.

Weapon.

Knife. There was one sitting on the countertop from earlier when she'd cut up a lemon.

Out the door.

Run. Run.

Down the elevator. No time for fear.

Get to him. Get to Maxim.

Run. Run.

She entered the alley where she'd seen them take him. There he was!

He was being held by two men while a third one hit him.

No! Not on my watch.

Running toward them, she raised her knife, thrusting it

down into the asshole's back. She'd put her full force behind it. She knew it would take a lot to get through his clothes to the skin below.

But her knife was sharp and he was caught by surprise.

He let out a yell while she started screaming. "Fire! Fire! Fire!"

The other two must have been taken by surprise, too, as Maxim managed to shake free from them and started fighting back.

"Aston! Run!" he yelled before she heard him make a pained noise.

Yeah, that wasn't happening. She didn't bother trying to pull the knife out because she didn't think she'd succeed. The asshole she'd stabbed turned on her, coming at her with a roar, and she took a defensive position.

He was more powerful than she was. But she was small and fast and she could take a hit. She dodged at the last moment, sticking her foot out to send him flying. Then she raced toward one of the two men on Maxim, jumping on his back with a yell.

"Fire! Fire!"

She'd once read that people were more likely to respond if you cried out fire rather than help.

She hoped that was true.

The jerk she'd jumped on tried to dislodge her, moving from left to right as she grasped him around the neck and tightened her hold.

He clawed at her arm. Pain slashed through her, but she didn't let go.

"Aston!" Maxim roared, right as someone grabbed her from behind and threw her against the brick wall.

Then there was the sound of yelling. Footsteps coming their way.

Someone had heard them.

"Hey! What's going on here?"

Two men grabbed the injured guy and started running down the alley.

She picked herself up with a groan. Ouch. She was going to feel that tomorrow.

"What's going on? Are you all right?" A big man stopped in front of her, staring down at her in shock.

"Just a mugging, I think," she said. "Thanks for helping."

She wasn't sure whether that was the truth . . . but then again, she didn't know that it wasn't either.

"Is your man okay? I'll call the cops."

"He'll be fine," she said quickly. "I'll call the cops myself. Thanks." She had an inherent dislike of the police and didn't want to be on their radar. "It's all good. Really. The city is getting to be a dangerous place."

"Uh, yeah. You sure you don't need my help?"

"No, thanks. You've done enough. I appreciate it."

"What about your guy?" He moved toward Maxim.

Maxim held up his hand. "Good thanks. Just winded. I've got it from here. Thanks."

With another wary look at them both, he left the alley. They didn't have much time to get out of there. She didn't want those guys to come back, but she also didn't want their rescuer to call the cops.

"Maxim! Maxim, are you all right?"

He was sitting, leaning against the wall, and his hand was over the side of his stomach.

She stared down at him in horror. There wasn't much light back here, but there was enough to know that things weren't right with him. He definitely wasn't just winded.

"What is it? What's wrong?" She kneeled next to him, reaching for his hand.

"Baby. I've been stabbed." His voice didn't sound right. It was fainter than usual. Like he was fast losing energy.

"Oh God." She hadn't panicked while he was being attacked. Or while she was fighting a man twice her size. But she could feel the panic looming. "I need to get you to the hospital."

"No hospital."

"Maxim, now is not the time for you to be Mr. Macho."

He let out a low laugh, then groaned. "Don't make me laugh, baby."

"Sorry," she replied. "I'm so sorry. Maxim, you need the hospital."

"Just need to be stitched up."

"Yeah! At the hospital!" she screeched. "Shoot. We should get out of here, though. Before those guys come back." She wished she hadn't sent their good Samaritan away now.

"What did you do to the one hitting me?" he asked.

"Not important. Can you move?"

"Yeah, baby. You help me; I can do anything."

She rolled her eyes at that. She would be lucky to get him to the street, let alone the hospital.

Shoot! Where was her phone? She'd had it in her hand when she'd gotten down here.

"I need my phone."

"Take mine. Search for it." He pulled his phone out of his pocket and handed it to her. She used the flashlight to spot her phone and picked it up before returning to him.

With his arm flung over her shoulder, somehow, Aston managed to get him onto his feet, though she stumbled under his weight.

"Holy heck balls. You don't look like you weigh this much."

"It's all this muscle, baby. Pure muscle."

"Uh-huh, come on, muscle man. Let's get you out of here." After that, she wasn't sure what she was going to do with him. But she'd figure it out.

She had to. Because she wasn't about to let him bleed out. She was not losing him.

"You've got to get me to my brother."

"What?" she asked.

"My brother. Get me to his place. He'll get a doctor."

She wanted to protest, but she wasn't a fan of hospitals, either.

"You're sure?"

"Sure, baby."

"All right. I need to call a taxi."

"We're taking my car." They'd reached the road by now, and she was looking around in worry. She really didn't want to stand out here and wait for a taxi, but what choice did she have?

"Uh, Maxim, hate to tell you, but you're barely standing. You can't drive."

"You can."

"I don't know how to drive!" She couldn't do it. No way. What if she crashed? What if she hurt him?

"Baby, it's automatic. Easy-peasy."

"Easy-peasy? You're nuts. You've lost too much blood, which is obviously affecting your brain." After saying that, she felt ill. How much blood had he lost? They were under the streetlights now, so she could see that his navy blue shirt was damp with blood.

Shoot. She needed to stop arguing and help him.

"I'm going to drive you," she muttered.

"Thanks, baby. You're being so brave."

"Don't be nice to me right now. I'm freaking out. You can't be nice or I might cry."

"All right, baby," he murmured. But she could tell he was just humoring her.

Jerk.

They reached his car and he leaned against it with a groan,

studying her. "Baby, you all right?"

"What? Yes, of course."

"You don't look okay. They hurt you? I'll kill those bastards." Maxim tried to move, as though he seriously thought he was going to go after some guys that were long gone to punish them for hurting her . . . when he was the one who'd damn well been stabbed. Not to mention the beating he'd taken.

The guy was nuts!

"I'm fine. Where are your keys?"

"Pocket."

Oh boy. She moved around to search in his back pockets, but he shook his head. "Front, baby."

Oh boy, oh boy.

She patted his front pockets, found his keys and dug her hand in deep.

"Just want to point out . . . pain makes things shrivel," he said as she brushed her hand against something while she was drawing his keys out.

"What?"

"Not a fair representation of what I got going on . . . in there."

Alarm filled her as his words started to slow. His eyes fluttered shut.

Then she realized what he'd said.

"Are you seriously worried about what I'm thinking about your . . . your dick size while you're standing there, bleeding out?"

"A man is a man, baby."

"Then a man is an idiot."

He chuckled, then groaned. "That I am. And stop being funny."

"Not trying to be funny, jerk," she muttered as she made short work of opening the passenger door and helping him into the seat.

Shoot. He looked so pale and there was a sheen of sweat over his face.

"Really think I should take you to the hospital," she said as she leaned over him to do up his seatbelt.

"Really think that if your tits are in my face, you should be naked."

"Maxim! I'm trying to do up your belt."

"Don't."

"You need it buckled. It's against the law to drive around without a seatbelt on."

"Baby. I've got a stab wound in my stomach. Cop pulls us over, doubt they'll care whether I'm wearing a seatbelt."

"It's not safe."

"It'll be fine."

"But I don't know how to drive! What if I crash?"

"Rainbow, look at me."

He waited until her gaze turned to him and she braced herself for some sage advice. "Don't crash."

"That's it? That's your advice? Don't crash?"

"It's good advice, baby."

It was idiotic advice; that's what it was. But she gave up trying to buckle him into his seatbelt, mainly because she was scared the belt would hurt the wound on his tummy.

Also, because her hands were shaking so hard she didn't think she would manage to buckle him up anyway.

Closing the door, she ran around the side and climbed in. She didn't bother with her belt either.

"How do I make the seat go forward?" She could barely reach the pedals.

"To the side of the seat. Button. Press the forward one."

The seat slid forward. Fancy.

"Where is the key? Where's the key hole thingie?" Oh Lord, she was losing her mind.

"Keyless start. Put your foot on the brake, and press that button. Then, move the stick to drive. But first, buckle your belt."

"I don't need my belt on."

"Baby. Belt. Now."

"So darn bossy. You'd think being stabbed would make you less bossy."

"You'd think wrong."

She rolled her eyes but didn't fight him. She followed his instructions until she was driving. Holy. Crap.

She was driving.

"This is insane. I'm driving."

"Yep, you're driving. Now, you think you can press on the accelerator a bit more? Because at this rate, I won't have any blood left by the time we get to Regent's place."

"Oh, right. Sorry." She pressed on the accelerator and the car shot forward.

Aston yelped.

"Ease back!"

"Oh my God!" she cried, reaching for him as he made a pained grunt. Her sudden acceleration had obviously jolted him. "I'm so sorry."

"S'all right. Should have said, ease your foot down. Got a touchy accelerator."

"I can't do this, Maxim. I can't! This is ridiculous. I'm going to crash."

"Hey, where is that badass baby who rushed . . . to my . . . rescue?"

Oh no. His words were slowing down again.

She had to do this. There was no one else. She had to save this man, who she was certain owned a part of her soul. She glanced down at where his hand was pressed to the wound in his stomach.

"I got this."

"You got this, badass baby."

"Be quiet and save your energy. Shoot. Except I need to know where I'm going."

He rattled off an address that meant nothing to her.

"Phone? I need your phone, Maxim!"

No answer.

"Fuck. Fucking hell. Fucking, fucking, fucking hell."

"Whoa, baby. You're saying fuck."

"Oh my God. I thought you'd lost consciousness."

"Might have for a bit. Then some angel swearing up a storm woke me."

"If there's a time to swear, it's now. I think we should call your brother and let him know we're coming. I need your phone, I don't have his number."

"Bluetooth, baby."

"What?"

"Call Regent," he commanded.

And the screen on the console suddenly started calling Regent. Okay. She should have thought of that. She wasn't completely ignorant.

"Maxim?" a tired voice asked. "Everything all right?"

She glanced at Maxim. Oh, shoot. He was out again.

Not good. Not good.

"Maxim? Maxim, are you there?" The person on the other end was getting worried.

"This is . . . this isn't Maxim."

There was a beat of silence. She closed her eyes.

"Idiot, he knows it isn't Maxim," she muttered to herself.

"Who is this?" the deep voice demanded. And the voice he used . . . well, it would take someone far stronger than her to deny him.

"This is Aston." She winced again. Like he'd know who she was. "I'm—"

"I know who you are, Aston," he interrupted, surprising her. "Is there a reason you're calling me on Maxim's phone at three-thirty in the morning?"

"Ahh, yeah, so I need to know how to get to your house, and I also need you to call a doctor now. Though I don't think doctors do house calls anymore, do they? Can you get one? Please tell me you can get one."

"Aston, can you do me a favor?"

"Uh-huh, sure."

"Take a deep breath. Hold it. Now let it out."

Okay. Wow. She felt calmer now.

"Now, tell me what's going on."

"Maxim got attacked. Three guys dragged him away from his car and into an alley, and I ran down to help him. The guys ran off, but he's been stabbed. He didn't want to go to the hospital, so now I'm in a car I can't drive, taking him to a house I don't have the address for, and he's not w-waking up."

"Okay, sweetheart," he said calmly. "I'm going to help you, all right?"

"That would be nice."

"That would be nice. Right. Where are you?"

"I don't . . . I don't know." She glanced outside. "Oh, Sal's Pizzeria. I just drove past. It's supposed to have good pizza."

"It does. You make your way safely here with my brother and I'll buy you a whole pie, all right?"

"All right, but Maxim's brother?"

"Call me Regent. And yes?" he asked.

"I don't know how to drive."

"Are you driving right now?"

"Yes." She guessed she was.

"Then you can drive, sweetheart. I'm going to give you directions. Are you ready?"

"Yes."

He told her where to go next.

"You'll have a doctor waiting?" she asked as she turned down a street. All right, she'd managed to successfully turn this thing. Go her.

This was so darn terrifying.

"Contacting him now," Regent told her.

"You can multi-task? My brothers can't multi-task. Once, one of them tried to drive while picking his nose and nearly took his own eye out."

There was silence.

Oversharing, Aston.

"I can see why he likes you."

"He told you about me?" she asked.

"Yes, sweetheart. He told me. Now, are you all right? Are you injured?"

"No, I'm fine."

"Good girl. Here are the next directions."

To her shock, she pulled up outside a vast mansion ten minutes later. There had been actual guards at the gate. What the hell?

Maxim hadn't mentioned that his brother was filthy rich.

Right. Like you've told him everything about your brothers?

True.

Her brothers were something she'd rather forget than talk about, though, and it was obvious that Maxim was close to his brother.

Also, Maxim had bought a whole building so maybe it wasn't just his brother who was filthy rich.

She tried to turn the car off, but it made a strange noise. What was wrong with it?

The door to the house opened and a man stepped out. Nerves filled her. She could barely see him, and yet she felt intimidated. He rushed to the passenger side of the car, opening the door before taking in Maxim, then her.

"Hello, Aston. I'm Regent. Are you sure you're not injured, sweetheart?"

"I'm really not. Please, help Maxim," she begged.

"I will." He looked over his shoulder. "Look after Aston. I've got Maxim."

She jolted. Who was he talking to? Then she saw someone else walk around the car. Holy heck.

She must have been out of it to miss this guy.

The door opened and she shied away from the man leaning down.

"It's all right, Aston," Regent said calmly as he drew Maxim out of the car. "This is my bodyguard, Jose. He'll help you in."

Bodyguard? Seemed like she'd landed in some strange new world.

"Can you put the car in park?" Jose asked.

"I don't . . . I don't know how . . ."

He reached over her and shifted the stick into park before hitting the button to turn the car off. He even undid her belt.

"Do you need help walking? Are you hurt as well?" he asked calmly.

"N-no."

"Would you like to come inside?"

"Do I have a choice?"

Silence was her only answer.

Yeah. That's what she'd thought. She looked from his serious face to the huge mansion. And then, she realized that Maxim was in that mansion.

So there was only one place she wanted to be.

"Let's go."

22

Aston paced back and forth across the room.

Jose had led her to a really nice living room. It had a big sectional in front of a huge television. The decor was a bit old-fashioned for her tastes, but it suited this house.

But she couldn't settle.

She'd been there close to an hour and no one had told her anything.

Where was Maxim? Was he all right? What if he wasn't? Panic flooded her.

"I want to see him." She whirled to where Jose was standing guard by the door. He might look relaxed, but she knew that if she made a move to leave, he'd stop her.

Aston didn't like that.

"Regent will return when he knows something," Jose told her calmly.

"I should be with Maxim." What if his injury was worse than she'd thought? This wasn't good enough. She strode to the door. She wouldn't let herself be intimidated by this behemoth of a man.

Jose stepped smoothly in front of the door. "You need to wait."

"I don't like waiting! Get out of the way, Colossus."

Jose's eyebrows rose just as the door behind him opened.

Oh heck. Her heart stopped as she looked at the enormous man entering the room. Jose moved out of the way to let him in. What was bigger than colossal? Immense? Gigantic? Humongous?

And this guy didn't seem as friendly as Jose. Which, considering that Jose was about as warm as an ice cube, was saying something. Swallowing heavily, she forced herself to push her fear deep. Showing fear would be a mistake. She'd learned that the hard way.

"Is there something in the water around here?"

The new guy tilted his head.

"Giant water," she muttered.

Did his lips twitch? Impossible, right?

"Aston, I'm Victor," the gigantic man said. "Maxim's brother."

"Right. I'm Aston. But you already knew that, since you said my name."

Urgh, chill, Aston.

Taking a deep breath, she straightened her shoulders. "I want to see him. I helped save him, drove him here while he was bleeding out next to me, yet now I've been shut in here with a man who would win the silent game every time. And I've run out of patience. I'm done being nice. So I want to see him."

"All right."

His reply surprised her.

"All right?" she said faintly. She'd been gearing herself for a fight, and all he'd said was 'all right'. "Yeah, all right. Now?"

"Sure. I'll take you to his bedroom now."

She narrowed her gaze at him. "That's what you came in here for, isn't it? To take me to him?"

He just stared at her without a word.

"Yeah, you were coming to take me to him."

He gestured with his head at the door, and she followed him as they moved out of the living room and to the stairs.

Why does there need to be so many stairs?

God, she was so tired. Plus, her feet were really starting to hurt. She hadn't felt them before, but the adrenaline rush had faded, and now she could feel every ache.

"Sorry I had to get grumpy back there," she said. "I should have let you talk first before jumping on you. But I'm tired. And worried. Not that it's an excuse. But I just want to know that he's all right."

Victor shot her a look she couldn't decipher.

"He is going to be all right, isn't he?" she asked, worriedly.

"You care."

"Of course I care! I wouldn't have raced out of my apartment in my pajamas and bare feet armed with just a knife if I didn't care."

He stilled and stared down at her. Then his gaze moved over her, taking her all in. He grunted.

She wasn't fluent in grunt, so she wasn't sure what he was trying to say.

"Knife?"

"Ah, yeah. I grabbed it from the kitchen. I really wished I'd grabbed my Mace too."

"What happened to the knife? Was that the same one that was used to stab him?"

"No," she whispered hoarsely as they reached the second floor. Her breath was coming in short pants. "Sorry, I'm not unfit. Just . . .uh, what did you ask me? Oh, the knife. No, that ended up in one of his attackers' backs."

Another grunt. Did he disapprove? But he didn't know the whole picture.

"I had to stab him. He was beating on Maxim. I don't know when he got stabbed. I'd do it again if I had to."

He gave a nod. Was that in approval or disapproval? Maybe he didn't believe her. Perhaps he thought she was a psycho who went around stabbing people.

They stopped in front of a door and he opened it, walking in. She guessed she was supposed to follow.

Inside was a massive bed against one wall and two men were standing off to the side by the windows, talking. One of them was Regent.

The other one was a stranger. But then her gaze left them, snagged by the man lying in the bed asleep. He was hooked up to monitors as well as an IV.

"How much blood did he lose?" she whispered hoarsely.

"Quite a bit." She glanced over to find the stranger talking. "I'm Doctor Edwards."

Victor placed his hand on the small of her back.

She jumped, but it gave her the prod she needed. She stepped forward toward Maxim.

It was hard to fight back her tears. But she didn't know these men and didn't want to show them any weakness.

Weaknesses could be exploited.

"Is he going to be all right?" she asked.

"I've stitched him up, but the knife was likely dirty," the doctor continued. "We'll keep an eye on him. He'll sleep for a while yet, and when he wakes up, he'll still need a lot of rest to recover from the blood loss. Luckily, it didn't tear up too much muscle."

Don't cry. Don't cry.

But her hands shook as she reached out to cover his hand with hers.

God. It could have been so much worse.

"Sit."

She glanced behind her to find that Victor had pulled a chair over for her. "Uh, thank you." Then she looked to Regent to find he was giving Victor a strange look.

"Doctor, could you give us a moment?" Regent asked. "I'm sure Gerald has some coffee on."

The doctor nodded, and Regent showed him out. She took hold of Maxim's hand, hating how cold it felt.

"He's going to be fine," Victor told her gruffly.

She nodded. Of course he would. "Do you live here as well?"

Victor nodded. "Yep. We built a house outside the city, but we live here most of the time."

"Oh, that's nice." She didn't know why she was trying to make small talk with this man. Aston guessed she just needed some noise to fill the room so that she didn't focus on the fact that Maxim was lying unconscious in the bed.

"He'll be okay, right?"

"Course he will."

The words settled her nerves. Of course he would be. Because she couldn't stomach the idea of him being anything but all right.

The door opened once again, and she glanced over as Regent walked in. He wasn't as big as Victor, but there was something even more intimidating about him. It was in the way he held himself.

This man wasn't used to losing. Or hearing the word no.

She remembered Maxim telling her that there were things she didn't know about his family. Things he needed to tell her.

Yeah, she was wishing now that he'd gotten around to telling her those things.

Licking her dry lips, she forced herself to keep her gaze on Regent, even though she wanted to look away.

"We need to talk," Regent told her. "I need to know everything that happened tonight."

She nodded. A shiver ran through her. A sense of foreboding.

Regent's eyes narrowed. "Are you injured?"

"I'm fine."

"I think the doctor should look you over to make sure," Regent decreed.

She shook her head. "I'm fine."

"Let's go to my office so we don't disturb Maxim," Regent suggested.

She tightened her hold around his hand. "I don't want to leave him." What if something happened to him while she wasn't here to look after him?

"The doctor will be back soon," Regent said.

"You trust him?" she asked.

Regent's eyes flared open. "Yes, of course. I wouldn't have him work on Maxim if I didn't."

She nodded, but she still didn't want to leave him.

The door suddenly flew open and a petite woman wearing a dark blue robe walked into the room. She gasped in horror as she saw Maxim.

"Oh my God! Why did no one wake me up?"

"Baby, he's fine."

She turned to look at Victor who moved toward the blonde woman.

"Victor! He's not fine! Gerald just told me that he was stabbed!" She glared at Victor.

"Gerald is a dead man."

She poked a finger at Victor. "No. Gerald is the only one around here who tells me anything. Why didn't you wake me up?"

"You were sleeping."

"Victor Malone, if something happens to one of our family, you wake me up."

Wow. This woman was tough. She couldn't imagine ever scolding a man like Victor.

"Little one, you need your sleep." His hand came to rest on her shoulder and the woman's face softened. Then her gaze moved to Aston.

"Hello. Who are you?"

"Um. I'm Aston."

The woman came toward her, holding out her hand. "Hi, I'm Gracen. I'm that big lug's fiancée." She pointed at Victor.

"That's brave of you," Aston commented without thinking.

Gracen grinned. "Don't let the outside package fool you. He's a marshmallow on the inside."

"Little one," Victor growled.

He might be a marshmallow for her, but Aston was willing to bet he wasn't like that with everyone.

"You're here with Maxim?" Gracen asked.

She nodded.

"She helped him when he was attacked, then drove him here," Regent explained in a surprisingly gentle voice.

To her shock, Gracen reached out and hugged her. "Thank you. We'd all be lost if something happened to Maxim."

"You're welcome." She couldn't remember the last time she'd been hugged. Well, by anyone other than Maxim. And while this wasn't the same as one of his hugs, it did help.

"You're freezing and you're in your pajamas! Why haven't you gotten her a blanket or something to wear?" Gracen demanded of the two men, pulling back with her hands on her hips. "Have they even offered you a drink? I baked blueberry muffins yesterday. Would you like one?"

"I, uh, um."

"I'll find you something to wear. Here, do you want my robe?" She reached for the tie as Victor growled in disapproval.

"No, no, I'm fine," she said hastily, not wanting to get offside with the big guy who was looking at his fiancée like the sun rose and fell on her.

"Gracen, we need to talk to Aston. Will you stay with Maxim?" Regent asked.

"Course I will." Gracen patted her shoulder. "Don't worry, I'll watch over him for you."

Aston felt tears form. This woman understood. Aston had never really had a friend. Other than Gretchen, whom she guessed wasn't much of a friend.

She would like a friend like Gracen though.

"Thanks," she said hoarsely.

Gracen nodded and took her seat when she got up. "He'll be fine until you get back. Promise."

Aston watched as Victor kissed the top of Gracen's head, then she followed Regent out the door and down the stairs.

Awesome. That meant she got to climb the stairs again later.

She was so tired, and she'd started limping slightly. She could really, really feel the pain in her feet now.

"Regent," Victor said as they entered an office that she guessed belonged to Regent. She didn't know why she thought that. Maybe because Victor didn't seem the type to have an office.

Regent looked to Victor and they seemed to share a silent conversation.

"Go get him," Regent commanded with a nod as he led her to a comfortable-looking sofa. "Please sit."

She nodded, grateful to sit. Another shiver ran through her and she watched as though in a daze as Regent pulled a blanket from a cupboard, and then wrapped it around her shoulders.

"Oh, thank you. That's kind of you."

He gave her a strange look. "Actually, sweetheart, it's probably the least I could do. And I should have done it already. I should have seen to your comfort."

There was definite censure in his voice, which was odd. Why would he see to her comfort? He didn't even know her. Maxim was his brother and injured. He should always come first.

She shook her head. "No. You were looking after Maxim. That was more important."

"Was it?" he asked, moving to the armchair across from her.

She frowned, confused at the question. "Of course it was. He was stabbed. I'm fine. And he's your brother, I'm just . . . Aston."

"Just Aston, are you?"

Either she was exhausted, or he just wasn't making sense. She wasn't sure which. She rubbed at her head as Victor and the doctor returned.

She stiffened. Why was the doctor here?

"The doctor's going to check to make sure you're not injured," Regent explained in a gentle but firm voice.

"I don't need that." She shook her head, stiffening.

"It will only take a moment. But he should have seen to you earlier."

Huh? She didn't understand. "I didn't need him. Maxim was stabbed and beaten."

"So they didn't touch you?" Regent asked.

"Ahh." Crap. She was trying not to lie. "Not that much."

"Uh-huh," Regent replied skeptically.

"You might be hurt and not know it," Victor told her.

She frowned. "I'd know."

"Adrenaline can trick your mind."

That was true. And now that she took stock, she was feeling bruised and sore. But nothing that she needed to see a doctor for.

"One of them threw me against a wall. That's it. I don't need to be checked over."

The doctor looked to Regent, who studied her.

"Her feet," Victor said.

"What?" she asked.

"Check her feet."

Great. They were the part that was hurting the most. She really wished she'd stopped to put on shoes. But then, perhaps those guys would have stabbed Maxim again.

So, a bit of pain in her feet was definitely worth it.

The doctor kneeled in front of her and held his hand out.

"Feet," Victor repeated insistently.

She huffed out a breath and raised her right foot. The doctor hummed as he checked her right foot, then her left. "They're filthy, and there are a couple of cuts that need to be cleaned and bandaged. Nothing deep enough to need stitches, though."

"I'll get Gerald to get some supplies," Regent said.

And she ended up having to put up with some strange man washing her feet, then disinfecting them and putting bandages on them.

"Stay off them as much as you can for at least twenty-four hours," the doctor ordered.

Sure. She'd get right on that.

He left and she stared at Regent wearily. "Can I go see Maxim again?"

Regent leaned forward. "I need you to tell me everything that happened first."

She drew in a deep breath. "All right." Then she told him it all. Seeing Maxim getting attacked, then grabbing a knife and racing down to help him, stabbing one of them and a good Samaritan helping them. And having to drive him here even though she didn't know how to.

Afterward, both men were quiet. What were they thinking?

"You ran out of the apartment in bare feet, dressed in your pajamas, with a knife?" Regent repeated.

"Um, yeah."

Lord, she was so tired that her head was thumping.

"Take these."

She opened her eyes, not having realized that she'd shut them, and saw Victor standing there, holding out two pain killers. The ones the doctor had left for her.

She shook her head. "I don't need them."

"You do. Take them."

"No. Thanks," she added, not wanting to be rude.

"Take them, or I'll tell Maxim when he wakes up."

She gaped up at the big guy. "You play dirty."

Victor grinned. And wow, that changed his face from terrifying to just scary. "Yep."

She swallowed the pills, then stuck her tongue out. "We good?"

"We're good."

"Have you always been a tattletale?" she grumbled.

"See why he likes you."

Weird. That's what Regent had said earlier. And what did that have to do with him being a tattletale? It was nice to hear though.

Letting out a deep breath, Aston tried to reassure herself yet again. "He'll be all right."

"Course he will." Victor repeated the same line from before. He would be all right.

He had to be.

Because she couldn't handle him being any other way.

23

"Do you know the men who attacked him, Aston?" Regent asked her, pulling her attention back to him.

Frowning, she shook her head. But something was tugging at her mind. Something that wouldn't leave her alone.

"Would you recognize them if you saw them again?" he asked.

"I don't know. It was too dark and it all happened so fast. But one of them does have my knife sticking out of him. There was also something about him..."

They were both silent, waiting her out.

"He smelled like timber."

"Like...timber?" Regent asked.

"Yeah, you know he smelled like he works with timber or maybe had some wood chips still on his top or something. I work for a construction company, and sometimes, the guys come in smelling like that to meet with my boss."

"Right." Regent and Victor stared at each other. "Has Maxim told you much about us?"

"No. He said he had something to tell me but then he ran out of time because he got a text from one of you and had to leave. Then yesterday, he was busy. We were supposed to spend today together." She gulped, swallowing back tears.

"It was brave of you to wade in like you did, sweetheart," Regent told her. "However, you shouldn't have risked your safety like that."

What?

"I had to. They were *hurting* him."

"And they could have hurt you. Maxim told us that you're important to him. That means you are important to us."

"So you expected me to sit by while he was being hurt?"

Victor grunted. "Gracen wouldn't."

Regent shot Victor a look, before turning back to her. "Anything like that happens again, you call me."

"They could have killed him," she whispered. "Before you got there."

Regent didn't look happy so she decided to change the subject.

"He wouldn't let me call an ambulance."

"They would have to report his injury to the police, which wouldn't have been ideal."

"Why not?" she asked. Although she had a feeling she might know. "You don't like the cops?"

"No, we don't," Regent replied calmly.

"I get that."

"You do?" There was surprise in his voice.

She winced. "My dad and brothers were often in trouble with the police."

"Were they? For what?" Regent asked.

She shrugged. "Assault. Burglary. They're dumbasses."

Shoot. Aston was tired. There was no way that she would have told them all that under normal circumstances.

"Is that so?" Regent murmured, looking pensive.

"It's all right. I don't have anything to do with them anymore." They were probably worried she was going to drag Maxim into that world. When the opposite was true. She didn't want him anywhere near those assholes.

"You've told Maxim about them?" Regent asked. He seemed to be the talker of the two brothers.

"No," she whispered, bracing herself. "I don't like to talk about them."

"Regent. Pajamas. Bare feet. Knife."

She looked up at Victor in confusion at his words. Regent nodded. "I know. It seems both you and Maxim were protecting each other from your families."

"Why would Maxim protect me from you guys? I mean, you're a bit scary, sure. And this place is kind of intimidating, but I know he's close to you all." She'd heard the pride and love in his voice when he'd spoken about them.

"Aston, have you seen anything odd going on with your employer?" Regent asked.

Why was he asking about Dayton? What did he mean, anything odd?

"I don't know what you're asking," she said cagily. Something strange was happening in the company, but she owed Dayton her loyalty.

"What I'm about to tell you might come as a shock, but I need your word that you won't discuss it with anyone," Regent told her.

She licked her lips and looked from Regent to Victor. "All right."

"There was a death at Maxim's club several weeks ago."

"I never heard about that."

"We tried to keep it quiet. The last thing we wanted was the police trying to shut the club down. Especially after we discovered that this person had taken a bad batch of a drug called Mixology. Have you heard of it?"

"No."

"We found the person selling it at the club. They told us who gave it to them to sell, and we followed the trail back. It led to your boss."

"My boss?" she asked faintly. "But why would it lead back to him? He's in construction. He's not into drugs. I'd have noticed if he took drugs."

"I'm not saying that he takes the drugs, sweetheart," Regent told her. "I'm telling you that it looks like he imports and sells them. And that a bad batch of the drug has killed several people across the city."

She sucked in a breath. Not good.

But she still couldn't believe that Dayton . . . no. "He's a good man."

Regent didn't try to argue; he simply nodded. "He might be a good man. Good men can do things that are against the law. But that batch of Mixology killed people, sweetheart."

Right. Aston stared down at her shaking hands. She'd stabbed a man tonight and she didn't even feel bad about it.

Maxim had been hurt.

And now his brothers were talking to her about her boss and drugs . . . why? What did this have to do with anything? And why tell her this?

"Why are you telling me this?"

Regent looked to Victor.

"Pajamas. Bare feet. Knife."

"Why do you keep saying that?" she asked Victor.

"He's reminding me that we owe you. That you belong to Maxim, which means that we need to look after you. Not put you in any more danger."

"What danger? What do you mean? This was just a simple mugging, wasn't it?"

"Three men drag a guy into an alleyway to beat him up and stab him at three in the morning," Regent said. "Sure, it could be random. Did you see these men approach before they attacked him?"

"No," she whispered. "But earlier I thought I was being watched as I walked home from the pool. So maybe they were lurking around."

Regent straightened. "You were followed home?"

"Maybe. I don't know. I didn't see anyone. But it could have been them, right? So it could be they were looking for someone to mug."

"I don't like this," Victor muttered.

"What time was that?" Regent asked.

"Around eleven."

"You went swimming on your own at night?" Regent asked.

"Umm, yes."

"That won't happen again," he told her.

Sheesh. Bossy.

Regent ran his hand over his face. "Did they seem to be looking for his wallet, his keys?"

"No." Oh God. She felt ill. Her mind raced, trying to pull this all together. "Do you . . . who do you think attacked Maxim if it wasn't random?"

She couldn't understand the connection between them telling her about her boss and this attack. She wasn't sure she believed what they were telling her about Dayton either.

Although . . . Dayton was acting weird lately.

"Aston? Are you all right?" Regent asked.

"You should have waited," Victor said. "He's not going to be happy."

Regent sighed. "I wish I could. But the sooner we discover

who attacked him, the better. I can't wait. I don't have that luxury."

"Does Maxim know what you suspect about my boss importing and distributing those drugs?" she suddenly asked.

Regent stiffened.

"Fuck," Victor muttered.

"Well? Does he know?" And was that the reason he'd gotten close to her? To see what she knew? A few weeks ago, someone had died at his club. The timing worked out.

It had seemed too good to be true that he might be interested in her.

Seemed it was.

"Yes, he did," Regent replied. "But—"

"You need someone to spy for you," she blurted out, finally connecting the dots. "On Dayton. To see if he's importing drugs."

"Well, yes, but—"

"Dayton has been good to me. He hired me without any real references. And he's never done anything to betray me."

Unlike Maxim.

Oh God. Had he ever wanted her?

"You need to listen to me, Aston," Regent said firmly.

But she was beyond listening. She didn't want to hear his explanation. Standing, she limped toward the door, trying to ignore the pain in her feet. Fury and hurt battled for supremacy.

"I want to go home now. I don't have any money, but I figure you owe me that much."

"You need to stay off your feet," Regent told her.

"I don't care. I want to go home."

Regent ran his hand over his face. "I know what you're thinking, but Maxim only recently learned about Dayton's involvement in the drug trade. He didn't get close to you in order to use you."

Okay, that soothed some of the hurt. But that didn't mean that he wouldn't use her to spy on Dayton now that he knew.

"He didn't know?" she repeated.

"We only discovered it a few days ago, we told Maxim on Friday night."

Did that have something to do with why he'd been busy all day?

She frowned as she looked over at Regent and Victor. "I don't know anything about Dayton being involved with drugs."

"All right, that's good." Regent didn't look happy about that though. "In all likelihood, he wouldn't mix his legitimate and illegal businesses together."

Shoot. Crap.

She didn't want to go against Dayton. And yet . . . there was a bad batch of drugs out there killing people.

Victor moved to her. "You need to sit."

She sighed but let him lead her back to the sofa. Once she was back sitting down, she wrapped the blanket around herself again.

"Do you think there some of that bad batch is still out there?" she asked.

"It could be," Regent said carefully.

"And more could come in," she muttered. "Hurting more people."

"That's true." Regent nodded.

"And you want me to spy on him for you? Because of this bad batch of drugs?"

Regent frowned. "That thought had crossed my mind, but that was before."

"Before what?" she asked.

"Bare feet. Pajamas. Knife," Victor muttered.

Huh. Oh.

"You . . . you wanted to use me to spy on Dayton, but now you don't because I helped Maxim?"

"When we told Maxim about Leeds' possible involvement with the new drugs, he told us about you."

"And he told us that there was no way he would involve you in this," Victor said.

And the wound closed up further. He didn't want to use her. Hadn't used her.

"Maxim made it clear that he cared about you. A lot. And now we also know that you feel the same," Regent explained. "We won't be risking you."

"Was he pulling away from me?" That's how it had felt yesterday. And even though she'd tried to pretend otherwise, it had worried her.

"If Leeds is involved in bringing this new drug in and he sees you with Maxim that could endanger you," Regent said carefully.

"Why? Why would it matter whether I'm with Maxim or not?"

"Because Maxim is a Malone."

So? She still didn't get it.

"She doesn't get it," Victor said, as though reading her thoughts.

"I can see she doesn't," Regent said gently. "Sweetheart, we're not interested in Leeds simply because we're worried about a bad batch of drugs."

Well, she had thought it seemed a bit strange. But she'd figured it had something to do with a man dying at Maxim's club. But now, that dark sense of foreboding was back.

"I don't know if we should tell her this," Victor said. "Maxim should tell her."

Regent nodded.

"I need to know," she insisted.

"No, Victor is right. This isn't our place."

"If I agree to spy on Dayton for you, will you tell me?" she asked.

Victor opened his mouth.

"Do not say it," she warned him.

"She can't," Victor said to Regent.

"Of course not," Regent replied. "I don't think we should let her work for him anymore. Maxim wanted her away from him."

"Agreed."

What the heck? These guys were insane. This was obviously where Maxim got his bossiness from.

"Whoa. Wait, no. Not agreed. You guys can't decide that. That's my job and I'm not quitting."

And what if Dayton is a drug dealer?

She swallowed heavily.

"It could be dangerous. I can't allow that," Regent told her seriously.

He couldn't allow that?

Was he for real?

"I only just met you guys," she pointed out.

"Bare feet. Pajamas. Knife," Victor reminded her.

She sighed. "How has Gracen not smothered you in your sleep?" Then, she instantly regretted that. "Sorry, didn't mean that."

He grinned. "Yeah, you did."

"I'm losing my mind." She ran her hand over her face. She was done in, so exhausted that she could barely think. And all she wanted was to curl up next to Maxim and just listen to his heart beat.

To remind herself that he was alive.

"I'm not quitting my job just because you think Dayton is distributing drugs in the city."

"You will if we think you're in danger," Regent said arrogantly.

Wow.

"Have you got a fiancée or wife?" she asked.

He looked surprised. "No."

"Hmm. I can see why."

Victor chuckled. "Yep. Definitely see why he likes you."

Regent gave her a stern look. "Aston, you can't work there anymore. It could be dangerous."

"How? You don't know that Dayton is guilty. And until you have proof, I don't think it's fair to vilify him."

"And what if he is bringing in drugs that are killing people?" Regent countered. "What if he's the one who sent men to hurt Maxim tonight?"

"What?" she whispered. "You think that Dayton is behind the attack on Maxim? Why would he be?"

"Because he might have heard that we've been trying to find out who is bringing Mixology into the city when we banned it," Regent told her.

"Banned it? How can you ban it?" she asked in confusion.

He and Victor looked at one another.

Seriously. They were so frustrating.

"Dayton might have seen you with Maxim," Regent added. "He might be worried that Maxim is using you to spy on him."

She shook her head. He can't have seen her with Maxim . . . right?

Though Gretchen might have seen them together that time Maxim picked her up. But would she mention it to her dad?

"He would have just fired me." Wouldn't he? "I doubt he knows I'm with Maxim. This is . . . we're new."

"You could be right," Regent said carefully. "But if he's panicking, he could act rashly. Therefore, you can't be anywhere near him."

"You really think Dayton could have sent men to attack Maxim?"

"It's a possibility."

"Because he's worried that you guys will discover that he's brought in Mixology. Something you banned."

"Yes. Maxim needs to explain the rest to you," Regent told her.

When he woke up. If he woke up.

No. He would wake up. She wouldn't accept anything else.

"I want to go see him. Can I do that before I have to go home?"

"Go home?" Regent asked.

"Yes. Go home. I can go home whenever I like, right?" Because she wouldn't handle any other answer. She wasn't going to be a prisoner. Not ever again.

"Once I'm sure it's safe."

She sucked in a breath.

"Maxim would be upset if he woke up and found out we'd let you leave, especially when we don't know if you're safe," Regent told her. "You're not a prisoner."

She wasn't so sure. But she decided to take him at his word. And did she really want to leave him, anyway?

No.

"I want to go back to him."

"I'll take you," Victor told her.

She nodded. But she hesitated for a moment, thinking things through. "Actually, here have been a few strange things I've noticed at work. Invoices that don't add up. A huge order for concrete that we overpaid for."

"Did you tell Dayton about what you found?" Regent asked.

"The first time I did," she admitted.

"And how did he react?" Regent asked.

"Strangely," she admitted. "So I didn't bring it up again."

"Could be how he's doing it," Victor said. "Smuggling the drugs in with his legitimate supplies."

Regent nodded. Then he looked at her with a tired smile. "Thanks, sweetheart. Go to him now. He needs you."

Did he? She wasn't so sure. But she knew that she needed him.

24

Fuck.

It felt like he'd been hit by a car. Everything damn well hurt.

Opening his eyes, Maxim stared around the room. Well, he tried to open his eyes. Only one of them co-operated.

Where the fuck was he?

Shit. This was his bedroom at the mansion. What was he doing here? And why was his side aching like a bitch?

Then, there were all the other aches and pains he was suffering from. Not to mention the fact that his right arm was numb. He glanced down that way and saw it was numb because someone had their head on it.

And something clicked inside his head. Memories rushed back.

He'd been coming home from the club, gotten out of his car, and that was when they'd attacked. They'd caught him by surprise.

Idiot.

He should have been paying closer attention. But he'd been

thinking about his girl and how he was going to have to pull back from her to keep her safe for a while.

And how much that was going to fucking suck.

Then he'd been pulled into an alleyway. He'd fought back, but three against one weren't great odds. Especially when one of those bastards had a knife.

"No!"

He stiffened as his girl cried out.

"Baby?"

"No! Maxim! Oh God! Maxim!"

Shit. Was she having a nightmare?

"Baby, wake up! Aston, wake up! You're safe." He tried to reach across his body with his other arm, but pain shot through his side.

"Fuck! Motherfucker!" he swore.

Suddenly, she sat straight up, staring down at him like she had no clue who he was.

"Baby, you're all right. You're safe."

"What . . . what are you trying to do?" she asked as he attempted to reach for her.

"I was trying to hug you."

"Don't do that."

He narrowed his gaze. "Excuse me?"

"You'll hurt yourself. You shouldn't be moving like that or you could rip your stitches. You needed fifteen stitches, Maxim."

"That's not so many." Fuck. One of those assholes had stabbed him.

"It's fifteen too many." Her voice was rising with a tinge of hysteria.

He watched her closely, taking in the large dark rings under her eyes and the messy mass of hair around her shoulders.

His girl wasn't doing so good. And it was up to him to take care of her. Had she gotten hurt when she'd jumped in with those assholes? Someone better have seen to her, and before they'd seen to him if they knew what was good for them.

"Come here, Rainbow." He held out his good arm, the one she'd been lying on.

Her eyes widened. "Didn't you just hear what I said? You need to lie still and not do anything that might pull at your stitches. That includes hugging me."

"I heard what you said, baby, and it's bullshit. You need a hug and I'm going to give you one. Now, either you make that easier on me by coming here, or you make me chase after you and force-hug you."

"Force-hug me?"

"Force-hug you."

"You know that could be considered assault, right?" she asked, that tinge of hysteria in her voice again.

"You planning on calling the cops on me for forcing you to hug me, Rainbow?"

"You know I'm not."

"Come here, baby. Even if you don't need a hug, I could sure use one."

Just as he'd thought, that did it. She ended up plastered against his chest. She came at him faster than he'd expected, so there was some pain as she landed heavily against him. But there was no way he'd ever say anything to her.

She shuddered against him. "You suck."

"I know," he soothed.

"You really, really suck."

"I do," he agreed as he ran his hand up and down her back, hoping to ease the trembles in her body. "I suck big time."

"How dare you get stabbed? You asshole."

"Total asshole."

"You got beaten up, you jerk."

"Lay it on me, Rainbow. Tell me how you really feel," he teased.

"And you need to stop being so reasonable. I don't like it."

"I'll stop," he promised.

"Making me drive you here while you were bleeding out. You nearly bled to death and I didn't know how to drive. Total jerk move."

He wasn't sure it'd been that dire. Although he noticed that he had an IV drip. Had he needed blood as well?

"So inconsiderate of me."

"Completely inconsiderate. You owe me some new pajamas."

He stiffened.

"Pajamas?"

"Yes, I was wearing my pajamas. I couldn't sleep and I went out onto my balcony for some fresh air. And then I saw . . . then I s-saw you being attacked."

Jesus. His poor girl. He could only imagine how terrifying that had to have been for her.

"Baby, you should have stayed safe in your apartment."

"They were beating you up, Maxim! You got s-stabbed."

Christ. He wished to hell he'd killed those fucking bastards. How dare they upset his girl?

"Now those p-pajamas remind me of them. I had to t-throw them out. Luckily, G-gracen gave me some of her c-clothes. But they were my favorite!"

Oh, his poor girl. He knew she didn't care about the pajamas. No, that was just the thing she'd decided to focus on.

A sob broke free from her mouth and he felt terrible.

"I n-need new p-pajamas now," she sobbed.

"I'll buy you pajamas, baby. As many as you want."

"Those h-had sloths on t-them."

"We'll get you more pajamas with sloths on them." He'd say

or do anything to stop her from crying. Turning his head, he kissed her forehead.

All of him hurt. The kind of hurt that he knew wouldn't go away in a day or two. But his physical pain had nothing on the pain in his heart right now. The pain he could hear in her voice.

"Baby, please stop crying," he begged. She clung to him and he could feel her tears against his bare skin. Someone had stripped off his clothes, so her face was pressed into his bare chest.

Under other circumstances, he'd be fucking ecstatic to have her in his bed with him. But he'd never imagined or wished she'd be sobbing her heart out like this.

"Shh, baby. You're all right. You're safe. Everything is okay."

"I'm not worried about me, you . . . you dipshit."

She didn't swear often. He had a vague recollection of her swearing while she drove him here. He winced at the memory. God, she must have been terrified. She didn't even know how to drive and she'd had a crash course on driving in the dark with him injured and passed out next to her.

Yeah, he could understand how that would make her swear.

"You could h-have died."

"Shh. It's all right, my baby. I'm okay. I'm so sorry you got scared, that I frightened you, but it's going to take more than a few assholes to take me out."

"They might have. They m-might have k-killed you."

The truth was, she was right. He didn't think they'd been trying to mug him. They'd wanted to cause him pain. One of them had stabbed him.

Fucking asshole.

And then she'd come racing in, ready to help him even though he'd told her to leave.

"You took my back."

"What?"

Anger mixed with fear inside him. "Soon as I'm feeling up to it, you're getting your ass spanked," he growled at her.

"What? Why?" She drew back from him and he didn't like that. But he had to tell her this. And then he could tug her back where she belonged. Next to him.

"You ran into danger, Aston. You aren't supposed to run toward assholes. You run the fuck away from them."

Her eyes widened. "You. Are. Kidding. Me."

He could see that she was angry. But he didn't care, since he was now mad too. The memory of her racing into the alley, and jumping on that asshole's back . . . yeah, that wasn't going to leave him anytime soon.

And she obviously needed a lesson in self-preservation. Which he was only too happy to give her.

"Not joking. Not even a little bit. And this is going to be a punishment spanking, Rainbow. So prepare yourself for that. You won't like it, but I will get my point across. You do not put yourself in danger. Not ever. Not for anything or anyone. Do you understand me?"

Her mouth dropped open, and she gaped at him. "They were attacking you!"

"Yep."

"You expected me to just calmly sit on my balcony and let you get beaten up?"

"I should have given you my brothers' phone numbers. I'll do that for next time."

"Next time? Next. Time. Are you kidding me right now, Maxim Malone?"

He winced. He blamed his slip-up on his blood loss because, typically, he wouldn't have made such a mistake.

"I just meant that if there's ever trouble, which is unlikely, you'll need my brothers' numbers so you can call them."

"That's what they said too," she muttered.

They had?

"Maxim?"

"Yeah."

"Even if I'd had your brothers' numbers, I still would have done what I did."

He stiffened. "What?"

"They were at least fifteen minutes away. I was right there. You . . . you didn't have fifteen minutes."

No, he hadn't. That didn't mean he wanted his girl getting mixed up in shit that he couldn't protect her from.

Then something else occurred to him. She'd been awake at three in the morning when she'd seen him being attacked.

"Baby, you couldn't sleep?" he asked softly.

"No. No. Nope. You do not get to go all sweet on me now, Maxim Malone! You can't go from telling me you're going to spank me to speaking to me in that voice. If it wasn't for me, you might be dead!"

"I had it handled." Yeah, he wasn't so sure of that. Not once they'd stabbed him.

"You did not have it handled you . . . you arrogant toad!"

Ooh, she was getting wound up. She was gorgeous when she was angry. But she still had to learn that he was in charge of her safety. And he would never allow her to put herself at risk.

"You can argue all you like, baby. You're still getting that spanking. Because, at the end of the day, you aren't to put yourself in danger for any reason."

"Not even to help you?"

"No. Not even to help me."

"That's . . . that's bullshit."

He reached up and cupped her cheek, wincing slightly at the movement. Her eyes narrowed and he knew she was about to lecture him again, so he pressed a finger to her lips.

"My life wouldn't be worth living if something happened to you, baby. I don't ever want you to get hurt."

She heaved out a breath, her face softening. He moved his hand back to her cheek, cupping it.

"I don't want you to get hurt either," she told him.

"I know you don't. And I'm glad you care about me. But I need you to understand something. You are more important than I am."

She gaped at him again.

"Baby? You all right?"

"Uh, yeah, just wondering what to say to that . . . that load of codswallop."

"Codswallop?"

"Yes, Maxim. Codswallop."

"Is that even a word?"

"Yes, it's a word. It means bullshit."

"Then why not just say bullshit?" he asked, deliberately winding her up.

"Because I'm trying not to swear!" She raised her hands in the air. "While still trying to impress on you that what you are saying is bullshit! I am not more important than you!"

"Baby, you are."

"Why?"

"Because without you, I don't think I'd want to keep breathing."

She stared at him in shock. "Maxim . . ."

"And because I'm a Malone. And I've told you this: Malone men take care of their women. Therefore, you are more important than me. Your safety is important. If you put yourself at risk, then you get your ass spanked so that the next time you go to put yourself in danger, you'll remember that spanking. And then you'll remember the man who gave it to you. And you'll remember that man thinks you're the most important thing in the world. Because you are his world."

Tears dripped down her face.

"Shit, baby. I didn't mean to make you cry."

"It . . . it's too soon to say those things. Who says things like that? People don't say them. Men don't say things like that."

"You think I'm going to get my man card revoked for saying things like that?"

"What? No!" She gave him a fierce look. "And if anyone tries, they'll have me to answer to."

He laughed, then groaned, placing his hand on his side. "Fuck, whatever drugs they've got me on, they aren't good enough."

"I'll get the doctor. Shoot. I should have gotten him straight away instead of losing it like I just did."

"No, you shouldn't have. You did exactly what you needed to do. You needed to get that out, and I'm glad you did."

"Maxim, you need to stop," she begged. "We haven't known each other long enough for you to say such lovely things."

"I have to know you a certain amount of time before I can say nice things to you?" he asked.

"Yes," she told him.

"Baby, I've known you for months."

"But you don't know everything about me. There might be things that you don't like about me."

"I know you, Rainbow."

"Not everything," she insisted.

"I know enough. Now, come here and kiss me."

"I should get the doctor."

"Kiss me," he demanded.

"Your brothers."

"They don't want to kiss me. I don't want to kiss them. I want you to come here and kiss me."

"You're nuts," she told him.

"Luckily, so are you."

He reached up and grabbed her around the back of her head, pulling her down to him. "Kiss me."

And so she did.

It started sweet and gentle, but then it deepened into something more. And to his surprise, he wasn't the one who took it deeper. When she drew back, the tension and worry had eased from her face.

"Come lie with me."

"I shouldn't. I should go and get—"

"Baby, that wasn't a suggestion. It was an order. Lie with me. Now."

She shot him a look.

"And don't be giving me any of that Rainbow sass. No sass while a man is lying on his death-bed."

Her eyes grew wide and he immediately winced, seeing his mistake. "Too soon to joke about that, huh?"

"News flash, it will always be too soon to joke about that."

"Got it. Come lie with me, baby, so I can hold you."

She finally settled into his side. Where she belonged. He kissed the top of her head, hoping that this would help her relax. Maybe even get some sleep. His poor girl was exhausted and had had a really rough night.

"I still don't think I'm more important than you," she whispered.

"It isn't something you need to think about, baby. It's just a fact of life. Are you all right? They didn't hurt you, did they?" Fuck. Why hadn't he already asked her that? He was doing a poor job of taking care of her.

"I'm fine."

"You sure? Because if I find out later that you're not and you were lying to me . . . you won't just be feeling my hand on your ass, you'll feel my belt."

"You have got to stop threatening to spank me."

"If you behave yourself, then you won't get spanked." He shifted around, looking for water.

"What is it? What do you need?" she asked.

"Is there some water anywhere?"

"Oh God! I didn't get you any water! I'll get you some."

Okay, he needed to nip this in the bud. This guilt trip she seemed to be on wasn't acceptable.

"Rainbow, look at me," he commanded as she rolled over to grab a glass of water off the nightstand. "Aston."

"I'm getting your water."

"Look at me."

She looked at him. Well, glared at him. But he'd take it. "I'm okay, baby. A bit sore and banged up, but I'm going to be all right. Understand? There's nothing you have to feel guilty about. And you don't need to run yourself ragged looking after me. In fact, I'm going to be upset if you do."

She huffed. "I think there should be a rule that if you're injured, you don't get to be bossy."

"Baby, I'm not just bossy. I'm *the* boss. And nothing will change the fact that I'm always the boss."

"You're out of control. Were you like this as a child?"

"As a child, I had little control over anything," he said darkly, taking the glass she held out. "My mom died when I was young and my dad . . . well, let's just say that he only really had time for Regent since he was the oldest. But that was a blessing for us and hell for Regent because our father was a cold, egotistical bastard."

"I'm sorry," she whispered. "I know a thing or two about having a bad father. My mom took off when I was young. I don't really remember her."

He squeezed her hand. "I'm sorry you had a similar experience to me growing up, baby."

"Yeah. But even though he was a terrible dad and person, I still wanted his attention," she said.

"I understand that. I was the same. But when he gave me his attention, I regretted it."

"Did he . . . did he hurt you?" she whispered.

"Sometimes. But more with his words than anything else. Regent shielded us all as well as he could, but that meant he had to grow up quickly. It's also made him overly protective of us all."

"Yeah, I kind of caught that."

"Has he been looking after you?" he asked in a low voice. Regent took care of his family, but outside that tight circle there were very few others that he paid attention to or cared about. And he'd just met Aston.

Regent didn't know that she needed handling like she was made of glass. That under that tough exterior, she was fragile.

"He's been looking after me. He had the doctor look me over."

"And?"

"I told you, I'm fine."

He grunted. All right. He would take her at her word. For now.

"You need to sleep, baby. Snuggle into me. Let me help you."

She eyed him. To his shock, she just nodded and slid closer to him.

Hmm. What was she playing at now? Well, whatever it was, he guessed he didn't care since it got him what he wanted.

Her in his arms.

25

Aston didn't need to sleep.

Well. That wasn't true. She did. She was completely and utterly exhausted. However, seeing as it was close to midday and she was now wired, she knew she wouldn't be able to. She'd gotten a bit of a cat-nap before. That would tide her over for a while.

However, Maxim needed sleep.

His body desperately required sleep in order to start repairing itself. He'd lost a lot of blood. And she knew that he was more likely to sleep if he wasn't worrying about her.

So she curled up next to him, holding him carefully.

He was silent for a long time, so she figured he'd fallen asleep. She should get up and shower. She was wearing some of Gracen's clothes, but she'd really like to get some of her own. She felt exposed like this. Her clothes were part of her armor and being without them left her vulnerable.

Should she stay here? She didn't want to leave Maxim. However, she couldn't get what they'd told her out of her head.

Was Dayton doing something illegal? Had he sent those men to hurt Maxim?

If he had . . . she wanted to know. Needed to know.

Which might mean that she needed to do some investigating on her own.

Which wasn't going to go down well.

These Malone men were really something else.

"Do you have nightmares often?" he asked in a rough voice.

"I thought you were asleep."

"I was dozing. Baby, do you often have nightmares? You were having one earlier, just before you just woke up. You called out my name, so I'm guessing that nightmare was about what happened last night. But do you have other nightmares often? Is that part of why you have trouble sleeping?"

"Yeah, I have a lot of trouble falling asleep," she confessed. "I can't seem to turn my brain off. I get into bed and I start going over everything. All the stuff that happened in my day. Things I could have done differently. All my regrets. Stuff about my family. And yeah, sometimes when I do get to sleep, I have nightmares."

"What are those nightmares about usually?"

She stiffened.

"Anything you tell me is safe with me," he told her. "I'd never use it against you, never tell anyone else without your permission. *You're* safe with me, baby."

"I know. You . . . you make me feel safe in a way I never have before."

"Except for what just happened when I couldn't protect you," he said bitterly.

She leaned up on one hand to glare down at him. She had to brush back her hair, which was such a tangled mess that she knew it was going to be a real pain to tame it. But that was a problem for later.

"Maxim Malone, it was three against one. Those odds weren't in your favor, and you were still more worried about keeping me safe than you. I'd say you protect me just fine."

He opened his mouth.

"And I don't want to hear another word about it."

A THROAT CLEARING had Maxim looking over at the door as Regent, then Victor, walked in. Regent looked serious, while Victor was grinning. Which was decidedly strange.

They were followed by Doctor Edwards, who Regent kept on retainer.

Immediately, the doctor moved to his side, checking his vitals and then taking a look at his injury. Which hurt like a bitch, but he didn't let on because he didn't want to upset his girl.

Or his brothers. Who could be over-protective.

Regent had his gaze on the doctor. Victor winked at him.

Seriously. What was wrong with him?

"You should have called me the minute he woke up," the doctor snapped at Aston, who tensed and tried to climb off the bed.

He held her tighter to him and then turned to scowl at the doctor. "Get out."

"What?"

"You're fucking fired. Leave now. And be grateful that I'm in no state to throw you the fuck out."

"Maxim," she whispered.

"Hush, baby. Let me take care of this."

"You can't fire me!" the doctor blustered. "I don't work for you. And you need me."

"I don't need you," Maxim retorted. "I can go find another doctor. One who knows how to talk to a Malone woman. And that means with fucking respect. You're fired. Leave now before Victor makes you leave."

The doctor swallowed heavily, growing pale. Then he glanced over at Victor. And he grew even paler.

"Mr. Malone?" The doctor turned to Regent. He was probably panicking because he realized his cushy job was about to end. Regent paid him well to be on call. And he wasn't called on that often. So, he spent most of his days dining out and playing golf.

So yeah, he was likely panicking.

"You heard my brother. You're fired. Take anything that belongs to you and go. But I know I paid for most of this equipment, so I expect you to take very little," Regent said coldly.

"This is . . . this is ridiculous!" he almost shouted. "I saved your brother, stitched him up, and now you're going to fire me just because she should have used her brain and called me in once he woke up."

"If I was in pain, feverish, feeling ill, she would have called you," Maxim told him. "But I'm none of those things and she could see that. Because she was using her brain. Unlike you. You were not using your brain when you snapped at my woman or when you just insulted her. So now you can get the fuck out. Now!"

"Maxim, it's okay," she whispered.

"It's not okay, baby. No one talks to you like that. And you thinking that it's okay, that's also not all right with me. You should expect to be treated with respect. All the time. And if anyone doesn't give you the respect you deserve, you'll come to me, understand?"

To his shock, tears filled her eyes. He heard the doctor thump out of the room, but his attention was only for her.

"I love you, Maxim Malone."

Thank fuck.

There she was. His Rainbow. His bright spot on a dull day.

"That's good because I love you too, Aston Symonds."

And then he kissed her. Because that's what you did when the woman you loved said she loved you.

She drew back and gave him a decisive nod. "Good. Then you'll understand what I'm going to do."

"What you're going to do?"

"I'm going to spy on Dayton Leeds."

26

Malone men were sexy.
Malone men were bossy.
They were overprotective.

They could be a touch controlling, but in that good way, which meant they just wanted to take care of you.

But also, Malone men were stubborn, argumentative, and they could be really, really frustrating.

"You are not," Maxim told her sternly, glaring at her from his one good eye.

Every time she saw his face, saw him wince in pain, she wanted to murder someone.

And if her boss had anything to do with those men attacking her man . . . well, the Malones weren't the only ones who could be protective.

"I am," she said calmly.

"No, baby. You are not doing this. End of discussion."

"Just because you say it's the end of the discussion, doesn't mean it's the end of the discussion."

"Do you love me?"

Dear. Lord.

It took a lot of patience to be with a Malone man . . . she'd known that already. But now she was definitely experiencing it.

All right, so she'd known that her statement would meet resistance. But she was hoping to talk them around.

Didn't seem that was going to happen.

"You know I love you," she replied.

"Then it's the end of the discussion."

"No, it is not."

"Aston," he grumbled.

"Honestly, I think I liked it better when you only paid attention to me when I was right in front of you."

He shook his head at her. "You were on my mind more often than that and you know it. I thought about you all the time. Mostly, when I was in the shower, jacking off."

"Maxim Malone!" Aston slammed her hand over his mouth as she felt her face growing red. She kept her gaze down, ensuring she did not look at his brothers.

Victor let out a deep laugh and Maxim tugged her hand away.

"You all right, big guy?" he asked, looking at his brother strangely.

"Yep. Just enjoying the show."

"Glad we could provide entertainment," Maxim muttered. He shot her a look. "My brother thinks you're funny."

"He thinks everything is funny." She frowned at Victor who stared back at her warmly.

"Ah no, he doesn't."

"Sure he does. I've seen him smile at least a dozen times since I got here."

Maxim stared at her, then Victor. Then he relaxed with a smile. "He likes you."

"Of course I like her," Victor replied. "Bare feet. Pajamas. Knife."

She sighed and glared at Victor. "Are we really back at that?"

"I'm never going to forget what you did for my brother, girl," he told her.

"None of us are," Regent added in a low, firm voice. "Which is why we can't allow you to put yourself in danger."

Maxim relaxed further. "She's family."

Regent nodded. "Yes. She's family."

There was some subtext to this conversation that she didn't understand. "What does that mean that I'm family? I'm not family."

"Of course you are," Victor said matter-of-factly. "You're family. Bare feet. Pajamas. Knife."

"Victor Malone, you better stop saying that or . . . or . . ."

"Or what?" Victor raised his eyebrows.

"I'm gonna tell Gracen."

Victor's eyes filled with amusement. She didn't understand why Maxim said he didn't smile much. He seemed to be constantly amused. Often, she thought, at her expense.

And yeah, she knew her threat was pretty empty. What was she going to tell Gracen? That her crazy fiancée kept saying the same words over and over again.

"I didn't do anything that amazing."

Regent walked forward and sat in a chair next to the bed while Victor leaned against the wall at the end of the bed. She hadn't taken much time to look at the bedroom. It was masculine but still warm, done in navy blue and maroon tones. A couple of really comfortable blue armchairs and an enormous bed were the main furniture in the room as well as two big bookshelves that framed a large TV on one wall. And there was an attached bathroom.

It was comfortable and nice. Welcoming.

"You don't consider saving my brother to be that important?" Regent asked.

"That's not what I meant. I just . . . I . . . don't want to make a big deal of it."

"Well, unfortunately for you, I do feel like making a big deal of it. You helped save my brother, you brought him to me even though you were terrified. That makes you family. And when you're family, you have to follow the rules."

She rolled her eyes heavenward. "More rules. If you threaten to spank me, we're going to have a problem." She pointed at Regent.

"Can see why you like her," Victor said to Maxim.

"Uh, thanks. But why do you keep saying bare feet, pajamas, knife?" Maxim asked.

"Because she was brave enough or foolish enough, depending on how you look at it, to rush into a fight to save you with bare feet, wearing pajamas, and armed with a kitchen knife."

"What the fuck? No one said anything about a knife!" Maxim roared.

Uh-oh. She tried to inch her way off the bed. Maxim turned to her, then hissed in pain.

She froze. "Do not move!"

"A knife?"

"Maxim—"

"You rushed in with a knife? You picked up a knife, but didn't bother with shoes?"

"No time for shoes."

"No time for shoes?" he yelled.

She hated to think how painful it was for him to yell with a hole in his side. All right, the wound had been stitched, but still. He needed to be calm.

"It's not a big deal," she told him.

"Wrong play," Victor muttered.

She glared at him. She thought he'd helped enough.

And by that, she meant that he hadn't helped at all.

"It's really not. I couldn't even feel my feet. I didn't notice."

"You could have stepped on anything. A bit of glass. A rusty nail. You could have cut your feet up, so it is a big deal."

"Maxim, you were being beaten up in an alley! You were stabbed! You had a huge hole in you. A small cut on my foot hardly matters."

His good eye narrowed. "You cut your foot? Show me."

"It's barely a scratch."

His gaze moved to Regent. "Did she get seen to by that asshole?"

Regent nodded. "He washed her feet and put a few bandages on them. None of them were deep enough to need stitches, but she's supposed to keep off them as much as possible for a few days."

"I carried her back up here after we learned that she'd hurt them," Victor offered.

"I didn't need to be carried," she muttered.

That had been embarrassing. Especially when Gracen had greeted them in the bedroom. She'd thought the other woman might get mad that her fiancée was carrying her around. But she'd been full of concern. And then she'd hustled to get Aston some clothes. Which were a bit small on her since Gracen was so short, but they were better than wearing those pajamas.

She'd never had anyone take care of her like that. Fuss over her. Well, other than Maxim.

And it had been lovely.

It'd made her wonder what it would have been like if her mom had stuck around. Or if she'd ever had anyone in her life that had actually cared about her. Even just a little bit.

"Did you not hear the doctor when he said that you had to stay off your feet?" Maxim asked her.

"Yes, but I had to walk on my feet to get you to the car. I also walked on my feet to get into the house, then to go up the stairs to see you, and then down the stairs again to talk. So I think I would have been fine to walk back up again."

It wasn't until she finished talking that she realized he'd gone tense. His face was hard. He was upset.

No, more than that. He was mad.

She froze for a moment, worried that he was mad at her. But his anger all seemed to be aimed at his brothers.

"Why didn't my woman get seen to first?" he asked in a low rumble.

Huh? What did he mean?

"The doctor should have seen to her first," Maxim said.

Oh crap. They were back to the 'my woman is more important than I am' conversation.

"Maxim, you were bleeding out. And unconscious. Of course the doctor saw you first. I just had a couple of cuts on my feet and a few bruises on my back. There's no way I needed his attention before you."

"What bruises?" he asked.

"Lord help me. What happened to the easygoing, doesn't have a care in the world, Maxim?" she muttered.

"He got himself a trouble-attracting, too brave for her own good, sassy woman. That's what happened."

"Jardin is going to be pissed," Victor commented.

What? Who was Jardin?

"That's my other brother." Maxim had obviously seen her confusion. "He's in Texas visiting our cousins. They've got some legal issues. They often have legal issues."

She wondered what that meant.

"So pissed to miss this," Victor said.

"You're not helping, Victor," Regent said firmly. "Maxim, it was my fault."

"Damn straight it was."

"You need to calm down," she told Maxim. "You're getting worked up over nothing."

He slashed his gaze to her. Well, his good eye went to her. She hated how bruised he was.

"You're injured. You should be resting, not worrying about any of this. Maybe we should all leave you alone."

"You step one foot off this bed and I'll have Victor tie you to it."

She gaped at him.

Fudge, he was serious.

"What if I have to pee?" she asked.

"They make adult diapers, don't they?"

"Maxim Malone!" She was incapable of saying anything more. She couldn't believe he'd said that.

Nuts.

Her guy was completely nuts.

"You are going to do exactly what the doctor said and rest your feet. That means the only reason you get out of this bed is to go to the bathroom."

"I have other things to do."

"No, you don't."

"I need to get some of my things from my apartment if I'm staying here."

"You're definitely staying here, and Victor can get your things. He'll take Gracen so he's not touching your underwear."

She groaned.

"No interest in touching her underwear," Victor said. "No offense, Aston."

"None taken," she said faintly. "What if I want to eat? Or tomorrow when I need to go to work?"

"I think we already had this conversation."

"We really didn't. I'm going to work, Maxim."

"You're quitting."

"I'm not."

"Again . . . I'll repeat it in case you didn't understand me before. I will have Victor tie you to the bed."

"Victor won't do that."

"He will, baby. He's a Malone man."

She groaned and flung herself on her back on the bed, her arm over her eyes. She was too tired for this. Her head hurt. Her feet hurt. And she couldn't out-stubborn a goat.

It was impossible.

"Are you all right? Do you need some painkillers?" Maxim asked her, his voice gentle now. Cajoling.

She sighed. She could say no. But she wanted to say no because she was annoyed at him. And saying no would only hurt her. So she nodded.

Victor looked at his watch. "Yeah, it's been a while since her last painkillers. I'll get some." He pushed away from the wall and moved into the bathroom. He returned with a bottle, shaking two pills out to give to her.

"Thanks," she muttered.

"We're just trying to look out for you, little sister."

Those words felt like a punch to her stomach. She had older brothers, but they weren't good older brothers. She'd read so many stories where the older brothers looked out for their little sisters. And she'd wanted that with a desperation that bordered on obsession. Yet she'd never had it. And her two brothers were never going to give that to her. Hell, she'd have been happy if they would have just ignored her.

Rather than torment her.

But the way Victor was looking at her. It didn't feel like the words were something he was just saying. It felt like he meant them.

Which was ridiculous when he barely knew her.

But still... she could feel herself getting teary.

"This is ridiculous. I hardly ever cry." She wiped at her eyes angrily.

"You've had a rough night," Regent said. "It's to be expected. Also, I'm guessing you're not used to people looking out for you?"

"I've never had that."

"So it's like you've gone from zero to a hundred then," Regent said. "Because we don't do things by halves."

"You sure don't," she muttered.

Maxim squeezed her thigh with his hand. "Take your painkillers, Rainbow. Then lie back and rest, okay?"

"It's a bit hard to rest when you were beaten and stabbed. I don't like that."

"We don't like it either," Regent told her.

"I can't believe you grabbed a knife and then ran down to help me in bare feet," Maxim muttered.

"You're all fixated on my bare feet for some reason." She swallowed her painkillers.

"You're family now. We protect our own," Regent said. "And we owe you for saving our brother."

"I don't know much about being part of a family," she told them. "My brothers and dad are complete assholes. But I'm guessing that family doesn't ever owe family. They just have their backs. Always. Am I right?"

"Yes, sweetheart," Regent said softly while smiling warmly at Aston. "You're right."

Victor nodded.

She wasn't sure how she'd ever thought the two of them were

scary. Because right now, the way they looked at her, they seemed anything but.

Or maybe it was because they were only scary if you weren't family.

Wow. How had her life turned around so completely?

Actually, she didn't need to know that. She had the answer.

The answer was Maxim.

She turned her face into his arm for a moment.

"Baby? You okay?"

"Just need a second," she whispered.

"Okay, you take your second."

God. For all that he could be a stubborn, pain-in-the-ass, bossy man. He could also be so freaking sweet.

Killing. Her.

"Can you take us through what happened last night?" Regent asked Maxim. "Maybe something will come back to you that you missed."

"Yeah, okay."

She didn't like how tired Maxim sounded. She wished she could tell them to leave so he could rest. But this was important and needed to be said.

So she held onto him and listened as he went through everything.

"So you've never seen any of them before?" Regent asked.

"Not that I recall. But I didn't get a really good look at them."

"Did Aston tell you that she felt she was being watched on her way home from the pool tonight," Victor said.

"What? No! What time was that?" Maxim asked.

She glared at Victor. "Tattletale."

His lips twitched.

"Um, I don't know," she lied.

"She said around eleven," Regent added.

"You are both off my Christmas card list!"

"Aston, please tell me you weren't swimming at eleven at night!" Maxim yelled.

"You need to calm down," she scolded.

"Aston."

"Fine. Yes, I was. But I usually swim that late at night, I just haven't been doing it lately. And I've never had a problem."

"You are never swimming that late at night again without me," Maxim decreed.

She decided that in order to get him to calm down she better agree with him. "All right."

"Gonna spank your ass for that too."

"Maxim!" she protested, going red. Yikes.

"So there's no way to know if these guys belonged to Leeds or not," Regent mused.

"But it's not likely this was random, right?" Maxim said. "Someone sent those guys to attack me. Leeds or someone else."

"Someone else?" she asked, moving her head to look around at them. Her moment was over. "Like who?"

"You're thinking about Patrick?" Victor rumbled.

Who was Patrick?

"I haven't heard that he's back," Regent said. "He ran after we got rid of the Ventura Gang and Santiago. As far as I'm aware he no longer has any allies here."

"Doesn't mean he couldn't pay some assholes to go after Maxim," Victor pointed out.

"But why go after me?" Maxim asked.

"Because he can't get to Regent or me," Victor said.

"Thank fuck he didn't go after Jardin," Maxim muttered. He turned to her. "Thea, my brother's fiance, has custody of her two brothers, Ace and Keir. If he had the kids or Thea with him when he was attacked..."

Right. She got it.

No, it was better that they'd gone for Maxim. At least he had her watching his back.

"I still don't think this is Patrick's work," Regent said. "It's too straight-forward for him. He's more of a snake, hiding in the long grass, ready to strike."

"So our best guess is Dayton," Maxim said grimly. "That fucking asshole must know we're on to him."

"We told Aston that we've been looking into Dayton because of the bad batch of Mixology on the streets," Regent explained. "And because someone died from taking some of that bad batch in your nightclub. But we haven't explained our other reason for looking into him."

"Right," Maxim said, then glanced at her. "That might be a conversation for the two of us to have in private."

She stared at him before gazing around at them. "I don't know what you do for a living, but you obviously have money. And you have armed guards at your gate. Which means you likely have enemies. Also, you didn't seem all that shocked when I called you in the middle of the night to tell you that Maxim was bleeding from a stab wound."

"Baby," Maxim said gently.

Regent stared at her for a long moment. It surprised her that Maxim stayed quiet. But she knew Regent was the oldest. And he was obviously the head of this family. She saw this in the way he held himself. How people listened to him. Deferred to him. And she hadn't known him long, but it seemed like they didn't do it out of fear. Which is the only reason she'd been brave enough to say what she had just said.

"I think we need to get this out in the open," she said. "Because if . . . if Dayton is behind all of this, then I'm guessing he could come after all of you again. Which means he could come after Jardin and his family. Or Gracen. Right?"

"Nobody is touching Gracen," Victor rumbled.

"Or he could come at you," Regent said.

"Nobody is touching Aston either," Maxim said in that same tone that Victor had used.

Badass alpha voice.

"Am I right when I say that you don't always operate on the right side of the law?" she asked.

Maxim tensed before letting out a sigh. "Our family runs the largest criminal syndicate in Louisiana. For years, the Malones have owned New Orleans. Our father groomed Regent to take over, just like his father did to him. And his father before him. And all of them, apart from Regent, have been fucking psychopaths. I hope you understand why I hesitated to tell you all this. It's not something I can tell just anyone. Well, many people know what the Malone name means. But still . . . it's one thing to hear rumors and another to have your man come straight out and tell you that his family has been in the crime business for years."

"Do you . . . do you all hurt people?"

Maxim grew even tenser. Victor straightened and stared down at her. But it was Regent who her gaze went to.

"You're family now," Regent told her.

"Right," she whispered.

"Family first. Everyone else second."

"That's your motto, huh?" she asked. Did that mean they harmed people who weren't family?

"That and don't fuck with the Malones." Victor's lips twitched.

"Baby, we don't have to do this now." Maxim claimed her hand in his.

"No, I want to do this now. Do you hurt people?" she repeated.

"Only those that deserve it," Regent said quietly. "My father used to rule using fear and threats. He would extort people for money and send his men out to shake people down for protection money. His crew ran the streets of New Orleans with knuckle dusters and guns."

She gulped.

"I don't run my city the same way. We have as many legal businesses as we do illegal. That isn't to say that we'll ever be completely legit. We're not. But all of Maxim's clubs are free and clear. We don't do any business there. If anyone is found dealing drugs, they're out. They're banned. Anything else, they're gone."

"Right," she whispered.

"Maxim isn't involved in any of this beyond being part of the family and having our backs. Just like we have his back."

"That doesn't mean I wouldn't jump in feet first if you needed me to have your back. Like I will with Leeds. Not only because his shit is killing people or because he might have sent men to beat on me, but because he's close to Aston."

"He's never done anything to me," she protested.

"That doesn't mean you're safe from him, baby."

"But I think I am. He can't touch me at work. There are people in and out all day. And that means I have a chance of finding something."

"No."

The other two nodded again in agreement.

Regent leaned forward, tilting his head. "You've said a few things that make it sound like you're not close with your family."

"Uh, no. You could say that. They're a bunch of liars and assholes." Why was he bringing her family up?

"My girl doesn't swear much. So when she does, it has more meaning," Maxim told them. "Why are you asking questions about her family?"

"I was worried about her reaction to learning about what we do," Regent murmured. "A lot of people would be understandably upset."

And she wasn't. Yeah, she could see how that would confuse him.

"Do you ever hurt women and children?" she asked.

"Definitely not," Regent replied in a cold voice.

"Regent," Maxim warned. "Watch your tone. She's not asking that as an insult."

She wasn't. And she was glad that Maxim understood that. Still, she was trembling slightly as she went to ask the next question. She was certain she knew the answer and didn't really want to ask.

Actually, maybe she should wait until it was just the two of them to ask specifics. Regent didn't seem like a man she wanted to piss off.

Regent sighed. "I apologize, sweetheart. I messed up. I know you didn't ask that because you've jumped to the worst conclusion about me. It's just . . . we have a sister."

"Lottie," she whispered.

"And I have spent my life looking after her. Protecting her. When she was younger, she was kidnapped. Terrorised. And she is . . . she needed protecting."

She nodded, eyes wide.

Lord, she wished she had had a fraction of what Regent had given Lottie.

"I would never do that to a woman or child. Ever. We are involved in criminal things, yes. We are not saints. But we never get involved in the skin trade. We do not own strip clubs or brothels. We do not shake hard-working people down for protection money. And we try our best to keep the streets clean from hard-core drugs. If anyone wants to deal in this city, they are supposed to come through me. So I can ensure that shit isn't getting sold to kids. And that it's not mixed with other shit."

"Right. And Dayton bypassed you."

"Yes, but the main reason I want to stop him is because he

doesn't seem to care that he sold a bad batch of that shit. In fact, he has his men giving away free samples of it and it's killing people."

She nodded. She thought she understood where he was coming from.

"My father isn't a good man," she blurted out. "He works for another bad man. And this man . . . he sends my dad and my brothers out to collect payments. And when those payments are short or not ready . . . well, I don't think I have to tell you what they do."

"Fucking hell. My baby." Maxim drew her in close, kissing the top of her head.

"It's all right."

But they all knew she was lying. It wasn't all right. It was crap. And her family were jerks.

"They're not good people. They're criminals. I ran away from that life. From them. I don't want to be like them."

"Fuck," Maxim muttered. "If this is your way of saying you want to step away from me because we're like them—"

"What? No. No." She sat up and shook her head, looking right at him. "It's not. Really. If one of my brothers got injured, my dad and my other brother wouldn't care unless it impacted them. Oh, they might go searching for revenge, but only because it meant they got to be violent. They love being violent."

"They hurt you?" he growled.

"Mostly with their words. But sometimes . . . yeah. I tried to stay quiet and hidden. If they didn't notice me, then they couldn't go off at me. But there were times I'd do something that would draw their attention. I didn't have anywhere to hide." She looked around at them all. "I'm not going to tie myself to that again."

"And you won't be," Maxim said. "Malone men take care of

their women. They put them up on pedestals. Protect them. And they don't let shit touch them. Ever."

"Yeah, I've got that. Loud and clear." She cupped his face with her hand. "I know you're not like them. The way you talk about your sister . . . I know you're not. I wouldn't love you if you were."

Relief filled his face and that floored her. That he cared so much.

For her.

"But Malone men need to understand that their women aren't helpless and that they might want to help. Especially if they've been working for a criminal without knowing it. Maybe helping that criminal without knowing it. And especially if that person they work for sent men to beat up their man."

"Still not happening."

"I'll be perfectly safe," she argued. "I could even tell Gretchen, his daughter, that we hooked up, but that you broke things off or that it was only sex. I could make it sound like I hate you. That would cover my butt if someone has seen me with you, right?"

All three men were shaking their heads.

"Think about it. I'll lay the groundwork. I could call her tonight. Tell her that I slept with you, that I thought you were the one, but you blew me off. Then I'll ask her if she thinks her dad will give me tomorrow off because I'm a mess. That will mean my feet will have time to heal, so I'm not limping when I go back. Then I can have a sneak around. See what I can learn." She thought that was a great plan.

"Nice thought. Not happening." Maxim gave her a stubborn look.

Grr. He was so irritating.

"You'll call in the morning, and tell them you're not coming in ever again," Maxim dictated.

"I'm not just quitting. I have bills to pay."

"No, you don't, because I'm covering you."

Oh, she so didn't think so.

Regent cleared his throat and stood. "I think it's time for us to go. I need to go find a new doctor. As soon as possible." Regent eyed him. "Rest. Both of you. It's close to dinnertime. I'll have Gerald bring up some food soon."

"Appreciate it," Maxim told them.

She gave them both a small smile. Then she waited until they were gone to turn to look at Maxim.

She took in his tired face. He looked done in. Pale, with dark marks under his eyes.

"You need to sleep." And he didn't need to be arguing with her.

"I need to take care of you."

"You always take care of me." Leaning in, she kissed him lightly. "Always. Now, let me take care of you." She attempted to move from the bed, but he grabbed her thigh.

"Where are you going?" he asked.

"I was going to let you sleep."

"I'll sleep better with you next to me."

"Okay, honey. Then I guess I'm sleeping next to you." She snuggled in next to him.

"You aren't doing this, baby," he murmured.

Yeah. They'd see.

It took less than five minutes for him to fall asleep. It took her another ten minutes to slowly and carefully get herself out of his hold. She moved to the bathroom first because she really had to pee.

Adult diapers.

Ha! The guy was insane.

After she had taken care of business, she grabbed her phone, chewing her lip.

Did she want to do this? It wouldn't be right to lie to Gretchen, would it?

But had Gretchen been lying to her this whole time? Deceiving her?

Gretchen wasn't always that nice. And there were times she got the feeling that she was using her. Like all the times she asked her to help with work that Gretchen should be doing herself, not Aston. Work she'd often had to stay late to complete.

So yeah, maybe Gretchen wasn't that nice.

Letting out a deep breath, she sent her a text.

Aston: *Hey, I have to take tomorrow off. I'm not feeling great.*

Gretchen: *But I needed your help with some marketing tomorrow.*

Aston's temper stirred. That's all she cared about? Was she not concerned about how Aston was?

Aston: *Right. Sorry.*

Suddenly, she didn't feel so bad about lying.

She looked at Maxim's bruised face. Sometimes, being nice didn't get you anywhere.

And truth be told, she was kind of sick of people walking all over her. Maxim needed someone strong. Someone tough.

She put her phone down. Now, she just had to convince Maxim that she was tough.

That she could do whatever was necessary to take care of her man.

27

"You're not eating your breakfast, Rainbow." It was the following morning and Maxim had slept for most of the night. Regent's new doctor had already been in to check on him and had also checked his girl's feet. He'd said that both were healing nicely.

"You never explained why you call me that," she said, clearly trying to distract him.

He'd let her do that for the moment.

"It's going to sound cheesy."

She leaned forward in the chair. She had insisted that he needed room to eat.

He had no idea why. What he really needed was her pressed up against him.

"A rainbow appears after the rain. You have a storm and then out of the gray something beautiful appears. And that was you . . . you were just so beautiful that it was like the clouds opening on a stormy day to let the sunshine pour in."

Sounded cheesy as hell. But it was the truth.

"Darn it, Maxim Malone. Just when I think I'm out of tears

and you can't get any sweeter, you go and say stuff like that." She wiped at her eyes.

"I'm not sweet, woman. I'm an alpha male."

"You're that too," she agreed. "But you're also the best thing to happen to me. I don't . . . I don't want anything to happen to you."

Maxim knew this had shaken her. He could see it in the way she constantly watched him. He got the feeling that she hadn't slept much.

That worried him because she didn't seem to get enough sleep as it was, which wasn't healthy.

"Baby girl, when was the last time you had a full night's sleep?"

She looked at him in surprise, probably wondering at the change in topic.

"Uh, I don't know."

"How long have you had trouble sleeping?"

"A long time." She sighed, looking into the distance. "You know that saying 'sleep with one eye open'?"

"Yeah?" he asked, not sure he was going to like where this was going.

"I feel like I've had to do that my whole life. I just . . . my brothers, if they got bored, well, they enjoyed doing things to me when I was asleep."

"Like what?"

She stared at him in shock, probably because he'd just yelled. "Oh. Oh, nothing like that."

"Then what was it like?" he asked through gritted teeth. He wanted to demand she tell him everything. But he knew that could make her clam up further. She had trouble opening up. Which was something they'd need to work on. Because he wanted to know everything about her.

"Pranks. One night, they cut my hair. Another night, they

drew something on my face. Stupid crap like that."

"Why didn't your father stop them?"

"Because he thought it was funny. As soon as I could, I put a lock on my door at night and used it every night. But my sleep never improved much."

"How much sleep do you usually average a night?" he asked.

"About three or four hours."

Fuck. Really, really not good.

"Baby, that's not healthy."

"I know. Every so often, it will all catch up on me and then I often sleep for at least twenty-four hours."

"What?" he asked, shocked.

"Yeah, it hasn't happened in months. Thankfully, last time it happened, it was a Friday evening and I was home. I collapsed on the sofa and woke up Saturday afternoon."

"What the fuck? You didn't even have time to get into bed?"

"I suppose I could have forced myself. I'm like a kid that's gotten overtired and hit the wall. And then I just sleep."

"So that shit could happen anywhere?" He was not liking this. At. All.

"I guess so. But it's never happened anywhere other than in my apartment or my bedroom at my father's house. So . . . that's something."

That's something?

"We are going to need to do something about this. That's not happening again. You need to sleep. And I do not need to be worrying about you walking along the street or riding the bus and collapsing."

"I'm sure that wouldn't happen."

"Not that you'll be riding the bus anymore," he added, ignoring her.

"Uh, we talked about this already. I'm going to be riding the bus during the day."

"Changed my mind. I'll get you a car and a driver. That's better than teaching you to drive anyway. Safer." Satisfaction filled him. He didn't know why he hadn't thought of that before.

"No, you aren't."

"Baby, did you say you loved me?" he asked.

Anger filled her face and he had to hide his smile. He didn't want her to think he was laughing at her. But she was gorgeous when she got all riled up.

"Yes, I love you. However, those words don't give you carte blanche to take over my life."

"I disagree."

"You can disagree all you like, Maxim Malone. But the fact of the matter is that I'm an adult who can make her own decisions."

"Like your decision to leave the house barefoot, armed with a knife, and attack men twice your size?"

She huffed out a breath. "Yes. And just so you know, if I had to make that decision again, I'd do the same thing."

"Aston."

"Maxim."

They glared at one another.

"Lord, you're stubborn," he told her.

"Me? *I'm* stubborn?" she asked.

"Yep, stubborn and reckless. It's good you have me."

"Is it? Please, tell me all the ways it's good that I have you?" she asked.

"Because I won't let you get away with shit."

"What the heck does that mean?" she demanded.

"It means, baby. That you now have someone who is going to hold you accountable. Who is going to ensure that you take care of yourself. And when you don't, I'll step in. That's what it means."

"I can take care of myself."

"Swimming on your own at night at a public facility until you're so exhausted that you can barely walk isn't taking care of yourself. Neither is running toward violence. Or not getting enough sleep at night. Or bending over backward to do everything for everyone around you without asking for help in return when you need it. I'm not letting you run yourself to the ground anymore, Rainbow. And I'm definitely not going to let people take advantage of you anymore. Understand me?"

"I . . . I don't let people take advantage of me."

"You do, baby. That neighbor of yours, she's a piranha. I understand it must be nice to spend some time alone with your husband, away from the kids, but how often does she ask you to look after them?"

"Used to be once a month, then once a week. Now, it's several times a week." She had grown pale.

"And it doesn't seem like she's asking anymore. Does she do anything for you in return?"

"No," she said starkly. "You really think she's taking advantage of me?"

"Yeah, baby."

"She never does anything for me. She doesn't . . . she doesn't even like me, does she?"

Fuck. Fucking hell. He thought about what she'd told him of her life. Her brothers and father sounded like violent, horrid people. Had she had anyone in her life who had cared for her?

"A friendship has give and take. It's not all take, take, take. You understand what I'm saying?"

"I think so. You're saying that no one in that building is my friend?" she whispered.

"Come here."

"No."

"Aston, come to me."

"You haven't finished eating."

He was more concerned about the fact that she'd barely touched her plate and that she was looking completely and utterly defeated.

"Right, I knew we weren't friends. I know what having a friend means. I've seen it on the TV, read about it in books."

Fuck.

Fuck. Him.

"Have you never had a proper friend?" he asked gently.

"Well, I have Gretchen."

Gretchen Leeds. Right. The same woman who'd left her at Glory on her own to get hit on by assholes. The same one she'd confessed to him often asked her to help with work and caused her to have to work overtime without pay.

Great.

He needed to help her find better friends. Gracen would love another friend.

"And now you think I'm pathetic, don't you? Because I've never had a proper friend. And because I thought that everyone in the building that I was helping, that I'd babysit for, lent money to, gave away my things to were my friends, and so now you think I'm pathetic."

She said most of that without taking a breath and he was hard pressed to put all her words together.

But he got the gist of it and he didn't like it.

He especially didn't like the way she kept calling herself pathetic. That wasn't happening.

He grabbed his plate, then hers, and set them away on the other side of the bed. Then he took her hand.

"I'm not repeating myself. Come. Here."

Her gaze went to his. Then she finally moved, climbing up on the bed so he could gather her to him.

"You are not pathetic. And I never, ever want to hear that shit out of your mouth again. Understand me?"

"But I am pathetic."

"Oh, you've done it now."

"I've done what?"

"You earned yourself a spanking for putting yourself in danger. And for swimming late at night alone. And now, you've earned one for calling yourself pathetic. You're not going to sit for a week."

"Don't try to joke with me, Maxim."

"I'm not joking, baby." She'd find that out soon enough. "Now, listen to me. The fact that those assholes didn't have the good sense to treat you properly when you were trying to offer them friendship is a reflection of them, not you. Got me?"

"I haven't always been a good person," she confessed. "I did some bad things to my brothers. When they were mean, I'd retaliate. I cut a piece of Benny's ear off."

"You really did that?"

"It was after he'd cut my hair. I loved my hair. It was so long and shiny. He chopped this huge hunk off. So I decided to do the same to him. Only I sort of slipped and cut off a bit of his ear instead. Not a huge piece, but yeah . . . so you see, I'm not a good person. And I need to make amends."

Fuck.

He wanted to laugh. But he couldn't. Because there was so much about what she'd just said that he needed to clear up.

"Okay, first things first. Good."

"Good. What's good?"

"I'm glad you cut off a piece of his ear. He sounds like a complete asshole. You should have aimed for his dick instead."

"Maxim!"

"What?"

"That would mean I'd have to touch his dick." She pulled a face.

"True, you wouldn't want to do that." But if he ever met the asshole, he'd make sure there was no chance of him ever fathering kids. He didn't deserve them.

"As for the rest of that codswallop that you just recited, that doesn't make you a bad person. And you have nothing to atone for. You certainly don't need to atone by letting people take advantage of you."

"I just want to be a better person."

"Baby, you're a good person. Did you ever hurt someone? Did you ever shake someone down for money or beat them up when they didn't have it?"

"No," she whispered. "But once, I slashed my dad's tires and let him think that one of my brothers did it."

"You did?"

"Yeah. I heard him talking about how he was going to have to get forceful with Mrs. Tiles. She was this lovely older woman who owned the butchery in our neighborhood with her husband. But he'd just died and she couldn't pay the protection fee. And my dad . . . he was going to hurt her. So I slashed his tires and snuck out to warn her oldest son. I knew him from school."

"And you think that makes you a terrible person?" he asked incredulously.

"No, what makes me a terrible person is that I slashed them with my brother Hugh's knife, then left it lying by the car for my father to see."

"There a reason why you did that?"

"Yeah, Hugh had locked me outside the house the night before when Dad wasn't there. It was after ten and freezing cold, and I only had a nightgown on. I had to go and hide in the woodshed. It was small and dark and scary."

"Motherfucking bastard," he spat out. "Is that why you're scared of small, dark spaces? Like the elevator?"

"I wish I could say yes. Unfortunately, I have more experience with smaller, darker spaces than that woodshed. And I could leave the woodshed anytime I wanted so it wasn't so bad."

"What does that mean?" he pressed. "What small, dark place couldn't you leave?"

"I don't . . . I don't want to talk about it."

Fuck.

This girl.

His girl. There were so many layers to her. It was like he peeled one away and there were a thousand more underneath.

You'll never be bored.

That was the truth. Frustrated. Happy. Horny. Tormented.

He'd often be those, he was sure.

Even after being beaten and stabbed, he couldn't stop his dick from getting hard around her. And that was a pain in the ass, seeing as he couldn't take care of it. He'd gotten up twice to pee, but it wasn't like he had the strength to rub one off. Even if he could have done that, with her waiting on the other side of the door, grumbling at him for getting up when she thought he should use a bed-pan, it would've been impossible.

Like fuck he was pissing in a pot and letting her empty it.

Not until he was on his deathbed.

Likely, not even then.

"Aston. Tell me. What small, dark place?"

Frustration filled him when the door opened and his two brothers walked in. He tried to hide that frustration when Gracen followed them.

She was practically glowing with happiness. Maxim liked seeing that. He'd like it even more if his woman smiled like that every morning.

She would once all of this had settled down. He'd wake her every morning with his mouth, his fingers, or his dick.

Yep. They'd both walk around with smiles on their faces like Gracen did.

"Morning!" she said cheerfully. Then her smile started drooping as she looked at them both. "What's wrong? Maxim? Are you in pain? Aston? Are you all right? You look like you didn't get any sleep at all again last night."

"Oh, I'm fine. Thank you." Aston's voice was stilted.

He leaned into her. "Gracen will never take advantage of you. Any friendship she offers will be genuine." He whispered it to her so the others couldn't hear.

She nodded, relaxing slightly.

"Did you guys not like your breakfast? I could make you something else. I make some delicious crepes, don't I, Victor?"

"You sure do, baby." Victor drew her to him and kissed the top of her head. "Why don't you take Aston downstairs with you? Get her some coffee and something to eat."

Gracen frowned slightly. "What's going on?"

"Nothing for you to worry about," Regent told her.

Gracen bit her lip, looking worried, but she nodded.

However, he should have known Aston wouldn't let them brush her off with that. It was undeniable something was going on. Victor wanted to shield Gracen as much as he could from the bad things that happened.

He understood that sentiment because he felt the same with Aston. He wanted her life filled with happiness, not worry and fear.

Only problem with that was Aston. She sat up, staring at his brothers with a frown. "What's happened?"

"Nothing for you to worry about," Regent repeated.

Uh-oh.

He and Victor shared a look. Regent was protective and was used to getting his way. He'd guarded Lottie and cared for her like she was the finest of china. And Lottie had needed that for a time. But now that she was gone . . . well, Maxim thought his oldest brother needed someone else to coddle and look after.

"If it's anything to do with Dayton or Maxim, then I want to know," Aston said.

"You might want to know, but that doesn't mean it's in your best interests to know."

She turned to Maxim, looking confused by Regent's words.

"He's being protective," he explained. "He has something to say and he's worried that you'll be upset."

"Which is why I'll tell Maxim first and he can decide whether to tell you," Regent said.

"Uh, no. I don't think that's the way it should go. I want to know. I've been through a lot of crappy things in my life so I'm not going to collapse. And you owe me the truth. Don't hide things from me to protect me." She turned to Maxim, glaring at him.

Maxim studied her. He was in two minds over this. He knew how strong she was. But he also knew how fragile she could be. And he wanted to be there for her. To give her everything she'd never had.

"Maxim?" she whispered, staring at him with confusion.

"You don't have to do it all on your own anymore, baby."

Her eyes flared, understanding filling them.

"You have me now. All of us. You don't have to do it all yourself. I know you're tough, you're strong. But it's okay to be weak sometimes too. You can go to sleep with both eyes shut, because I'll be here, watching over you. Keeping you safe so you can rest."

"Damn it, Maxim. Stop saying nice stuff to me." A tear slid down her cheek and he reached up to brush it away.

"Never. You're not alone. You've got a family. A proper one. We're fucked up in our own ways, but we look after one another. Always. And you've got me. I'm not going anywhere."

"Do you promise?"

"I promise."

She wiped at her cheeks.

"I want to stand between you and all the bad things in the world, my baby. I know I won't always be able to do that. But it's something I need to do. It's what I want. I want to be that for you. Can you let me?"

"I . . . I don't know. I can try. It will take some getting used to, though."

"I get that."

"Do you get, though, that you could have died? And that I'm tied up in this in ways that you might not like, but that means I might be able to help. And I know you're protective of me, but I'm protective of you as well. So let me help. Or, at the very least, don't push me out. Because thinking and worrying is worse than not knowing."

Shit. Aston had him there.

He knew that she'd probably build whatever this was into something bigger than it actually was.

"What she said," Gracen piped up. "I wished I'd recorded that."

"Don't get ideas, baby," Victor rumbled.

Gracen reached up and kissed his cheek. But she only managed this because Victor leaned down for her.

"All right, you can stay. That does not mean you have permission to help beyond offering any insights. From the safety of this room," he warned.

She nodded, looking obedient.

Maxim wasn't fooled for a second. He drew her against him, ignoring the way his side burned. This morning, he'd refused to take any pain killers that might make him sleepy or cloud his mind. Which meant he was in more pain, but he needed to remain vigilant.

He was worried that Aston would sneak off and try to take

down Leeds all on her own. He definitely wouldn't put it past her.

Maxim was sitting up, resting against the headboard with his girl under his arm. Victor sat in an armchair, which wasn't like him. He usually liked to stand. But it was clear why he'd decided to sit as soon as he drew Gracen onto his lap.

Regent took the last chair, looking at both of his brothers like he didn't know how he was related to them.

Regent would find out one day what it meant to have a woman. And that careful balance between protecting them and allowing them freedom.

Hmm. But then, he'd probably just tip over that line and go straight for smothering them in protection.

The thing is, Maxim got where Regent was coming from. But in this instance, he also knew he couldn't fully protect Aston.

"What is it?" he asked.

Regent sighed. "Are you certain you want to discuss this in front of your women? I'm not sure about this. It's our job to protect our women and children." Regent looked from her to Gracen. "You're both family, which makes you both mine to protect."

Aston snuggled into him and he knew it was because she liked hearing that.

His family was the best. They might have had a fucked-up beginning, but it had only made them stronger. Tighter.

Nobody fucked with the Malones. Family first.

28

These guys were nuts.

Completely bonkers.

But they were the kind of insane she wished she'd had in her life forever.

"Understand?" Regent pressed.

"I think I'm beginning to," she whispered.

Gracen sent her an understanding smile. She was snuggled into Victor's huge chest like there was nowhere else she'd rather be.

And Aston understood that feeling too.

"Right. I'm going to lay it out, then. Three more deaths were reported this weekend. All of them are linked to Mixology."

"Fudge," she muttered.

"And those are the ones that we know for sure have links to Mixology. My guess is that there are more deaths," Regent added.

Shoot.

"It really doesn't help that they keep giving samples of this shit away," Victor grumbled.

"That means that more people will be accessing it," Maxim said. "People out having a good time who wouldn't buy drugs normally, but will take a free sample if offered. Fuck. This isn't good."

"People are starting to take notice. It's already being reported on local media and the police chief is feeling pressure from the mayor. None of this is good for business," Regent said.

Aston stiffened. "Is that the reason you care? Because it's not good for business?"

Regent shot his cold gaze to hers and she stiffened. Uh-oh.

"Regent," Maxim warned.

Oh no. She didn't want to come between the brothers. They were all close and Maxim seemed to regard Regent as more of a dad than a brother since his own dad had been a terrible person.

Something they had in common.

She should have kept her mouth shut. Probably should have left the room like Regent suggested.

"No. Contrary to what my father tried to turn me into, I am not an unfeeling monster."

Oh God. Now she felt terrible.

"I'm sorry," she rushed out. "I never meant to imply that. It's just . . . my father wouldn't have cared except for how it affected business. And I know it's unfair to liken you to him. I'm just . . . sorry. Do you . . . do you want me to leave now?"

"Leave?" Regent asked quietly.

"Your house." She pressed her trembling hands together.

Everyone was staring at her. She could especially feel Maxim's gaze on her.

"I want to know your father's name," Regent said bizarrely.

"S-sorry?" Why was he asking about her father?

"And your brothers. Where they live. Their details."

"Why?" she asked.

"Because I'm going to need to have words with them."

By words, she thought he might mean something else.

"You won't be having words with them until I'm out of this bed and can come too. Because those words are my right to have with them," Maxim said to his brother.

Okay, they definitely meant they were going to have something other than words.

Warmth filled her. Even though she didn't want them going anywhere near her father or brothers . . . their words still gave her the warm fuzzies.

"I like having words. I'll be coming along too," Victor rumbled.

"Me too," Gracen added.

"You definitely won't be going, little one," Victor told her.

Regent nodded and when she looked up, Maxim was doing the same.

Gracen pouted. "Well, get in a word or two from me, okay?"

"You got it, baby," Victor agreed.

Yep. They definitely weren't going to have words.

"Thanks for the sentiment," she said, feeling shy. "But it's all right. They're no longer a part of my life and they don't matter. I don't need anyone to *have words* with them for me."

She was still confused about how they'd moved from their previous conversation to talking about her family.

"They might not be here physically, but they're here in other ways," Regent said. "One thing you need to know though. No matter what you do or say, as long as you don't betray my family, you'll have a home here. And you will not be told to leave. I've reacted badly twice now when you asked me something. And that's on me. I apologize and promise to do better."

Oh shoot.

She'd overreacted. Again.

"No. There's no need to apologize. I keep making mistakes,

thinking that you might be like them. So I think I'm the one who needs to apologize."

Something warm filled Regent's face. He nodded. "I don't want anyone else to die, Aston."

"Me neither. I really wish I could help more. I feel like I could make a difference. Do something good." She turned so she could look at Maxim.

"You don't need to atone for anything," he told her.

She wasn't so sure of that. Even though her brothers might have deserved what she'd done to them, the memories still left her feeling bad.

"Every time someone gets hurt from these drugs, I'm going to feel it on me. It's going to feel like my fault."

"It is not your fault."

"Maybe, but it will feel like it. Most of the time, I was helpless to stop my father and brothers from hurting people. But this time, I can help. Please don't make me feel helpless again."

"Aston, you might be able to help in other ways," Regent said.

She turned to him.

"Is there anyone there that you think could be leaned on? Anyone who might know more? Or is there anywhere you think the drugs could be being held?"

"Gretchen might know more. What if I just met with her? At a public place. I could still tell her my story about you breaking up with me and see if she'll tell me anything?"

"I don't know, she's unlikely to say anything bad about her father," Maxim said.

Drat. He was right. Gretchen was probably going to remain tight-lipped about it all. If she even knew anything.

"I wonder if the drugs are being stored at one of his worksites," she said. "The last order for concrete was really off. I wonder if that has something to do with it. Also, there's something really odd about the sales Gretchen is making too. The houses are selling for far too much money."

"Money laundering, perhaps," Regent said. "How many worksites does Leeds have?"

"Probably over a hundred."

"It's a lot," Regent said. "But we could probably narrow them down. He'd need a big site to hide the drugs, but somewhere he could still get to them easily."

"I could make a list, help narrow it down." She could totally do that. "Would that help?"

"It would help a lot, sweetheart," Regent told her. "Probably more than going in to work."

"Okay. I'll do that."

Relief filled her. All she wanted was to help.

29

"Are you upset with me?" she asked a few hours later. They'd nailed down some more details before eating Gracen's delicious crepes. Then, Maxim had spent half an hour on the phone convincing his brother, Jardin, that he didn't need to cut his working holiday short to come home. It seemed to her that Jardin was looking for an excuse to come back early. Apparently, his cousins were a lot to handle.

"Come here." He patted his lap.

She frowned at him. "I'll sit here." There was no way she was sitting on his lap.

He gave her an unhappy look. "Get your butt here and straddle my legs."

"I'll hurt you."

"You'll be careful."

Well, of course she'd be careful. But she could still hurt him while trying to be careful.

"Get here. Now."

Aston very carefully placed her leg over his lap so she was

facing him. She didn't go anywhere near his wound. Or his bruised ribs.

"I'm over this."

"What?" Her? Was he over her?

"Being injured. Being stuck in this bed," he grumbled. "Over. It."

"I didn't realize you'd be such a bad patient."

"Well, I am. Baby, I just want to be able to take you into my arms and kiss you. I want to throw you over my knee and spank you until you can't sit for a week. I want to tie you to the bed and eat your pussy until you can't walk. That way, you'll stay where I put you."

"Stay where you put me?" she asked, outraged.

"Yep. Stay where I put you. Which will be somewhere very safe."

"I'm not in any danger, Maxim."

"You were when you came running in to help me. I could have painted a target on your back."

"Not intentionally. I'm just glad I can help in some way. I wish I could do more."

"This is important to you," he murmured. "Helping."

"Yes, but it's not more important than you."

"Fuck, baby. You just earned yourself a whole fucking bunch of orgasms once you're ready for that."

She felt herself growing red. "How about you just don't give me those spankings you say you owe me?"

"Oh no, I'm still giving you those."

Drat.

"I'm sorry I wouldn't let you do more, but the idea of you being hurt fucking kills me," he told her.

"I know. I just hope it's enough and I can help save people. That feels . . . important. It feels as though my life might have meaning if I can help save even one person from being hurt by those drugs."

"You don't think your life has meaning?"

"I was told continuously that it didn't. My dad's favorite thing to say to me was that he wished I'd never been born. That he should have smothered me as a child. Or that it was the one time he wished he'd worn a condom."

"That mother-fucking bastard." His face filled with fury. "I'm definitely having fucking words with him."

"He's not worth it."

"Protecting you is always worth it."

"I'm not in danger from him anymore. You don't have to worry. I ran from him as soon as I could. I had some money saved, but I also stole some of his cash, which I know would've pissed him off. I changed my last name and I cut ties off from them. They're all dead to me and that's the way it will stay."

Reaching out, he cupped the side of her face. "You are not worthless, useless, or anything else that fucker said to you. Understand me?"

"I know I'm not."

"I'm going to tell you how amazing, wonderful, and beautiful you are every day until I wipe out those words from your mind."

"You're an amazing man, Maxim Malone."

"Nope. Just your man." His face softened. "You never told me why you're so scared of small, dark spaces."

She glanced away. Shoot. She hadn't told him because she didn't really want to talk about it. She could feel herself starting to shake.

"Baby? Hey, stop. No one is going to hurt you again. I'm here now. I'm going to take care of you."

She swallowed heavily. "There was a small storage closet under the stairs in our place. It could fit a few boxes. And one scrawny kid."

"Jesus fucking Christ," he said, sounding horrified. "He locked you in there?"

"My mom took off when I was young and I guess he didn't want to bother with me when he had to go out and the boys were at school. So he'd lock me in there with a bottle of water, a box of crackers, and an old container in case I had to pee. No one could hear me if I started crying or yelling. When my brothers had to look after me, they'd do the same. But they did it to torture me."

"Fucking hell. Those fucking bastards. I'll kill them all." He drew her close to him, hugging her with one arm. And she knew she shouldn't let him. He was going to hurt himself.

But it felt so good.

"I'm sorry. So sorry that happened to you."

She was too.

"Come here, baby."

"I am here."

"No, I mean, get your lips on mine. Right now."

"I can't do that without hurting you."

"Don't fucking care if you hurt me."

"Well, I care, Maxim Malone," she huffed at him.

"Want your lips. Now."

She glared at him. Then she grabbed the headboard on either side of his head and leaned into him. He wrapped his hand around the back of her head and held her there as he kissed the hell out of her.

When he let her go, she sat back, feeling flustered and hot. She wanted more, but she knew he wasn't up to more.

He groaned.

"Oh no, you're in pain. I hurt you! Where does it hurt?"

"It's all right, baby. It's the sort of pain that will go away."

"Maxim."

"I'm all right," he told her.

He wasn't, though. And she couldn't work it out. Was it his side? His ribs? His bruises?

"Got to go to the bathroom," he muttered.

"I still think I should find you something to pee into," she said worriedly. "You're going to hurt yourself moving around too soon."

"I'm not peeing into a damn bowl, Rainbow. Hard limit."

She sighed and helped him sit up. As he stood, his hard cock brushed against her and she jumped, then glanced down at it.

"Oh."

"Just ignore that. It will go down. Seems he just gets excited whenever he's around you."

"You refer to your dick as a 'he'?"

"It's a guy thing."

"It must be," she muttered as she hovered around him while he moved to the bathroom. "I've never called my . . . my . . . well, *that* anything."

"Yeah? We can change that if you want." He gave her a wicked grin.

"I don't think we need to do that," she said hastily.

Leaning in, he kissed her. Then he groaned. "Damn it. I'll be back."

She stood outside the door as he walked into the bathroom. Then she realized she should give him some privacy. Except . . . she had a question.

"Can you pee with an erection?"

"I'm trying my hardest to get rid of it," he replied.

Her eyes widened. "You are?" Her voice was high-pitched as she wondered exactly *how* he was getting rid of it.

"Not like that!" he replied, amusement in his voice. "Seriously, baby. Do you think I'm in here rubbing one out with a stitched-up hole in my side and you standing on the other side of the door?"

She leaned her forehead against the door with a groan. She was such an idiot.

"I'm not experienced with these things," she told him.

"Peeing while you've got a boner? Didn't really think you would be."

More amusement. How could he speak so openly? She didn't think she could ever talk like this about any of her bodily functions.

And she hadn't been talking about peeing with an erection. She eventually heard the toilet flush and moved away from the door. But not too far, since she needed to be close in case he needed her while moving.

She knew her face was bright red when he opened the door.

"Baby, you gotta stop being so cute and funny. I can't take it."

"Sorry," she whispered. "I'll get right on that."

"What are you going to do? Start practicing mutism and wear a paper bag on your head?" he asked.

"Yes?"

"You'd still be fucking adorable and cute." He moved back to the bed and sat on the side with a groan. "I want a shower."

"Nope. No way. No shower for you."

"I need a shower."

"I'll give you a sponge bath then."

As soon as the words were out of her mouth, she wished them back. Well, sort of. She'd never bathed anyone before. Other than her brothers, she'd never seen a man completely naked. And she wished to hell she could wipe her memory clean of them. She had never touched a man's chest, legs, or anything in between.

So she really wondered how she was going to touch him without combusting.

"I'll have a shower, Rainbow. It's fine."

"What? No! You can't shower. You could slip over. Hurt yourself. You need to lie in bed and let me take care of you."

"Baby, you can't even say the word dick without going bright red. I don't think you need to be washing me. I'm not a fucking invalid."

Uh, actually, he was.

She gave him a look. "Get in that bed, Maxim Malone. Let me take care of you for once."

"You sure you want to touch me?"

"Not wanting to touch you isn't the problem."

He grinned. "It isn't? You want to touch me, Rainbow?"

"Since the first moment I met you," she confessed. "You looked like some sort of Greek god. Too pretty and perfect for this world."

"I'm not pretty," he grumbled. "I'm an alpha male. Handsome. Rugged."

"Yes, of course." Sheesh, the male ego was a fragile thing.

He grunted. "All right, since you're dying to get your hands on me, you can give me a bed bath."

So gracious of him.

She rolled her eyes.

"None of that sass or I'll have to punish you."

"Another spanking?"

"Hmm, I'm thinking that after my bath, I'll tease you until you beg me to let you come."

"Oh. That doesn't sound like a punishment. That sounds . . . nice."

Nice? Really Aston? That's a bit lame. Nice.

"It won't be *nice*. It will be hot and heavy. And I didn't say you were going to get to come. Just that you would beg to."

"What?" She stared at him wide-eyed.

"I think I might tease you, get you all hot and bothered, then stop."

"But . . . that would be . . ."

"Punishment."

Oh. Wow.

"What would stop me from finishing myself off?" she asked before she could stop herself.

His gaze grew hot. "You wouldn't be able to finish yourself off if I tied you to the bed."

Holy. Heck.

He was in no shape to do any of this . . . but a girl could fantasize.

"Which is what I would do if I caught you being naughty and trying to finish yourself off after you'd been punished. Very naughty behavior."

That shouldn't have sent a wave of arousal through her.

Shouldn't. Have.

But it did. The idea of being tied to his bed was one she liked. Far too much.

"You like that idea, don't you, baby?" he crooned.

"We should stop talking about it."

"Why? Because it's making you feel all hot and bothered?" he asked.

"Maybe," she said faintly. She was trying not to lie and besides, it was pretty obvious. "You're not up to any of this."

He raised his eyebrow. "You sit on my face, and all I have to do is lie there. The only part of me that would be getting a workout would be my tongue."

"Oh my God." She put her hands over her face. That was all she was going to be able to think about now.

He laughed, then groaned.

Immediately, she felt terrible. "You need to lie down."

She helped him lie back. Her gaze hit those delicious abs. His bare, smooth chest. But then her eyes landed on the bandage on his side and she felt reality crash through her haze of arousal.

He caught her hand as she went to move away, raising it to his mouth. "Love the way you look at me."

"Like a stupid virgin that's never seen a man before?"

"Rainbow, what have I said about the way you talk about yourself?" He gave her a stern look.

Well. Darn.

She was in trouble now.

"I think I'll just go get the stuff ready for your bath."

"You do that," he growled.

She rushed into the bathroom.

"Don't run around on your feet," he demanded.

"My feet are fine." It was kind of ridiculous for Maxim to worry about her feet when he had been stabbed.

"Just do as you're told."

She peeked back out of the bathroom door to look at him. "Seriously? Do as I'm told?"

"My life would be a lot easier."

"I live to make your life easier," she said sarcastically.

"That's what I like to hear," he replied. "So you'll be staying where I put you. You'll follow all of your rules and won't give me any sass?"

Grr.

"Don't hold your breath." Honestly. This man. He could try the patience of a saint. Something she knew she was not.

Aston found a small bowl in the cabinet. Cleaning it out, she filled it with warm water and got some shower gel, a cloth and a towel.

Then she paused at the entrance to the bedroom. She could do this.

She could totally do this.

Right?

Maybe.

30

Deep breath. You have this.

"Baby? You all right?" His voice was unbelievably soft, which melted her fears away.

This was Maxim. The man she loved. She wanted to help him. Touch him.

"Yep." She walked in, holding the stuff, she'd gathered and set it down on the nightstand.

"Come here."

"Oh no." She pointed her finger at him. "I know how this goes. You are not distracting me. The water is the perfect temperature. You distract me, and then it goes cold."

"Then you warm it up again. Come here."

"No. I'm bathing you. I am not getting waylaid by sweet kisses and sweeter words."

"Baby, you look like you're going to the dentist."

Oh, shoot. Did she?

"I didn't . . . I don't mean to look like that. Um, I'm not . . . it's not . . ."

"Put that stuff away, baby. You're not ready and that's okay."

She straightened her shoulders. "No."

"No?" He gaped at her like he'd never heard the word before.

"No. I am ready. It's just . . . I'm nervous and it's *ridiculous* and that really freaking *annoys* me."

"It's not ridiculous."

"It is! Because I want to touch you. I want to help you. I have been attracted to you since the first moment I saw you. But I've never dated a man. I'm twenty-four-years-old and I've only kissed three men, and they were really boys. When I was at school, I tried to remain in the background. But some boys did notice me."

"Of course they did," he murmured.

She didn't understand why he said that, but she kept going. "We snuck kisses at school. Would eat lunch together. But I couldn't technically date. My father wouldn't allow it without meeting the boy I was going out with, and I couldn't take anyone home with me."

"I'm surprised he cared."

"He cared because he saw me as an asset," she muttered. "And he didn't want that asset getting sullied up in the back of her boyfriend's car."

"What?" he whispered.

"He intended to marry me off. I didn't know about this until I finished school and he started taking me to gang parties. He started introducing me around and I got this bad feeling."

"Fuck," he muttered. "Is that when you ran?"

"It's when I started making plans. I needed to save some money first. He let me get a part-time job, but he wanted all the money I made. However, I managed to hide most of my tips from him. The night . . . the night I ran, he announced my marriage. To a man three times my age. I was three months from my twentieth birthday."

"Motherfucking bastard. Where did you go?"

"I moved around several times over the next few years, found someone to help me change my name, dyed my hair this color, and then I came here."

"Baby, I fucking hate that you had to live through all of that shit."

"Me too," she whispered. It hadn't been easy. There were times when she didn't know if she was going to make it.

But she had. And she was proud of herself.

"Also, so glad this isn't your actual hair color."

She snorted a laugh.

"You have to know that I'm not going to pressure you to do anything you don't want to do."

She nodded. "I know you wouldn't. You're willing to go slow with me."

"I'll take all the time you need me to."

"But like you said, going slow doesn't have to mean doing nothing, right?" she asked bravely.

"That still doesn't mean that there is any pressure on you to do anything."

"And if I want to?"

Heat filled his eyes. "Then that's an entirely different thing."

"It is, isn't it?" She picked up the cloth and dipped it in the water.

"You're sure?"

"I always told myself that if I met someone who cared about me, who was protective of me, that I wouldn't get upset. That I would feel grateful because I'd never had that. I've never had gentle. Tender. I've never even had a decent level of concern. And with you . . . I have all that and more."

"Is this your way of saying you're getting annoyed with me asking if you're sure? And to let you get on with it?" His lips quirked, so she knew he wasn't upset. In fact, his eyes looked like they were dancing.

"Yes."

"You should just tell me to shut up and take it, baby."

"That would be rude. But yes, shut up and let me touch you."

He started laughing, but then he groaned. "You're too damn cute."

"And you're going to be in trouble if you keep laughing like that," she scolded as she drew the blankets back. He was dressed in a pair of navy blue and white striped pajama bottoms.

Those would need to come off.

"Would you be able to lie on the towel if I lay it out for you? Maybe I should change the sheets on the bed too."

"You aren't changing my sheets. Lay it down, I'll get on it."

She set the towel down and he shuffled onto it.

"You'll have to help me with my pants, baby."

He'd managed to get some pajama pants he'd had in a drawer here on last night.

"Of course." She climbed onto the bed, and after some strain, Maxim raised his hips so she could shimmy them down until he was just in his boxers.

Lord. He was beautiful.

He seemed to think that beautiful wasn't a masculine word. But that's what he was.

"Like what you see?"

"Yeah. I do."

He grinned. "I like that there's no playing games with you, Rainbow."

"That's good. Because I don't know how to play any."

"You gonna touch me now or look some more?" he asked.

"I'd really like to do both."

"Do what you like."

Those were dangerous words. She settled next to him on the bed. He was lying closer to the side than the middle, so she could easily sit on the edge of the bed and reach all of him. Rinsing out the cloth, she started with his face and neck.

The easy parts.

Well, she'd thought they would be. Her heart raced and her hand trembled slightly as she moved down toward his chest. He had a swirling tattoo on the right side of his chest that went down his entire arm.

"Can I move your arm without it hurting?"

"So long as you're not going to yank anything, you're good," he replied. "Well, there's one thing you can happily yank."

She paused. "Maxim!"

"Aston." He grinned.

The truth was, she wasn't horrified by that idea. She was intrigued. And a bit worried since she didn't have any idea what she was doing. She raised his arm so she could wash along it.

Who knew that cleaning someone like this could be so . . . darn . . . sexy and intimate.

Maybe it wouldn't be, if it wasn't Maxim who she was touching.

"Would you like me to do that?" she asked as she moved the cloth over his chest. She ran it over his nipples, watching as he shivered. "Are you cold?"

"No." He was staring at her intently, his gaze filled with heat. Hunger.

Oh.

This was . . . it felt good knowing that he wanted her. Because she felt the same.

She moved to his other arm. That seemed safer than tackling his abs.

Lord, he was built.

"You didn't answer me," she murmured as she rinsed the cloth again, then gathered the courage to move down his stomach.

"About what?"

"Would you like me to take care of things for you . . . down there?" She could see his hard dick pressing against his boxers. It seemed that getting stabbed hadn't affected his libido.

He stiffened. "Down where?"

"There," she whispered.

"Baby, if you can't even say it, then I don't think you're ready to take care of anything."

Urgh, she was acting like an idiot. "Your erection. Your hard cock. Your dick. Would you like me to word it any other way?"

"No," he said tightly. "That works."

Shoot. Had she really just asked him that? What a dork she was.

"I . . . I need another towel. And to warm up the water." She darted back into the bathroom with the bowl, nearly spilling it.

"Baby, get back here."

"In a minute."

"Now. Or I'm coming to get you."

She returned with just a new towel, before she'd managed to warm the water. She glared as she saw him attempting to sit up.

"Stay where you are." She glared at him.

"I will if you will. Stop running around on your feet."

"My feet are fine," she told him.

"I will get Victor to tie you to the bed."

"You will not."

"Don't try me, Rainbow. Why did you run off?"

"Because . . . because . . ." She really wanted to lie. Her gaze went to her feet, unable to look at him. "Because I can't believe I just asked you if you wanted me to give you a hand job!"

Oops. She hadn't meant to blurt that out.

31

"Ahh, so you were offering that." She glanced up to find him smiling. "You weren't sure? No, of course you weren't sure. Because that's probably the most awkward offer you've ever heard."

"No. But it was the cutest."

"I wish I could be sexy rather than cute," she lamented.

"You can be both."

"Highly unlikely at this point."

"Cute can be sexy," he said firmly. "Come here."

"You say that a lot."

"Well, you spend a lot of time far from me. If you would just stay next to me all the time ,I wouldn't have to keep saying it."

She rolled her eyes but moved over to him. "I can't spend all my time right next to you."

"Why not? Would make my job much easier."

"Your job?" she asked. How would it make running a night club easier?

"Hmm, it's my job to take care of you."

"Dear Lord, help me," she said.

He took her hand and drew her even closer to him. "You need to finish the bath, but you also need to know that just because I have a hard-on, that doesn't mean you're obligated to do anything about it."

"Oh. That's good to know, but I wasn't asking out of obligation." She started sliding back toward his legs, but he grabbed her hand, halting her.

"You want to give me a hand job, baby?"

"I want to give you pleasure," she said. "I want to learn what you like. You'll need to teach me as I don't know what I'm doing. I just know that I want to *try*."

"Fuck me. Must have done something right in my life to earn you."

She blushed and looked down. The way he spoke to her . . . it was something she never thought she would have.

"How about this . . . you do whatever you feel comfortable with? Touch me, don't touch me, you run the show."

Her gaze shot up to his. "But what if I do something wrong?"

"I'll tell you. But I promise there's very little you could do wrong."

She wasn't so sure about this. She was pretty certain that plenty could go wrong. But she nodded. "I still need fresh water."

He was quiet as she got some more clean, warm water, and then sat back by his feet. As she washed his feet, he let out a choked noise. She glanced at him in surprise, smiling. "Are you ticklish?"

"I am when someone is running a cloth over my feet."

"Sorry," she told him. But she was grinning as she moved up his legs.

"You enjoyed that."

"I sure did," she agreed with a giggle.

"Sadist."

Another giggle escaped and the tension eased from her. This was Maxim. He was willing to go as slow as she needed. He was never mean or harsh.

And he was always protective.

So when she got to the bottom of his boxers, she put the cloth down and reached for the top of them, tugging at them.

"Sure?" he asked.

She shot him a gaze.

"Right. Got it."

He lifted his hips and she shuffled them down. When she was finished doing that, she forced her gaze to look at him.

Dear Lord.

She hadn't expected that.

"It's so big," she blurted out.

He let out a chuckle, followed by a groan.

"Sorry," she muttered, feeling herself turn bright red. "That was dumb."

"Don't," he warned. "Nothing you say or do is dumb."

She disagreed, but she didn't want to argue.

"You haven't seen many dicks, huh?"

"Just my brothers, and I wish I could erase that memory. Oh, and porn."

"Porn?"

"Hmm, my brothers watched a lot of porn. I learned not to look, but sometimes, I couldn't help seeing it. And those men were always pretty well endowed. You could be a porn star."

"Thanks, I think," he said dryly.

"You're pretty too," she teased. "You'd have been popular."

"Brat," he grumbled. "You really want this, don't you?"

Want it? She more than wanted it. She craved it. But all she managed to do was nod.

"Then go for it, Rainbow."

She ran the cloth along his shaft and he groaned. "Fuck."

"I didn't hurt you, did I?" she asked with alarm.

"I'll tell you if you hurt me. And no, definitely not."

Oh, so he liked it.

She lifted his dick out of the way to carefully wash his balls. She knew she had to be careful.

He parted his legs to help her. When she was finished, she sat back, satisfied with her efforts. He looked even harder, if that was possible.

She ran her hand over the shaft.

"Fuck, baby. Your hands are so smooth. Warm. Just squeeze me a bit harder. Fuck, yes."

"Are you sure I'm not going to hurt you?" she asked tentatively. "What about your stitches?"

"What stitches?"

"The ones in your side," she said with exasperation. "What if we tear them?"

"A man would put up with a lot worse than a few torn stitches to feel your hands on him."

Oh. That was nice.

If nuts.

"But no other man is ever going to feel your hand on his dick, understand?"

"Of course not." She moved her hand slightly faster and harder, listening to his breathing grow deeper. He really liked this. And he was enjoying something that she was doing to him.

That kind of blew her mind.

"That's it, baby. Fucking perfect."

Yeah, he wasn't the only one who was enjoying this. She was feeling powerful. She wasn't sure she'd ever felt powerful before.

And she liked it.

"Can you move your legs farther apart?" she asked.

"I'd do anything for you, baby."

That was nice. But all she needed right now was some space so she could kneel between his legs.

He did as she asked and she slid between his thighs, moving her hand back to his dick before she decided to go for it. She placed one hand on the bed beside his hip and lowered her mouth to the head of his cock.

There was a pearl of pre-cum there and she licked it up, humming.

That wasn't as bad as she'd thought. It was definitely something she wanted to explore more. She took the head of him into her mouth and sucked.

Yum.

"Fuck, baby. You don't have to . . ."

Of course she didn't have to. She popped up and stared up at him. "I want to."

"Fuck me. I'm the luckiest man on the planet," he whispered. "My girl wants to suck my cock."

"It's a beautiful cock."

"I'll allow you to call my cock beautiful."

"That's big of you," she told him.

"I thought so. Take my dick back into your mouth."

With pleasure.

Although she did roll her eyes at his bossiness.

"Fuck, baby, yes. Wrap your hand around the base of me and take more of me into your mouth. Suck. Hard."

Okay, so his bossiness was actually quite helpful. Because she was discovering that she liked not having to think or worry about what she was doing.

She just had to do what he told her.

"That's it, baby, take me as deep as you can. You don't have to take me so deep it's uncomfortable. I want you to like this."

Oh, he didn't have to worry about that.

He wrapped his hand around her hair. "You're never to tie

this up when we're together, alone like this. Understand me? If you need it when you go out there, you can tie it back. But not with me. You don't need your armor with me, Aston."

She drew off his dick, blinking rapidly. "You're not supposed to make me cry while I give you a blowjob."

He grinned. "That a rule, is it?"

"It is." She nodded. "But also . . . that was very sweet."

"That's good. Because you're the sweetest thing I've ever met. Your mouth, fucking amazing. Your ass, gorgeous. And your pussy . . . I know it's going to be so damn sweet. Cannot wait for a taste."

Yikes.

That sounded . . . amazing.

"Let's do that. Once you're better. We should do that."

His grin widened. "We will."

She was glad he was looking healthier. Less pale. Although he was still bruised down his side and could barely open his left eye. Then there was the large bandage on his left side.

"Baby, I'm all right. I promise."

"I won't hurt you?"

"You won't. You okay? Do you need to stop?"

"I definitely do not." She moved her mouth to his dick, but this time she licked along it. "Such a beautiful dick."

"Fuck, baby. Fuck."

Aston pressed her tongue over the head of him, then took him as deep as she could without gagging. She cupped his balls, playing with them lightly.

"Fuck. Fuck. Fuck."

Wrapping her other hand around the base of him, she held him tight as she moved her mouth faster. Sucking harder.

"I'm going to come soon. If you don't want to swallow, you can pull back."

Did she want to swallow? The idea appealed to her, but she also wanted to see him come.

She pulled back. "Is it okay if I watch you come?"

"Christ, yes, baby. That's fucking okay with me."

"Oh, good."

She ran her hand up and down his shaft, listening to his breathing quicken. She liked the moans that escaped his mouth.

"I'm close, baby. Fuck. Yes."

She watched in fascination as he came.

Oh, yeah. She liked this. Even if it made a bit of a mess. Well, she knew what to do with a mess. He was panting as she leaned down to lap up his come.

"Fuck, baby. Are you kidding me?"

She froze and stared up at him. He looked dazed. There was a light sweat on his skin.

"Am I doing something wrong?"

"No, I just . . . I don't think it's possible for me to get hard again straight away. But watching you lick me clean just might do it."

"So I shouldn't do it?"

"If you want to do it, you should."

"Good." Because she didn't want to stop. She cleaned him, and he was starting to get hard again. But she drew back because he was also looking tired. After helping him into his boxers, she pulled up the covers.

"Shit. Can't fall asleep . . . so damn good, baby . . . I need to . . . do that . . . you . . ."

"Sleep." She brushed his hair back and kissed his forehead. "I'll watch over you."

32

This would be easier with her laptop. She even had some work stuff on it that might help. But for the moment, she had a pretty good list of possible worksites for Regent to investigate.

Standing, she looked over at Maxim, who was still asleep. She still couldn't believe she'd seen him naked. Touched his cock. Sucked it. Cleaned him up with her tongue.

And she wanted to do it again.

As much and as often as possible.

But right now, he needed sleep. Poor Maxim, she'd worn him out.

Standing, she checked herself in the mirror. Urgh, she really needed to go and get her stuff. She was grateful to Gracen for lending her some things, but they weren't hers.

The yoga pants were too short and slightly big around the waist while the T-shirt didn't cover her bottom. Her hair was a wild mess. She attempted to tame it, but she didn't have her brush. She pulled her hair back into a ponytail.

At least there had been a spare toothbrush in the bathroom cabinet. And she'd showered this morning.

With a sigh, she headed downstairs.

Where would she find anyone, though?

Regent's office.

Pausing, she knocked, moving from foot to foot nervously.

"Come in."

It was just Regent in the room, which made her more anxious. She realized that she'd gotten comfortable with Victor. Surprising, given his size. But then, he was just so cheerful it would be hard not to feel relaxed around him.

He raised his head, eyes flaring with surprise as he saw her.

"Aston? Is everything okay? Maxim?" He stood, looking like he was preparing to move past her and rush up the stairs.

"Oh no, he's fine! He's asleep."

"Good. What's wrong?"

"Oh, nothing is the matter. I'm really sorry. Perhaps I should have waited until Maxim woke up." She felt silly now. He had to have far more important things to deal with.

"Come and sit down, Aston." He moved from behind his desk and gestured to the sofa.

Would he get angry at her for bothering him? He didn't seem angry. But would that change? Why hadn't she thought of that before she'd knocked on his office door?

Idiot.

"Aston," he gentled his voice. "I promise that you're safe here with me. You'll always be safe with the Malone men. Okay?"

"Okay," she whispered.

And she sat. Mostly because she was feeling a bit woozy and out of it. He eyed her.

"When was the last time you got some decent sleep?"

"Probably 2013," she joked.

His eyes flared. "Are you serious?"

"I don't sleep that well."

"Maxim will have to change that."

She frowned at his words. "I don't think it's up to Maxim to deal with my sleep habits."

"Well, it is. Now, what did you need to talk to me about?"

"Oh." She jolted. "I'm sorry to interrupt."

"If you're family, you're never interrupting."

Wow. That was nice. All right, then. "I came up with a list of potential work sites you could investigate."

His lips twitched at the use of the word investigate.

"I think I should go with you."

"That's not happening," he said firmly but gently.

"Yeah, I guessed you were going to say that. I just thought I might help."

"It's likely that there are guards wherever he is holding the drugs. That could mean there will be some danger, and I can't take you toward the danger."

"Right. Well, what do I do about my stuff? Can I go and get some of it? I mean . . . I guess I'm staying for a while. If that's okay?"

"You can stay here forever if you like."

Well, that was nice. If a bit odd.

"But you'll be staying here with Maxim for the foreseeable future. I don't want him moving anywhere until he's at full strength. And I'd prefer you both stay here until we figure out who attacked him."

"All right. Then I'll need my stuff. And I don't know what to do about my job. I mean, there's a chance you're wrong, right? That he's not involved with the drugs?"

"A very tiny chance. Do you think you can tell Leeds that you're still ill? I'd rather keep him guessing at this point about whether you're involved with Maxim."

"I can do that." It was going to be scary, looking for a new job. But she didn't say any of this. It wasn't his problem. She had a bit of money in savings she could use to keep herself going.

"Is there anything else I can help with?" he asked.

Shoot. She was still sitting there. She should leave now. Let him get back to more important things.

She shook her head and stood. He stood as well.

"I know it's hard for you to give up your life for an unknown amount of time. If there's anything I can do to help, let me know."

That was so kind.

"Just find the guys selling this stuff."

"That I can do."

"Do you know if Gracen is around?" she asked.

"I believe Victor has taken her to her ballet lesson."

"Ballet? She likes to dance?"

"Yes. She goes to ballet lessons with her friend Sammy."

"Oh. That sounds like fun." She could do that. She knew she'd be great at ballet. Aston had natural dancing skills, after all.

"I'm sure she'd be glad for you to join her."

"That's a good idea."

"Thank you," he said solemnly.

"Do you think I could grab my things soon?"

"I'll try and arrange something."

"Thanks. I appreciate it. I hope you find the drugs tonight."

"So do I."

His phone rang and he moved to grab it as she headed toward the door.

"Maxim?" he asked.

She turned in surprise as he answered the phone. Then his lips twitched as he stared at her.

"Yes, Aston is here. No, she came down the stairs on her own.

Yes, I will make sure to scold her. Yes, I'll bring her back up immediately."

"That was Maxim?"

"Yes. He woke up, found you gone from the bed and that you weren't in the bathroom, and grew alarmed."

"Alarmed?"

"Hmm. I'm supposed to scold you for walking down the stairs on your feet and for not leaving him a note. Then take you back upstairs."

"Oh, you don't have to take me back upstairs. I can find my own way up."

"That's not the reason he wants me to help you. I'm going to apologize now."

"For what?" she asked as he came toward her.

"Putting my hands on you without permission."

Huh? Oh!

She found herself in his arms as he headed toward the door.

"You don't have to carry me."

"Actually, I have no choice."

"What?" she asked.

"I was told in no uncertain terms that if I didn't carry you back up to Maxim, he was going to come downstairs and carry you up himself."

"Good Lord. My feet are fine!" she said with exasperation.

"I can't comment on that. But if you were mine, and you were injured, you'd most certainly be in trouble for leaving the room without my permission."

Holy. Heck. Balls.

It was like she'd fallen into a different dimension.

One where the men were all nuts.

But she didn't say another word as he carried her up the stairs and into Maxim's bedroom. All without getting slightly out of breath.

He walked her right up to the bed where Maxim was sitting up, scowling at the doctor.

"I caught him trying to leave the bed," the doctor said as he stared at Maxim coldly.

Wow. Brave doctor.

"My woman was missing."

"I wasn't missing," she told him. "I was downstairs, talking with your brother."

Regent set her down on the bed and Maxim drew her against him. "You're not supposed to be walking too much on your feet."

"They're fine."

"You are forbidden from leaving this room without my permission."

"I think that's our cue to leave," Regent said.

The doctor nodded, his lips twitching.

"Maxim Malone. You cannot forbid me from doing something."

"Can. Did. Discussion over."

"Discussion is certainly not over!"

"You just added to your spanking. You're not sitting for two weeks now."

"Maxim!"

"Gave me a fucking heart attack. I woke up and you weren't here. I thought you'd run off to do something stupid."

Oh.

Shoot.

She turned to face him and saw the worry on his face. Her anger melted.

He was worried.

And that changed everything.

"I won't run off and do anything crazy. I promise."

"Yeah?"

"Yeah."

"Do you promise not to leave the room without my permission?"

"That I don't promise. Because that's nuts. But I will leave you a note if you're asleep so you know where I am."

"And you'll keep your phone on you. I tried calling you and discovered it was here."

"I'll do that too." She cupped his cheek with her hand. "Sorry I worried you."

"I'd apologize for forbidding you from doing something, but the truth is I'll probably do it again."

She just grinned, shaking her head.

33

She couldn't settle.

She rolled this way and that until he finally couldn't take it anymore.

"Baby."

She let out a gasp that had him drawing her close. "Shit. Didn't mean to scare you."

"That's . . . I thought you were asleep," she said.

"Hard to sleep while you're tossing and turning."

"I'm so sorry. I'll sleep on the chair. I told you I was happy to do that. I didn't hurt you, did I?"

"Baby, you are not sleeping in a chair. You are sleeping in a bed. My bed. With me. Forever."

"Forever?" she whispered.

Shit. Was he pushing too much? But she loved him. He loved her. She had to know this was about forever, right?

"Forever. Is that a problem?"

She wrapped her arm around his upper chest. "No problem at all."

"Good. I didn't think so," he said arrogantly.

"Maxim?"

"Yeah, baby?"

"Do you think they've found the drugs yet?" she asked.

"I don't know."

"If they find the drugs, if Dayton is a part of all of this, I'll have to find a new job."

And that was worrying her? Fuck. Why hadn't he realized she'd be concerned? His girl was a worrier. He had to get ahead of that shit and head it off before it could snowball in her mind.

"Is that a problem?" he asked.

"I like my job."

"I know, baby."

"What if I can't find another one? I don't have a lot of experience."

"You know you don't have to work, right?"

"Of course I have to work. I have bills to pay. I wouldn't like living outside in the cold."

"You're not fucking living outside in the cold." Did she seriously think he'd ever allow that?

"With how protective you are, I figured that," she said dryly. "However, if you're about to tell me that you'll cover everything for me, just stop. I like earning my own money. I never had any independence when I was younger. My father controlled everything. And I'm not saying I don't like that you're protective of me. I do. I like it a lot. But I also like having a job."

He understood that. Didn't necessarily like it. But he got it.

"Then we'll find you another job."

"I'll do it myself. If someone will hire me."

"Are you good at your job?" he asked.

"Not to sound arrogant, but yes."

"Then someone will see that and hire you. Everything is going to be all right, Rainbow. I promise."

"Yes. Yes, it will."

"And I don't know if they've found the drugs yet, but staying awake and worrying over it won't help."

"My brain won't let me sleep."

"Then let's see if we can find something to distract you. You'll have to help since I can't move around that easily. I want you to strip off, then feed me your breast."

"What?" she squealed.

"You heard me," he said sternly. "Strip. Feed."

He'd noticed that she liked taking orders earlier when she was sucking his cock. And he was only too happy to tell her what to do. He'd been controlling with some of his other lovers, but not to this extent.

But everything with Aston was different.

"Now, baby."

"I don't think we should do this."

"I'm going to count to five and if you don't obey me, as soon as I'm well enough, I'm tying you to this bed and teasing you all night."

She was stripped and on her knees next to him, with her breast above his mouth, by the time he got to three.

That was some fast moving. And she'd jostled him a bit, but he'd never tell her that.

Instead, he got to work, playing with her nipple. He sucked on it as his hand moved lower, toward her pussy. He ran a finger along her slit, satisfaction filling him as he found she was wet.

Fuck. Yes.

"Good girl, baby," he whispered after he let her breast go. "Getting all nice and wet for me. Part your legs farther."

He ran his finger along her slit and then flicked her clit as he took her other breast into his mouth. He sucked on the nipple as he toyed with her clit.

Fuck. What he wouldn't give to be able to bury his face in her pussy and eat her until she screamed.

He could feel her shaking, so he drew his finger back. She made a disgruntled noise.

"Shh, baby. Give me your mouth now."

She bent down so he could kiss her and his finger went back to her clit. Round and round. Then he flicked it until she was shaking again, her breath coming faster.

Moving his finger lower, he slid it gently into her, rocking it in and out. Fucking hell. So tight.

"Oh. Ohh." She leaned her head back and he pressed the palm of his hand to her clit as he kept moving his finger in and out of her pussy.

She cried out as she came, and he wished he'd thought to turn the light on first so he could see her when she found her satisfaction.

"That's it, baby. Give it to me. Come for me. Let me hear you cry out. Say my name."

"Maxim," she breathed out. "Oh God, Maxim."

"That's it. Good girl." He slid his finger free of her pussy just before she collapsed against him. He drew his finger up to his mouth and sucked on it. "Fucking delicious. Just like I thought."

"That was . . . amazing. Well done."

He broke out in a laugh and she glanced up at him.

"Fuck, baby. I don't usually laugh after sex or during it. But you're too adorable."

"Is it a bad thing? To laugh during or after sex?"

"No, baby. Not bad at all. Now, lay your head on my chest and go to sleep."

"I'll lie on your chest, but I might not sleep," she warned as she snuggled in.

He rubbed the muscles in her neck until he heard her sigh, relaxing against him.

Yeah, they'd just see about that.

34

She'd slept.

She couldn't believe it. And for more than just a couple of hours. She'd woken up pressed against Maxim.

Last night had been a night of firsts. The first time she'd slept for more than a few hours at a time in years. Other than when she hit a wall and slept for long stretches.

And the first orgasm she'd experienced that she hadn't given to herself.

She wasn't sure which one was better.

Actually, scratch that. She definitely knew which one was better.

Her man sure knew what he was doing. And he'd done it while injured using just one hand.

Imagine how he'd rock her world when he was at full strength.

"I like that smile on your face," he told her as he came out of the bathroom the next morning.

She'd already gotten up, showered, and dressed in some more of Gracen's clothes. Now she was trying to tame her hair.

She really needed her stuff. Desperately.

"Me too," she said.

He walked up behind her. He was dressed in just his pajama bottoms. She was beginning to find those pajama bottoms incredibly attractive.

"Shouldn't you be in bed?" she asked.

"Sick of being in bed, baby." He wrapped an arm around her from behind, both of them staring into the mirror she'd been in front of. He kissed her neck. "I liked making you come in my arms last night. But I liked it even more that you slept in my arms."

"I know," she whispered.

"I look forward to doing that every night."

She turned in his arms and carefully hugged him. "Me too."

There was a knock at the door and she tried to pull away, but he held her tight. "Come in."

She turned her head as Regent and Victor entered. They looked exhausted. Victor was carrying a huge cup of coffee. While Regent carried two pizza boxes.

"Pizza?" she asked.

"Sal's," Regent confirmed with a smile. "You earned it."

He hadn't forgotten that he'd said he would buy her one!

"I know it's a strange time to eat pizza, but I'm starving," Regent explained.

"Me too," Victor said.

"Jesus, did you guys get any sleep?" Maxim asked, moving away from her. But he grabbed her hand and led her to the bed. He sat on it, resting against the headboard, with her tucked in next to him.

"Nope," Victor said. "I'm heading there in a minute. Gotta

convince Gracen she needs a sleep-in." He yawned. Then he took a piece of pizza.

She took one too. Yum. Delicious.

"Did you find the drugs?" she asked after swallowing a mouthful.

"We found the drugs," Regent said with satisfaction. "Not only that, but we stole the drugs."

"Got it all?" Maxim asked.

"Yep."

"Shit," Maxim said. "He's going to be pissed. And his supplier will be even more pissed."

"Yes," Regent said. "But he should have thought more before selling in my territory. I've sent word to him that if he tries to bring any more drugs into my city, the same will happen. The police also ramped up last night. They arrested a lot of the street level pushers and sent another strong message to Leeds."

"The fucker is screwed," Victor said.

"What do you think his next play is?" Maxim asked.

"Well, unless he has the money to pay outright for those drugs, the cartel he is working with isn't going to be happy. I've got a lead on that too. It sounds like it's Perez who's been supplying the drugs."

"Fuck, he's bad news. He won't like this at all," Maxim said.

She had no idea who they were talking about. But she guessed she didn't have to know. All she wanted was for this all to be over and those drugs to be off the streets. She polished off a second piece of pizza and then sat back. It really was amazing pizza.

"My guess is that Leeds will try to run," Regent said. "And that's good news for us."

She breathed out. "So it could all be over soon."

"Very soon," Regent said.

"I don't know if this is a good idea."

"Did I eat your pussy last night?"

"Maxim Malone! You did not just say that to me!" She glanced around to make sure that no one else was around.

Three days had passed since they'd found all the drugs at one of Dayton's work sites. It had been one of the sites that she'd identified as the most likely to hold the drugs.

So, in a way, she had helped.

The day after the drugs had been taken, Dayton Leeds had been found dead in his home office. He'd shot himself.

She still felt strange about that. On the one hand, she'd stopped that drug from killing more people.

On the other hand . . . she'd played a part in Dayton taking his life.

Yeah, that was weighing heavily on her mind.

They still didn't know who exactly had attacked Maxim, which wasn't making any of them happy. But she didn't know if they'd ever figure that part out.

"I made you come three times last night. Twice with my fingers and once with my mouth." There was deep satisfaction in his voice as he slowly moved down the stairs.

"I'm not sure what that has to do with you walking down the stairs," she said to him with a glare.

The man was too much.

He had decided to get up and dressed today. And then walk downstairs. So now she was walking down in front of him to make sure he didn't collapse and hit his fool head.

"If I can make you come three times, then I can walk down the damn stairs."

"You seem to forget that you'll have to walk back up the stairs."

"I'll deal with that problem when I get to it."

Grr.

"Don't you want to go get your things?" he asked.

That's why he was walking down the stairs. Because he wanted to go with her to get her things. A couple of Regent's men were also going with them to carry whatever she chose to bring back with her.

"You don't need to come with me."

"If you're leaving the house, I'm coming with you. Trouble finds you."

She didn't point out that he wouldn't be a lot of help if trouble came looking for her. She knew better than to crush a male ego.

They were fragile things.

Instead, she kept moving down the stairs in front of him. When they reached the bottom, she let out a sigh of relief.

He drew her to him with a grin, kissing the top of her head.

"See? Easy."

"Easy, right."

Her phone started ringing and she drew it out of her pocket. She'd managed to do a small amount of online shopping, and Gracen had picked it all up for her. So she felt more like herself today in a long dress with full sleeves that ended in tight cuffs at her wrists.

She'd also bought some comfortable shoes and a good hairbrush.

Maxim had frowned when she'd walked out of the bathroom with her hair tied back in a bun, but hadn't said anything.

She frowned as she saw that it was Eva calling. It wasn't the first time Eva had called, but she'd been avoiding answering her calls.

With a sigh, knowing she couldn't really keep putting her off, she answered.

"Hello, Eva."

"Oh, Aston, hi."

"Are you all right?" she asked. The other woman sounded off.

"It's just . . . I haven't seen you around in a while. I was getting worried."

Was she really? Or was she concerned about losing her babysitter?

"I've been staying with a friend."

"Ahh right. The kids miss you."

"I miss them too." Which was the truth. "I'm coming to get some of my things now, I'll stop in to say hello to the boys."

"Now?"

"Uh, yes. Are you going to be home?" she asked, wondering why the other woman sounded weird.

"Yep, yep. How far away are you? My apartment is a mess."

"About fifteen, maybe twenty minutes. And I don't mind." It wasn't like it was usually tidy. "Bye, Eva."

"Bye."

She ended the call and turned to Maxim who crooked a finger at her.

She rolled her eyes but moved toward him, not wanting another 'come here' conversation. Because that conversation always ended the same way. With her 'going there'.

"You're a soft touch, baby." He drew her into him and kissed the top of her head.

"You think I should be mean to her? I know she's been using me, but I do like her kids."

"No. I think that you should be exactly what you want to be."

"But you think people take advantage of me when I do that."

"You didn't let me finish." With a finger under her chin, he tilted her head back. "You be exactly who you want to be,

Because now you have me, and I will make sure that no one walks all over you."

She smiled up at him. "You know, I was wrong."

"About what?"

"You don't suck."

He laughed until he groaned and she had to scold him.

∽

TWENTY MINUTES LATER, they were walking along the hallway toward her apartment. They'd had to take the elevator, which wasn't her favorite thing. But she couldn't handle Maxim trying to traverse any more stairs.

When they reached her apartment, Maxim frowned and took hold of her arm.

"What is it?"

"I don't know. I have a bad feeling." He glanced at her neighbor's door. "Why isn't she coming out?"

"She doesn't always come out."

"No, but she knows you're coming." He knocked on Eva's door. No answer.

All right. That was odd.

Maxim moved her behind him and sent a quick message off to someone. Probably Regent.

"Should we not go into my apartment?" she asked.

He shot his gaze to the two men with them, Rocco and Levin. Then they moved cautiously back down the hallway.

"Maxim?" she whispered.

"We're leaving, baby. I'm not taking you in there. No one is going in without more manpower behind us."

Then the door to Aston's apartment opened and Eva appeared. A tearful, fearful-looking Eva.

But that wasn't what made her heart stop. That had her

stomach dropping. It was the person behind Eva, holding a gun to her head.

"Gretchen," she whispered.

"Really, Aston. Have you not worked it out yet? You are a little slow, aren't you? Now, I suggest you all get in here before we're seen. Hands up where I can see them and nowhere near your guns or it's bye-bye neighbor."

Motherfudger.

Actually. This called for proper swearing.

Mother. Fucker.

"Stay behind me at all times," Maxim ordered her as they raised their hands.

She nodded as they headed into her apartment. Which had been trashed. It was like a tornado had gone through it.

Perhaps later, she'd get upset about that. But right now, she had more important things to worry about.

Like getting all of them out of this alive.

There was another man in the room, one who seemed vaguely familiar. He was standing behind her wrecked sofa with his arms over his chest.

"Bart, take care of them. Get the guns off them and tie their hands," Gretchen ordered, nodding at Rocco and Levin.

They looked to Maxim, who nodded. They both got on their knees and put up with Bart, tying their hands behind their backs and taking their guns. This wasn't looking good for them.

Bart moved to Maxim and patted him down, taking the gun from the small of his back. Then he turned to her, his grin evil.

A shiver ran through her.

"Touch her and die," Maxim threatened.

"You're not in charge here, asshole," Bart snarled back. "I'll touch her if I want to touch her. And I won't do it nicely, seeing as I owe her for stabbing Frank."

She sucked in a breath. "You were one of the men who attacked Maxim."

"Finally, you get it," Gretchen said drolly.

Bart grabbed her and Maxim pushed him back.

Oh God! Maxim couldn't get into a fight when he was still injured. She stepped between them as Bart reached for his gun.

"Bart! Calm down! Just leave her, she won't have a weapon. She's too much of a goody-two-shoes for that."

Bart stepped back with a snarl.

What was Gretchen thinking?

"Where are the kids?" she asked Eva, worried about the boys.

"D-daycare," Eva whispered. "I p-put them in before calling you."

Fuck. Fuck.

"Did you call Aston to find out when she was coming back?" Maxim asked sharply. "Did you tell Gretchen that she'd be here?"

"I had to! She threatened the boys. And I knew she meant it b-because she killed Dan!" Eva wailed.

Oh God! Gretchen had killed Dan? Aston was going to throw up. She just knew it.

Threatening children. Killing people. This was a nightmare.

Aston gaped at Gretchen. "Did I ever know you at all? I thought we were friends."

"Friends? Of course we weren't, you stupid bitch."

"You asked me to go out with you."

"Yes. At first, it was because I knew you'd make me look good," Gretchen sneered. "I couldn't take any of my other so-called friends. They would have one-upped me. Bitches."

Right. So she didn't have any real friends to take. Ouch. That still stung, though.

"And then it was a test. I was suspicious when I saw you getting into his car outside of work." She pointed at Maxim. "I knew the Malones wouldn't be happy with someone selling drugs in New Orleans. They don't own the city. Fucking bullshit. So I asked you to go with me to Glory. I wanted to see if you'd mention knowing Maxim. But you didn't."

Shit.

"I also wanted to go because the guy who'd been selling Mixology at Glory had gone missing, and I needed someone else to sell there for me. Unfortunately, I couldn't get anything on any of the staff to use to pressure them."

"You bitch," Maxim spat out.

"Biggest catch in the state . . . what a joke," she said, looking him up and down. "I mean, at one time, I thought about hooking up with you, but then I knew it would be too dangerous, getting that close to you and your family."

Maxim reached back and squeezed her hand. She didn't know why Gretchen hadn't tied them up, but she was grateful.

Why was he squeezing her hand, though? Oh, did he want her to keep talking?

"You must have a magic pussy to keep him this long."

"I love Maxim and he loves me."

Gretchen snorted. "That's a useless emotion. I loved my daddy. But when his time was up, it was up."

"W-what are you trying to say?"

"He didn't kill himself, did he?" Maxim asked. "You killed him."

What?

Aston didn't know how to feel about this. Relief? Sadness?

"I think he'd suspected what was going on for a while, but he was in denial that his darling daughter would use him like that. Then when your brother raided his worksite and took all the drugs and sent him that message, well, he knew for sure. He threatened to go to the cops and I shot him."

"You're a monster," Aston accused her.

"You'd know about monsters, wouldn't you?" Gretchen sneered.

"What does that mean?" she whispered.

Then the door to her bedroom opened and the biggest monster of them all stepped out.

Oh God. Oh no.

Her stomach dropped. She was going to be ill.

"Aston?" Maxim said urgently.

"Dad," she whispered.

Maxim crowded against her as Eva continued to sob quietly, and her father walked farther into the room.

His gaze was on her. And it was filled with malevolence.

"Wh-what are you doing here? How did you find me?"

"It wasn't hard to find out who you really were," Gretchen said. "After I grew suspicious of you, I did some digging and found out about your dear dad."

"Why didn't you just fire me?"

"Keep your friends close and your enemies closer. I thought about trying to use you to get the Malones to back off. Even had one of my guys watch you a few times. But then, I decided you weren't important enough. However, he was." She pointed at Maxim. "I had my guys send a message to his brother that he wasn't as invincible as he thought. That I could get to his brothers if I wanted to. But you just had to interfere, didn't you, Aston? You helped Maxim escape my guys, so I called up Robbie, your dad, and offered to pay for him to come down here."

"You stole from me, Aston," her father said. God, she remembered his voice. She loathed the sound of it. Fear tumbled through her, making her feel ill. "You ran from me, you stupid, worthless bitch. Messed a lot of things up. Time you came home and made things right."

"She's not going anywhere with you, asshole," Maxim snarled. "And do not speak to her like that again."

"You aren't in charge here," Gretchen snarled at Maxim. "And it isn't like you're walking out of here alive, so you won't need to worry about what happens to poor Aston."

"Come here, Aston," her father ordered.

She shook her head. Terror held her frozen.

Eva's sobs increased until Gretchen let out an annoyed noise. "Oh, shut up." She tossed Eva to the floor and held her gun up. "You're annoying. Time for you to shut up for good."

That's when Maxim moved. He shoved Aston to the side before throwing himself at Gretchen.

She screamed as she landed on the floor. She knew Maxim was still hurt. And Gretchen and Bart had guns. Plus, who knew what weapons her father had on him.

But Maxim obviously knew something she didn't. Because in the next moment, pandemonium erupted. She cowered behind what was left of the sofa, wishing she knew what to do. How to help.

And that's where he found her.

Her father.

"Come on. You're coming with me." He grabbed her wrist, holding on so tight that it hurt. Tears filled her eyes, but she refused to let them spill.

"No!"

"You are! Get the fuck up!" He drew her up and she fell into him. She took that moment to gather herself before she pulled back from him.

"No! Let me go!"

"Aston!" Maxim moved toward her, looking every inch the warrior. His shirt was ripped and he was limping slightly, which worried her. She glanced around, shocked to see Bart moaning on the floor, his hand over his stomach, which was bleeding.

Victor was undoing the ties on Levin and Rocco while Regent stood over Gretchen's prone body.

Eva was off by the wall, crying and shaking. If she could have, Aston might have felt bad about that. But she didn't feel much except worry for Maxim and anger at her bastard father.

"Is she dead?" she asked.

Regent gave her a slight nod as he stared at her father. "Let Aston go."

"No! She's not yours! She's mine!" he roared. "My daughter!"

"Like fuck she is! Let her go! Now!" Maxim yelled.

And she knew she had to do something before he did something rash and reopened his stitches.

So she turned to her father and glared up at him. "I am not yours! Because I have no father." Then she drew her leg back and kneed him in the balls. He let go of her arm and she rushed into Maxim's arms.

He held her tight against him as Victor moved to take care of her father. She heard him yell, heard something heavy smack into something solid. But Maxim's hand on the back of her head kept her face buried in his chest so she couldn't look.

And the truth was, she wouldn't have looked even if she could have.

"I think I've changed my mind," she whispered.

"What's that, baby?"

"I don't need any of my things."

"I'm going to buy you all new things, baby."

"And I'm going to let you."

35

"Spread your legs, baby. I want to taste you."

Dear. Lord.

"Aston. Spread."

She spread her legs because of his commanding tone of voice and because she wanted him to taste her.

She'd found she was rather addicted to him eating her out. But she was even more addicted to having him in her mouth. Which she'd already had that night. And every night since their run-in with Gretchen and Aston's father a week ago.

"I can hear you thinking from here. Obviously, I need to up my game." He grabbed her legs and pushed them back before spearing her pussy with his tongue.

Oh no, he definitely didn't have to up his game. They were in his room at the Malone mansion. She hadn't wanted to return to the apartment building, not even into his penthouse apartment.

And he was willing to give her that. He was willing to give her anything. They hadn't talked about where they would live. But for now, she was happy here.

Maybe she was hiding from life right now, but she figured

she was entitled. It wasn't every day that your supposed friend held a gun on your neighbor and you saw your estranged, violent father.

For now, she was going to let Maxim and his brothers shelter her from the outside world and just breathe for a while.

"Fuck, baby. You taste fucking delicious."

She licked her lips. Because so did he. And she wanted more.

"I want you in my mouth again," she demanded.

"I'm eating you now."

"But—"

"No."

"Maxim. Please."

He drew back from her, kneeling, and gave her a stern look. "I can see I haven't been firm enough with you."

"You're firm now." She stared down at his hard cock.

"Hey, my eyes are up here. I feel objectified."

"You don't like that?"

"I fucking love how much you like my dick. I like how much you enjoy it in your mouth. But you must realize that I like having my mouth on your pussy. And that's what's happening right now."

"What if I don't want that?"

"Yep. I've been far too lenient. Time for that punishment you're owed."

"I think I'm fine with your mouth on my pussy," she said hastily.

"Damn straight you are," he muttered. And he proceeded to show her just how much he enjoyed eating her out as she came with his name on her lips.

He kissed his way back up her body.

He wasn't fully healed yet, but he was getting there. And she was doing all that she could to get him to take it easy.

Including telling him that she needed a nap. Daily. And that she could only sleep with him there with her.

Which was actually true. And she often fell asleep during their naps, even though she hadn't intended to.

Although her sleep was getting better, her encounter with Gretchen and her father hadn't helped with her nightmares. Even knowing that Gretchen was dead. And that Maxim, Regent, and Victor had had words with her father.

Maxim had assured her she'd never hear from him or her brothers ever again. She wasn't sure how they'd achieved that, but she'd decided to take him at his word.

She felt his hard cock pressing against her as he moved onto his side next to her. His hand cupped her breast and she rolled into him, wrapping her hand around his thick erection.

"Fuck, baby. Your hand feels so good."

"You know what would feel better?" she whispered. "My pussy."

"I've got no doubts about that. But you're not ready."

He hadn't fucked her yet. Something that seemed very sweet in the beginning when he told her that he wanted her to be fully prepared before he did.

But now, it had become rather frustrating.

"I am ready." She pushed him onto his back, only able to do this because she took him by surprise, and then she straddled his lap, staring down at him. "I'm ready. Please. I need this."

"I want to give this to you, don't think that I don't. But are you sure?"

She reached between them and grabbed his dick, trying to guide it to her entrance. "I'm sure."

He rolled them back and kneeled between her legs. "Easy, baby. We're going to take this nice and slow and I need to get gloved up first."

"You know I'm on protection and I'm clean."

"I'm clean as well, you're sure?"

"Please. Do you need me to beg some more? Please, please."

"Hush, baby. No more begging needed. I want to give you what you need." He kissed her. Long and hard. And then his finger was at her entrance before he thrust it deep. It felt good, but it wasn't enough and she moaned her frustration. Then he moved to two fingers, which felt even better.

But still not enough.

Nothing was enough.

Then he slid his fingers free before his dick pressed inside her.

"Wrap your legs around me, baby. Hold on tight and tell me if it gets too much and you need me to stop."

No way was she doing that. With how protective he was, she likely wouldn't get to feel his dick inside her until she was eighty.

"You feel so good. God, baby. Just hold on."

There was some pain, she wouldn't lie. She was stretched to her limit and she didn't think she could take him.

And then his finger was between them, rubbing at her clit and he paused to kiss her. Gentle and sweet.

He pushed forward and she was taking him.

And it was epic.

By the time he was fully seated in her, they were both breathing heavily, and she knew she needed more.

"Move, Maxim."

"Your wish is my command."

He started slowly. But soon, his movements grew harder. Faster. It was almost too much. Too overwhelming. She could feel herself reaching for that peak but was worried she wouldn't get there.

"Just relax, baby. Let me do the work. You just lie back and let me take care of you."

Lord. This man.

He was the best thing to ever happen to her. And she wasn't ever letting go. So she relaxed and let him take her there. And when her orgasm washed over her, it was consuming and delicious. But it was even better when he joined her, thrusting deep, a shout of satisfaction coming from his mouth.

She latched onto him, holding onto him tight.

Not ever wanting to let go.

He must have felt the same because he rolled them over, so she was lying on top of him and his arms were tight bands around her.

She nuzzled into his chest. "I don't want to move."

"I don't want you to move."

She found the energy to lean up on her arms so she could look down at him. "I just have to tell you that you're the best thing that ever happened to me."

"That's good to hear, baby. Because I feel exactly the same way about you."

∼

She was sitting on Maxim's lap in the living room a few nights later when Regent stormed into the room.

She'd tried to sit on the sofa, but Maxim had other ideas, as he often did.

And she was in his lap.

But then again, Gracen was sitting in Victor's lap on the other sofa.

So she didn't feel entirely out of place.

"You're just in time, bro," Maxim said, turning up the news. For some reason, he'd insisted that she come watch the news with him. She wasn't sure why.

She stared at the familiar building on the screen as the news reporter started speaking. What was going on?

"Several members of the notorious Dark Vipers gang have been arrested after a large batch of the new drug, Mixology, was found in this building. Look! Several of them are being escorted out now."

She sucked in a breath as she spotted Hugh first, his gaze on his feet, his arms locked behind him as an officer led him to a police car. Then, Benny. He was glaring at everyone, his mouth moving as he no doubt spat crap at everyone. Last, there was her father. He looked shrunken. One side of his face was bruised and he shuffled along as though in pain.

She glanced at Maxim, then to Victor, then Regent. She knew where those drugs had come from.

"You all did this? For me?"

"Course we did," Maxim said.

"You're family," Victor added.

"It wasn't that difficult," Regent added.

Actually, she bet it'd been very difficult. But they had done it. For her. Just like they'd taken care of Gretchen, Bart and the other two guys who had beaten Maxim up. Regent's men had found one standing watch outside the apartment building that day. While the other guy had been recovering from his stab wound in Gretchen's apartment.

They'd left Gretchen's body in her apartment. Along with a lot of evidence that indicated she'd been using her father's business to import and sell drugs.

"Thank you," she whispered as Maxim hugged her tight.

"You're welcome, baby. I'm always going to take care of you."

She knew he would.

Regent reached for the remote, turning the television off before he turned to hold out a white envelope that she'd left on his desk. "What is this?"

Uh-oh.

Maxim tensed under her. "Baby?"

"That's for you," she told Regent.

"And why would you give me five hundred dollars?"

"Well, it's all I can afford right now. But I'm going to start looking into new jobs so I can pay my way while I'm here. I'm sure it takes a lot to run a place like this, and I've been eating your food and using the utilities, so I... thought... I..."

"Oh shit," Victor muttered. "Time for us to leave." He picked Gracen up and walked out with her in his arms.

"You gave Regent money?" Maxim asked in a strangled voice.

"Uh, yes. I don't know why the two of you don't seem too happy, but I should pay my way. Plus, I know that you gave Eva money to leave town." And she'd left a few days after her run-in with Gretchen. Aston felt bad about that, about Eva losing Dan, about everything she'd gone through.

Regent pointed at her, opened his mouth, then he closed it. "See to this, Maxim."

He stormed out, the envelope landing on the sofa beside her.

"He didn't take the money," she said.

"Nope."

"I get the feeling he's a bit upset."

"Yep."

"Because I tried to pay my way?" she asked.

"Yep."

"But why?" she asked.

"You're one of us now, baby. That means that I look after you. It means my brothers do too. That means you do not pay your way. It means you do not worry about getting money to pay your way. Understand?"

"I still think that I should help out."

"You might think that you don't help out, but that's not true. You make me laugh, you make me happy, and that means more to Regent than you paying your way."

"Oh." That was actually really sweet.

"Of course, now I need to spank your ass."

"What?" She gaped at him.

"Afraid so." He lifted her off him and then got up, grabbing her hand to tug her out of the room and up the stairs.

"You are not spanking me for trying to give Regent money."

"I have to. It's the Malone way."

"Maxim!"

He grinned at her as he tugged her into his bedroom. "Regent is expecting it."

"That's . . . that's ridiculous!"

He drew her over to the bed, then he sat and arranged her over his lap.

"You cannot spank me for this!"

"No?" He drew her bottoms down, along with her panties, baring her ass.

"No!"

"I still owe you a spanking for putting yourself in danger."

"I helped save you."

"You still put yourself in danger. And you put yourself down. So let's get your ass red so my brother knows you've learned your lesson. And so I know you've learned your lesson."

He slapped his hand down on her ass and she let out a small cry. She kind of thought he might be joking. That he'd stop after a couple and get down to other business.

But he didn't.

Oh no, he definitely meant business. His hand slapped down on her bottom until it was hot and sore. Throbbing. Until she was kicking and cursing him.

But she didn't stop him by saying her safeword. Because she knew there was a part of him that needed to make his point. And that point was that he wanted her safe.

Always.

And she liked knowing that he wanted her to be safe.

So she let him spank her. And then she let him hold her until she stopped crying.

After that, she let him give her three orgasms for making her cry before she let him fuck her.

And all of it, other than the spanking, was glorious.

Later that night, after another round of him fucking her, he tucked her into his chest and held her tight.

"You took my back."

"What?" she asked.

"You took my back when I needed it. You're loyal, sweet, kind, funny. Do you want me for me?"

"Of course I do!"

"My perfect girl."

That was when she remembered him telling her about what he was looking for in a woman.

And she fell asleep with a smile on her face.

EPILOGUE

T*en months later...*

ASTON STARED INTO THE MIRROR, brushing out an imaginary wrinkle in her dress.

This wasn't the sort of dress she was used to wearing. While there had been a lot of changes for her over this last year, some things were more difficult to change than others.

She and Maxim had continued to live with Regent for a few months until she'd found the most gorgeous house about three blocks away.

And seven months ago, they'd moved into that beautiful house with a turret and a wide front porch.

It was more beautiful than anything she thought she'd ever deserve. But according to Maxim, she deserved the world. So she'd let him give her this. And the best thing was, Victor and

Gracen had decided to move out and into their own place. Which was only three doors down.

She'd even found a job she liked. It was actually for one of Dayton's competitors. He'd bombarded her with job offers until she'd agreed to a trial run. She'd been working for him for six months now.

Life with Maxim was amazing. He was still ridiculously overprotective and demanding. But sometimes, she liked his demanding ways.

And she tried to never take for granted the fact that he loved her.

She ran her hand over her blonde hair. She'd gone back to her original color with Maxim's gentle coaxing.

She'd become more comfortable with wearing her hair down or dressing in clothes that didn't cover her from neck to toes. Mostly because she now felt safe and cared for with Maxim. But sometimes, she still grew nervous and wanted to fall back on her armor.

Like right now.

Because she was about to go downstairs in this gorgeous dress that revealed a whole lot of skin and walk down the aisle in front of a bunch of people, a lot of whom she didn't know.

Gracen and Victor were getting married at the Malone mansion today, and for some reason, Gracen had wanted Aston to be one of her bridesmaids along with her best friend, Sammy.

And so Aston was dressed in a silky blue dress with spaghetti straps that was tight around her chest and waist, then flared out. It was flattering and beautiful.

The door opened and she jumped, looking over as Maxim entered.

"I'm not sure you're meant to be in here!"

He grinned. "Pretty sure that only matters if you're the bride, baby."

She glanced down at the ring on her finger. It was a huge diamond surrounded by smaller diamonds. She'd joked that she'd be able to see the thing from the moon.

Maxim had told her that was precisely the point.

She couldn't believe that one day she would become Mrs. Maxim Malone.

"When we get married, can it just be the family?"

Understanding filled his face. "It can be whatever you want, baby." His gaze moved over her and heat filled his face. "Jesus, Rainbow. I don't know whether I want to show off how fucking gorgeous you look in that dress or cover you up in a sack so no one else can look at my girl."

"You think I look gorgeous?"

"Fuck, yes. Totally beautiful."

"You look beautiful too." And he did. He was dressed in a dark blue suit with a white shirt that was open at the collar.

"Told you, baby. I'm not beautiful. I'm an alpha."

"I know. You still look hot." She licked her lips.

"You keep looking at me like that and we're going to be late," he warned. "Which means Victor will kill me."

"We have half an hour." She moved toward him, slipping onto her knees in front of him. Then she undid his pants, pulling out his dick, before she sucked him down.

And it definitely didn't take her half an hour to suck him off.

So he ended up returning the favor, with her sitting on the bed, her dress up around her waist while he kneeled in front of her, eating her until she came.

So when she went down to join Gracen and Sammy, she had a smile on her face and a spring in her step.

Sammy grinned at her knowingly. Aston had been going to ballet lessons with Gracen and Sammy for the last eight months so she knew the other woman now. Also, she was killing it at ballet lessons. She could tell that everyone thought so.

"Lucky bitch," Sammy muttered.

Yes, she certainly was.

~

MAXIM SEARCHED FOR HIS GIRL. While the wedding wasn't a huge one, he knew it was likely too much for Aston.

He spotted Thea, Ace, and Keir laughing together. Carrick had his arm around Thea and was staring down at the boys with a warm smile. Jardin walked up to them, wrapping his arm around Thea on the other side.

Thea moved away from her men slightly and raised her camera, taking a photo of the boys. Maxim knew she'd been nervous when Gracen had asked her to be the wedding photographer. But she didn't need to be. Even though she'd only just started her photography business recently, she was already popular. It had taken a while for Jardin to find an assistant he was happy with, but he'd finally employed a lovely older lady. And Thea was free to pursue her dream.

Happiness filled Maxim as he took them in. Then he looked over to where Gracen was sitting on Victor's lap as she chatted with Lottie, who was sitting on Nico's lap. Liam was standing behind Nico, one hand on Nico's shoulder, his other hand on the back of Lottie's neck.

Gracen's niece wasn't there. He knew the rift between them hurt Gracen, but he hoped like hell that Gracen knew how much her family loved her.

He was certain Victor told her that often.

Finally, he spotted his girl. She was talking to Regent. She put her hand on his arm and then flung her other arm out, nearly taking out a waiter.

His grin grew. His girl had had a few drinks and she was utterly adorable.

Regent put his arm around her as she wobbled, and spotting him, he started to herd her toward him.

That was all right with Maxim. He had the urge to take her home to finish what they'd started earlier. As they grew closer, happiness filled her face as she saw him and she flung her arms out toward him.

"Maxy-Moo!" she cried.

Oh, fuck no.

He had thought, hoped, prayed she'd forgotten that ridiculous name. And now she'd cried it out in front of his entire family.

She was so getting her ass spanked.

Regent grinned at him, looking so happy it still shocked Maxim. Then his woman came up behind him, wrapping herself around him.

And well, Maxim could say more about that...

But that story was for another day.

Instead, he bundled his woman up and took her home, to their bed, where he proceeded to give her several more orgasms before fucking her and tucking her into his side to sleep.

And all of his dreams were filled with her.

His perfect girl.

Printed in Great Britain
by Amazon